CLAUDE

James D Eate

Author of:

Fiction:

The Tartarus Transfer

Non-fiction:

How to Photograph Wildlife Without Leaving Home

For
Jonathan, James and Richard
For no better sons could a man ask.

Contents

One

Wednesday 5th November

The clock was ticking.

Of that DCI Mike Pullman was well aware, the message made it clear; one hundred million pounds by the eleventh hour of the eleventh day of the eleventh month or people would die.

Twenty four hours had already passed since the first explosion and they were nowhere nearer identifying the extortionist. Five days and counting.

The demand note had been delivered, inside a box of fireworks, to Corrine Browne at the BBC Look North studios in Hull. She was on air at the time broadcasting her pre-8am slot on the national Breakfast programme. Katie Moore the weather presenter finished her forecast and Corrine handed back to Charlie and Louisa in Manchester. She had twenty minutes to prepare for the next slot although, unless something dramatic happened during that time, it would be exactly the same script and VT as the transmission she had just completed. The package had arrived wrapped in Manila paper sealed with brown parcel tape and simply addressed to *the lovely Corrine.*

Assuming it to be a gift from a fan she opened the parcel and found the note. Her immediate reaction was to assume it was a joke from the production team. The short, typed note read:

The explosion that demolished the empty properties in Preston Road yesterday was not caused by a gas leak as you reported. It

*was a little demonstration of my expertise and as a friendly
warning of things to come if I am disrespected.*

*Tell the good burghers of Hull that unless I receive £100 m by
11am on Tuesday 11th they too can expect fireworks.*

Nobody died yesterday but that will not be the case next time.

*Do not waste your time trying to second guess me. I will
surprise you.*

I will let you know how to deliver the money in due course.

Claude

When Corrine had finally accepted that the crew were not
playing a prank, she checked with reception and was told that the
parcel had been delivered by a motorcycle courier, just before she
went on air; Maggie Williams, the show's producer, called the
police.

Sperring bagged the box of fireworks. Forensics would give it
the once over along with the note. 'You don't remember anything
about him at all?' she asked the receptionist for the second time.

'No I've told you he looked just like any other motorcycle
courier. They're in and out of here all day long.'

Sperring knew that memories could be jogged with a little
questioning. 'About six foot you say.'

'Yeah I guess so; five eleven, six foot something like that. I
didn't really look up at him. I was taking calls; he didn't want a
signature so I didn't pay him any attention.'

'What was he wearing?'

'Black leather, one piece I think and a helmet with a black
visor. One thing I did notice was that his gloves weren't normal

gloves they just had two finger sections. I remember thinking when he put the parcel down that his hand looked more like a hoof.'

'No logo on the leathers or the helmet?'

'Not that I noticed. I'm sorry. Like I said I didn't pay him any attention,' she reiterated. She did however remember that he had a nice tight bum but she wasn't going to mention that. 'Jerry our security man might remember him.' She pointed towards a slightly built man standing just inside the front door.

'Okay thanks. If you do recall something else give me a call on that number.' Sperring gave the receptionist her card. She knew that the security man had already been interviewed by DC Sharpe; the conversation proved fruitless; he hadn't noticed the courier arrive at all because he'd been busy at the rear of the premises, supervising the arrival of some new office furniture.

Other than Corrine's, and those of the receptionist, forensic examination showed there were no fingerprints on the parcel or contents. The fireworks were a standard box which could have been purchased at any supermarket or independent retailer; their purpose was assumed simply to be an illustration of the extortionist's pun in the note and the day of delivery being November 5th, Guy Fawkes Day. The note had been produced on a computer using Times New Roman type face and was printed on ubiquitous 100gm laser paper.

A forensic team, senior fire officers and gas engineers had re-visited the Preston Road explosion site, to investigate the claim made in the note, but after further investigation they were unable to determine the exact cause of the blast. Humberside police

7

nevertheless had no option other than treating Claude's claim as genuine rather than opportunistic. Details of the threat were withheld from public announcement until its exact nature and extent could be determined.

The team checked all the known motorcycle couriers in the city, none of which had delivered a package to that address on the morning in question. That left two possibilities: either the person calling themselves Claude was the mystery courier or the parcel originated from outside the city. The civilian researchers on the team would now have the laborious task of contacting all courier companies within a twenty mile radius in the hope that one of them had made the delivery. Pullman knew it was an exercise in futility.

For almost two days there had been no further contact from Claude. No more messages meant that there was nothing more on which to progress the investigation into the extortionist's identity; unless another communication appeared Pullman's team was impotent.

In the meantime they had other matters to occupy their minds. Pullman didn't like the fact that Thomas Wethersby's killer was still at liberty; nor did the Chief Constable. She had insisted that he make every effort to rectify the situation. Pullman didn't need prodding; he was more than anxious that the killer should not escape justice.

Wethersby's headless corpse had been found on the promenade at Bridlington three weeks prior. When his head was found the following day it had the letters SOC scrawled on the forehead identifying his death as part of the wider investigations in a series of world-wide killings. Wethersby was a teacher in a six form college in Howden and had been suspended following allegations of sexual assault on two female students. During police investigations into the academic's death a forensic analysis of his laptop hardrive had shown him to be a sexual predator. He was a Hebephile, but that was not proof positive that he had assaulted the two students, Gemma Maxwell and Angela Carson, although Pullman was, by then, more inclined to believe their accusations. Perhaps Wethersby had targeted them after all, believing their reputation for promiscuity would make the young teenagers easy prey. His guilt or otherwise in those crimes would probably never be proven but that didn't mean he had not been involved in other sexual assaults on pubescent girls or that any less effort should be made to find his killer.

The unpleasant task of viewing the seven hundred or so pornographic images on Wethersby's computer had fallen to officers involved in Operation Oakwood, the follow-up investigation to Operation Yewtree. Many of the girls pictured, were known to have appeared on other computers seized during their on-going nation-wide investigations. Most of those computers belonged to many of the so called great and good of show business, child care and health, education and other professions that would have seemingly innocent access to impressionable children and young teenagers; Wethersby among them. As each new case emerged so the officers began to understand that they were just skimming the surface. The internet may have made the problem more accessible in recent years but the inherent depravity of mankind had been in existence since time immemorial. When most of the suspects and accused in Operation Yewtree were engaged in their odious acts the internet was just an unrealised concept; those acts had still occurred.

The blocking of search terms by the likes of Google and Microsoft would make it more difficult for novice sexual predators to gain access to child pornography but it would not deter those who were already aware of sites hidden in the dark recesses of the

World Wide Web. Restricted access would only make the predators compulsion to find those sites more urgent and compelling; making the Operation Oakwood officer's determination to identify and close such sites equally urgent and compelling.

At Howden police station, DS Peak's checking of the Maxwell and Carson families' alibis for the night of the murder had been completed; all members of both sides were cleared of any personal involvement. At Pullman's behest the DS was now in the process of verifying the CRB and DBS records of all staff at the college. Previous cases recorded by the Yewtree team had shown a propensity for sex offenders to cluster around establishments or specific areas. There was without question two distinct types of perpetrators; those that sought mutual protection and gratification amongst a group of the like-minded perverts and those loners who operated in a seedy world of their own.

There was still the little matter of the two thousand pounds retrieved from Wethersby's mini. His bank account records did not show the amount as having been withdrawn nor was it taken out on either of his two credit cards. It could have been loaned from a pay-day lender or from a pawn broker. There was no watch or jewellery on his body when it was found so hocking it was a possibility. What did he want two thousand pounds in cash for?

If it was a blackmail payment why had he not had it about his person; same if it was to purchase drugs? It was a question Pullman had pondered frequently during the intervening weeks.

DS Sperring had suggested that it may have been for the purchase of sex services; that he had arranged to meet a provider on the prom and was too afraid of being mugged to have the cash on him while he was waiting. Pullman didn't think that someone who got their rocks off on pubescent girls would be paying for sex.

10

Sperring's counter was that he could have arranged to meet a pimp providing young girls for clients with his sexual preferences; it was hardly an unknown trade.

His passport was still at his home in Clipton, ruling out the possibility that he intended to skip the country that night.

Both Pullman and Sperring were still intrigued by the tattoo on Wethersby's arm uncovered during the post-mortem. The letter H in outline with a separated drop shadow inside a circle formed by the body of snake had to mean something. Neither of them had come across anything similar and online checks failed to throw any light on the subject. On a whim Pullman decided to send a copy of the PM picture of Wethersby's arm to DS Peak. The H could have a connection with Howden in which case it may have some significance to Peak.

Two

Friday 7th November

Much to Pullman's utter dismay his review of the Wethersby case had been interrupted by a summons to another pointless 'whatif' meeting of minds convened by Pauline Crompton, the Chief Constable of the Humberside force.

The previous day she, Iain Thwaite the Assistant Chief Constable (Operations) — the post of Deputy Chief Constable being vacant for the past four months due to the incumbent Bob Cole's untimely suicide — and Pullman sat down to select a name for the operation. The national list of possible operational names from which they could choose contained some wholly inappropriate choices; Big Bang, Flash Dance, Boomtown and Touchpaper among them. Of those that were acceptable most were too feminine sounding to win Pullman's vote. In the end the ACC came up with the solution – Alligator.

The extortionist had signed himself Claude and Iain Thwaite remembered that on a trip to the States some two years previously he and his wife had visited the California Academy of Sciences, a museum come interactive wildlife centre in Golden Gate Park, San Francisco. One of his most vivid memories was of a captive albino alligator there called Claude. It was a perfect match – Operation Alligator needed to have teeth.

Crompton sat in the middle of the group on the long side of a highly polished oval wooden conference table. Directly opposite her was Muriel Hudson the Lady Mayoress of Hull; to her right

Frank Delaney, Chief Executive of Hull City Council and to her left Peter Monkton the Police and Crime Commissioner for Humberside.

On Crompton's side of the table was Iain Thwaite and Pullman. It was the second meeting in as many days.

Crompton opened the meeting. 'Let's get started shall we; I'm sure we've all got plenty to do. We've not heard anything further from the person calling himself Claude but if he is genuine then we can expect to hear from him very soon. His time stipulation is getting closer so he must make contact shortly to give us time to act. You agree Mike.'

It was more of a command than a question. Pullman nodded his head in agreement.

Crompton continued. 'Hopefully you've all found the time to think the matter through so that we can collectively develop our whatif strategies enabling us to react to the next contact. Iain.'

The ACC took the floor. 'Our extortionist has advised us not to try to second guess him but that's just what we must do. There are numerous possible scenarios and I'm not saying that our list is definitive by any means but we need to plan for all possibilities. I propose that we go through the list so that Operation Alligator is prepared for all eventualities; if anyone would like to add to the list please do so at the end.'

Pullman was deep in his own thoughts. Thwaite's voice was just an incoherent drone in the background. Expect the unexpected was the gist of Claude's comment so what was the point of drawing up a list of what they could expect? By its very definition an unexpected event was unpredictable; it would be unforeseen, unanticipated, a surprise. That's what the note had said *I will surprise you.* During the next two hours before lunch they would pontificate on everything they could *expect* might happen – an

13

exercise in futility; when, and if, Claude delivered his next message they could react to the circumstances. This meeting was political bollocks; it served no practical purpose; it was purely to cover arses; to allow the press office to inform the media that the top brass and city big wigs or as Claude had referred to them *the burghers of Hull* had been doing all they could, when in actual fact they'd done nothing constructive.

He was now beginning to re-think his decision not to accept a permanent placement at the National Crime Agency instead of returning to the Humberside Police.

The spell in London had helped him come to terms with his wife's death. He could now think of Jane without the ensuing depth of melancholy. Of course he missed her immensely but he was no longer crawling through the mire of despair and self-pity that he had wallowed in for the previous four months since her loss.

Three weeks working in the capital with Lynne Sperring for company had given him a new resolve not to regress into a depressed state. The sixteen years age difference between him and his Detective Sergeant made him realise how little he had in common with someone her age, indeed how little he had in common with any woman. In fact it made him understand his whole situation better; his life had revolved around shared interests with Jane. Now his life would be completely different. It was not the life he had planned or the life he wanted but it was the life he now had; he was determined to make a fist of it.

He certainly didn't want to waste hours in turgid think tanks. DS Sperring and the rest of his team had the Claude situation in hand. The extortion demand appeared to refer to the city itself so the natural starting point was council employees bearing a grudge. Most likely an ex-employee; possibly one of the six hundred or so made redundant in the previous year. They needed more to go on than one demand note. It would take forever and a day to interview all six hundred and Claude may not even be amongst them. It could be someone with a grudge going back years; such feelings can sometimes take a decade or more to fester in the mind or before the perpetrator had the wherewithal to implement their revenge. The list of ex-personnel had already been obtained from the council HR department and checking begun on the more obvious candidates. It could even prove to be a relative of an ex-employee; they wouldn't be on the list.

Alternatively Claude could be a council tax payer or member of the general public who had crossed swords with the local authorities. Perhaps his bin hadn't been emptied on time or pot holes in the road hadn't been repaired. The most trivial grievance can turn into all out conflict; although one hundred million pounds recompense was one hell of a peace treaty.

Pullman was content that they weren't ignoring the problem nor were they wasting their time on trying to predict the future. He'd prefer to let the intelligencia continue to look into their crystal balls while he and Sperring in particular focussed on the unsolved murder of Thomas Wethersby.

Pullman was suddenly aware that he had snorted in the first throes of sleep; he did his best at turning the oink into a cough which actually did make him splutter. Pullman ran his eyes over the attendees none of whom appeared to be paying him any attention. The ACC was still droning on; Pullman shuffled forward in his chair reached for the carafe of water and filled a tumbler. He swallowed half the tepid water then surreptitiously pinched his right thigh, digging his fingernails through the suit trouser leg into his skin as firmly as he could bear. The combination of movement and pain normally raised his concentration level. It worked once again but he knew the effects were transient. If Thwaite didn't quit

15

soon Morpheus would entice him away for a second time. Fortunately the ACC was in the concluding phase of his diatribe.

'So ladies and gentlemen that's what we can expect,' he said triumphantly.

The unexpected happened that night.

Sammy's Point was named after Martin Samuelson, a local man, who in 1857 built a shipyard on a triangular strip of land jutting out into the Humber Estuary at its convergence with the River Hull. Like so many boat building and repair yards in the UK it fell into disuse until The Deep was built on the site. Opened in 2002 the major award winning visitor attraction, with a claim to be the world's only submarium, had attracted millions of visitors over the previous decade or so.

On this particular dank autumnal evening, the last of the day's visitors had left the attraction and were now exiting the car parks. The exterior of the unique building was partially illuminated by the ambient lighting around the walkways and the blue gel spotlights which shone high up on the aluminium tiled super structure of the uniquely shaped building. Across the river tourist lingered in the Nelson Street Gardens to admire the architecture of the sparkling jewel rising towards the dark night sky like the bow of a leviathan vessel. The reflection of the illuminated building painted the murky water of the estuary, merging with the luminescence of the glittering red and green signal lamps on the jetties to form a rippling impressionist canvas.

Inside The Deep an army of cleaners was swinging into action to prepare the interior for the hordes that would descend the following day. Rails were being polished; glass cleaned; litter collected. Catering staff were setting out the tables for the Two Rivers Restaurant alongside the viewing windows for the 'Endless Ocean' display. The display was one of the attractions major exhibits; a colossal, floor to ceiling, circular glass tank representing the ocean with all manner of sea-life represented. Located in an area normally swarming with visitors the restaurant opened only on Friday and Saturday evenings; this Friday, like most Fridays, it was fully booked.

Ironically diners could enjoy their seared tuna or Seafood Linguini whilst watching live sharks, green swordfish and giant rays amongst the hundreds of other sea dwellers swimming around in the specially constructed giant tank. Understandably most sensitive diners forwent the Chef's Catch of The Day choice opting instead for the non-swimming hors d'oeuvre and mains.

The three waitresses had decided that the lone diner at table four had been stood up. The table laid for two had been booked two weeks in advance so he must have been expecting a guest to join him. Their conjecture was that it was an internet date that had not materialised. Not that the waitresses were surprised; he wasn't exactly God's gift; patently wearing an ill-fitting toupee and possessing a shark fin of a nose. He checked his watch frequently and fidgeted with nervous anticipation.

'Can I get you something to drink while you're waiting.' asked one of the three young waitresses on duty, according to her badge she had been christened Cheryl. Not that the diner noticed, his eyes were fixed on the menu.

'Sparkling mineral water, please,' he replied. 'Could I order?'

'You don't want to wait for your guest?'

'No. I'll order for myself if that's okay.'

'Your guest can always....'

17

'There won't be a guest,' he said abruptly. Cheryl wasn't to know that there had never been a guest attending. The non-showing date never existed; their conjecture had been well wide of the mark.

Cheryl returned to the waitresses' station with his order. 'Table four's definitely been stood up,' she whispered softly to her colleagues.

'Not surprised he looks a right saddo.'

'Perhaps his cheque bounced at the escort agency,' they giggled.

'She probably got a whiff of his aftershave it's that new one from Lavatory Garnier; Eau de Mestos.' They giggled again.

Saddo was unaware of their fun at his expense. He seemed transfixed on the inhabitants of the tank. A small shoal of Bluefin tuna swept past; the rhythmic oscillations of a three metre long Moray eel fascinated him as it weaved between the rocks representing the ocean bed. The hideous ugliness of an Anglerfish caught his eye as he mused how lonely it must be; the Joseph Merrick of the sea floor. He consumed his Chicken and Bacon Terrine followed by an eight ounce blue fillet steak with Jack Daniels sauce. The fish continued to swim past as if on a continuous loop, reappearing frequently on the same glide path. In different circumstances it would have been a soothing experience akin to watching a tank of tropical fish in a dentist's waiting room.

Another small, slim, blond waitress in her late teens approached his table to clear the mains plate. Her badge read Emily.

'Everything okay for you?' she asked with well-practiced politeness; trying hard not to show her fixation with his toupee.

'Yes fine, thanks.' The word thanks disappeared into his napkin as he wiped the bourbon sauce from around his mouth.

'Can I get you some desert?'

'What do you recommend?' he asked.

'The Tangy Lemon and Lime Tart is very nice or the Sticky Toffee pudding.' said Emily still unable to divert her gaze from his hairpiece.

The tart sounds good, thanks'

'Would you like cream or ice cream with that?'

'Cream.'

'Okay coming right up.' She turned her back to him and gurned in the direction of her fellow waitresses standing at the serving point. It was a well- practiced grimace usually applied by the three girls to no-hopers who tried to pick them up in nightclubs.

'Oh, excuse me,' he said. 'Could you point me in the direction of the toilets?'

She turned back and simultaneously morphed the look of disgust into one of enforced pleasure. 'Sure, just bear left at the steel column and it's on your right just before you get to the entrance.'

'Thanks. Is it alright if I leave my things here?' he indicated the rucksack under the table and his coat draped over the vacant chair.

'Sure, I'll keep an eye on them for you.'

He smiled to show appreciation. Leaving his padded jacket and his rucksack where they were, he walked towards the toilets went straight past them and out of the exit door. He walked quickly past the main entrance and turned left over the short footbridge across the River Hull; then left again along the footpath into Nelson Street Gardens by the side of Hull's, somewhat ambitiously named World Trade Centre. In the distance the silhouette of the Humber Bridge was visible against the last throes of the evening light. It took less than three minutes before he was mingling with the few remaining sightseers; he leaned on the guard rail; looked back across the river to The Deep, switched on his mobile phone and pressed the speed dial button.

In the Two Rivers restaurant the young Emily delivered the Tangy Lemon and Lime Tart to vacant table four. It was the last thing she ever did. The mobile phone in the rucksack connected, simultaneously triggering the detonator attached to the bomb. The device exploded with such ferocity that young Emily's life ended in a nanosecond; she literally disintegrated, kibbled. The intense force shattered the three inch thick plate glass walls of the submarium despatching a bore of two and a half million litres of salty water, roaring through the temporary restaurant; like a mining hush devouring all before it. The third waitress was speared through the neck by a fourteen inch wedge of table before being swept along in the tidal wave; diners she had been serving were sliced open by shards of three inch thick plated glass; several died instantly. Others, some with missing limbs were washed away by the tidal wave; choking and screaming hysterically as water filled their lungs. Giant rays, jelly fish and other deep sea creatures were swept along with the unrelenting torrent barrelling through the corridors. The power failed, plunging the chaos into darkness; save for the low level illumination of the ceiling mounted safety lights; casting a moon like glow over the pandemonium.

The impatient, angry river rushed along sluicing around bends, demolishing displays until it hit the main glass entrance doors, straining against the sheer weight of the tidal force; a wave backed up, turning direction and swirling around the gift shop. The water found its own level; turning the entire ground floor into an impromptu aquarium. Panicking swimmers hauled themselves onto display cabinets, clambered onto exhibits and counters to get their bleeding limbs away from the blood thirsty sharks. They were not in the state of mind where they could reason that the fish would not

20

harm them; these were not Great Whites or Piranhas – their ferocious appearance belied their passive nature. No longer able to dam the water, the main doors finally breached under the weight of pressure; a tsunami burst out of the building, across the almost vacant car park; sweeping the few parked cars before it and uprooting the ornamental trees.

Almost as suddenly as the furore had started a quiet calm descended for a moment; then shock set in, followed immediately by the realisation of what had happened. Those that could, started to scream hysterically at the sight of missing limbs, crying out in pain; others sobbed with fear. Slowly as the water level dissipated, floundering fish, flapped wildly, fighting for oxygen; bodies and flotsam lay in pools. The scene resembled that of the aftermath of a tropical storm.

The catastrophe had taken less than four minutes to unfold; the consequences, for the victims, would last a lifetime.

Three

It would take several hours before the police would be able to confirm that five innocent diners and two young part-time waitresses, with their whole lives ahead of them, had died that night.

Pullman and his team had been on the scene for a little over an hour during which time he was able to do little more than assess the extent of the chaos. An initial examination by gas engineers together with a forensic officer had determined that the devastation had not been caused by a gas explosion; meaning that it was likely to have been caused by an explosive device of some sort.

Pullman knew he needed to give a statement to the media circus outside. It was his least favourite part of the job. He stepped out to face the clambering wolf pack. Microphones were being thrust into his face from all directions and heights. Camera flashes were strobing the scene. TV cameras took pole position. A fleet of ambulances and police vehicles congested the road outside the stricken building; four fire tenders were in attendance; flashing blue lights reflected all around. Pullman took his reluctant presidential stance in front of the assembled journalists.

'I can confirm that an explosion occurred at approximately eight fourteen tonight.' His tone was sombre and matter of fact. 'There have been a number of fatalities and several people have been taken to Hull Royal Infirmary, some with severe injuries. We have not yet established the cause of the explosion. We hope to be able to issue a further statement at nine o'clock tomorrow morning. Until then there is nothing more I can tell you.'

'Chief Inspector can you tell us if it was a terrorist attack.'

'No.'

'No it wasn't or no you won't tell us?'

'No I *can't* tell you because we don't know yet.'

'BBC, Inspector Pullman, we understand that thousands of fish have perished. Is that correct?'

'Yes.'

'Do you know the names of the casualties?' asked ITV.

He wanted to say that Nemo and Willy weren't amongst them but he wasn't doing stand-up so kept it straight. 'No. We are trying to establish identities so that the next of kin can be informed. This will be done before any names are released to the media.'

First of all they had to find the fatalities and match the jigsaw of body parts. They would check the computerised booking system for the names of diners then cross reference that with the names of the living but there was no guarantee that everyone who booked had turned up; or that someone hadn't wandered off into the night concussed. The pathologist and the mortuary staff had a busy time ahead of them.

'Do you have any suspects Chief Inspector?'

Pullman took a deep breath to compose himself. He detested having to deal with the media; he had just told these morons that he didn't know the cause of the explosion and they ask him if he has a suspect.

'We don't know yet if a crime has been committed so we would hardly have a suspect would we. That's all for now, thank you. We'll hopefully know more at nine o'clock tomorrow morning.' He turned away from the throng and re-entered the building.

The fire service officers were in the last throes of pumping out the residual water, straight over the embankment into the river Hull. Distraught staff estimated that ninety percent of the fish had perished or were in the process of doing so. The remainder they had managed to re-house in the smaller coral tank exhibit and other vacant tanks in the quarantine, acclimatisation and breeding sections.

The police forensic team were preparing to examine the scene and gather evidence. It would be a painstaking process and unlikely that they would have definitive answers any time soon. At this early stage there seemed no doubt the explosion was the result of a bomb having been detonated.

John Hansen the senior Forensic Scene Investigator beckoned Pullman over to the centre of the action. Pullman stepped carefully between the carcasses of stranded fish as he answered the summons.

'We're going to need to call in a bomb expert on this one. I can handle things up to a point but I'm already thinking that this will be pushing my expertise to the limit.'

'Anyone in mind?'

'I have as it happens. James Jamieson he's professor of chemical engineering here at Hull Uni. I've met him a few times; he's written several papers on explosives and their criminal uses. He was called in to look at the bombings at Catterick Army base a couple of years ago and the explosions up at the ICI chemicals plant in Redcar.'

'Okay, I'll see what the boss has to say. I presume he'll want paying.'

'Who doesn't?'

'Are you sure it was a bomb?' Hansen said he was pretty sure. Pullman called Pauline Crompton at home; she was just preparing to leave the house having been informed of the incident. He filled her in on the situation and requested the services of Professor James Jamieson. To his great surprise the Chief Constable agreed immediately and said that she would take care of it personally.

The blast had devastated the entire restaurant area; just the rubble of a war zone endured. The viewing window was completely gone along with all but a small remnant of the walls on either side of the epicentre. Shallow pools of water inside the tank were alive with flapping fish desperately fighting to extract oxygen from the remaining brine. A gaping chasm where the laminated floor had been exposed the basement below. The furniture was little more than kindling.

Water stained displays and interactive exhibits throughout the ground floor were ruined. The attraction would not be a magnet for anyone, except the curious, for several weeks or possibly months. As a charity it would need more lottery funding or a successful public appeal to raise restoration funds.

The only available witness to the event was a waitress who had wandered into the kitchen at the moment of the explosion. The aluminium swing doors of the kitchen were buckled and hanging from their hinges, having absorbed most of the impact, protecting the kitchen staff in the process.

DS Sperring walked across to Pullman with the waitress in tow. The young girl, dressed in a black blouse and skirt over which hung a short white apron with frills around the edges, was clearly distraught. Tears mixed with black mascara trickled from reddened eyes, flowed down her cheeks and pooled below her chin.

'Sir this is Cheryl Baines one of the waitresses.'

'Hi, I'm DCI Pullman are you sure you're okay?' he was genuinely concerned.

'Yes I think so. I didn't get injured or anything. I just can't believe that....'

'Yes I'm very sorry about your friends.'

'Em was my *best* friend since nursery school.' Her tears flowed faster.

Sperring comforted her as best she could and said to Pullman. 'Her name was Emily Taylor 18 years of age. The other girl was Nishtha Khumari. Cheryl and Emily are from the area but Nishtha comes from the Midland's. I've got the addresses. They'd all just started their first semester at Uni.'

Pullman nodded. 'If you don't feel like talking we can do this tomorrow.'

'I'll try.'

'Do you remember seeing anything suspicious; an unattended bag or package of any kind?'

'No, nothing like that.'

'Anything strange; out of the ordinary?

'Well the saddo was a bit strange.'

'The saddo?'

'We reckon he'd been stood up. He just looked odd. Wore a naff hairpiece and he had a nose like Adrien Brody.' She choked. 'I'm sorry.'

'That's okay, take your time. Can I get you a cup of tea or something?' asked Sperring comforting her again.

Cheryl shook her head she took a deep breath in an effort to compose herself.

Pullman had no idea who Adrian Brody was or what his nose looked like; he could be a friend of the girl but more likely he was a pop star or an actor. Sperring probably knew but rather than ask, he made a mental note to look up an image on his smart phone a bit later. He thought he'd push the young woman's composure with one more question. 'Did he have anything with him, a bag or...?'

'A rucksack; it was dark, black I think'.

The colour was immaterial there wouldn't be much of it left now. Pullman didn't think there was anything to be gained by asking for any more descriptive features for the time being. The strange man's hairpiece would make that pointless; it would no doubt by now be gracing a polystyrene wig stand. He guessed the distinctive nose would be back in the putty jar.

Cheryl's dad arrived along with Emily Taylor's parents. Mr Baines was relieved to see his daughter. He put his arms around her.

'Where's Emily?' cried Mrs Taylor the anguish spreading across her drained face. 'Cher where's Em?'

Cheryl sobbed uncontrollably and hugged her best friend's mother. Mrs Taylor realised the significance of Cheryl's inability to answer her.

'Oh dear god no. Please no.' Despite being a generation apart the two women cried together.

Mr Taylor stood alone, head bowed, lips quivering. He knew he'd lost his only child. 'Can we see her?' he asked quietly.

How do you tell a parent that there was nothing to see, their daughter was virtually vaporised; not even sufficient pieces to form a human jigsaw; there would be no remains to bury. Pullman didn't know the answer. It fleetingly crossed his mind to tell them that she would have felt no pain, known nothing about it but he didn't think the words would comfort them. No words had comforted him in his hour of need. He knew only too well how they were feeling. The sense of loss. The numbness. He didn't have the words to ease the pain so he ignored the father's question. Instead he took them to a seating area that had escaped damage and arranged for tea to

27

be brought to them. He would leave the reality of the situation to the bereavement counsellor.

Sperring spoke to Mr Baines. 'I think Cheryl ought to go to the RI for a check-up. It doesn't look as if she was injured but you can't be too careful.'

'If it's all the same to you I'll take her home and if there's any problem I'll whip her down to A&E. It must be chaos down there at the moment; you normally have to wait hours anyway with this going on we'd be there all night.'

'Okay that's up to you.'

Half an hour later Cheryl and her father said goodbye to the Taylors and made to leave. As the sole surviving waitress passed Pullman she stopped, turned back and said, 'Don't know if this means anything but Emily said the customer smelt of bleach. Made a joke about it, said he must live in the same care home as her Nan.' She shrugged, turned and walked away with her head resting on her dad's shoulder and his arm around hers.

The Taylors sat in silent grief, comforting one another.

Nishtha Khumari's body was assumed to have been found. The corpse of a young Asian girl wearing the same waitress uniform left little doubt. The wooden stake had sliced through the vertebra in her neck and the blast had severed her lower left arm and most of her thigh.

Pauline Crompton called Pullman back on his mobile to tell him that Jamieson would be there by 10.30 that night. She had said the morning would do but despite the late hour he was keen on seeing the scene immediately. She, herself would be there in around twenty minutes, the car was on its way to her. Pullman checked his watch it was just before 9.30pm.

The kitchen staff were very kindly making tea and sandwiches for the hardworking emergency service personnel, he figured that it

28

included him and his DS so he left a member of the submarium staff with the grieving couple, while he and Sperring availed themselves of the hospitality and waited for Jamieson to get there from Beverley.

The Chief Constable arrived at 9.50 pm. Pullman took her around the scene. There wasn't a lot she could do but she hung on until the professor duly arrived at 10.20. He was younger and taller than Pullman had envisaged. There was no logical reason why he had imagined the academic would be in his seventies, five foot seven with Einstein hair; in reality he was about the same age as Pullman; possibly late forties max, six feet tall and well-groomed in his casual shirt and brown leather bomber jacket.

Pauline Crompton greeted him and after introductions to Pullman, Sperring and Hansen; he set about wandering through the debris, observing the scene and recording photographs on a very compact camera. The police personnel left him in peace for ten minutes then curiosity got the better of them. Crompton and Pullman walked over to Jamieson who was busily engaged in collecting fragments of material from the debris.

'Any thoughts?' asked Crompton.

'Definitely a bomb. There's no gas service in the immediate area so we can rule that out. Pretty powerful too as we can see,' he said indicating the crater, 'probably bigger than it needed to be considering it was such a confined space.'

DS Sperring joined them.

'Depends what the intention was,' said Pullman. 'Any clues to what was used?'

'Not yet probably Semtex but it could have been home made. You can get all you need to know off the internet these days.'

'Apparently there was a guy sitting in the epicentre who smelled of bleach. Is that significant?'

'Really,' he thought for a moment. 'That's a possibility,' said Jamieson. His brow furrowed as he looked around consumed in thought.

'What's a possibility?'

'Acetone peroxide,' he pinched his nostrils and rubbed the tip of his nose in a professorial gesture. 'An organic peroxide and highly explosive; it's a white crystalline powder with a distinctive odour of bleach.'

'Could he have got hold of that?' asked Crompton.

'No problem. It was widely used by terrorists a few years back; maybe it still is. Triacetone triperoxide or TATP for short is one of the few high explosives that doesn't contain nitrogen so it became a staple with terrorists; they used because it could fool security scanners designed to detect nitrogenous explosives.'

'So this TATP is common place.' said Pullman.

'I wouldn't exactly say common place. You can't get it in the local supermarket or on EBay but it's quite easy to make and relatively cheap. It's known to have been used in numerous suicide bombings in the Middle East over the past few years. It was used in London car bombs. You'll remember Richard Reid who was dubbed the shoe bomber – the guy who tried to light a fuse in his shoe on a plane – he used TATP. The seven-seven bombings in London were implemented with the same home-made explosive. It's believed that the four perpetrators had something like ten pounds of the stuff between them, enough to have killed fifty-two people and injured hundreds more.'

'So, if it was this guy who smelled of bleach, he could have had enough in his rucksack to have done this.' It was more of a statement than a question from Pullman.

'Way more than enough, a couple of pounds would be plenty.'

Sperring was perplexed. 'Why would a suicide bomber want to blow up a fish tank?'

'Assuming he did commit suicide,' said Pullman. He could have just planted the bomb. We can't be sure either way.'

'He'd have had to be careful though, it's notoriously unstable stuff. Some terrorist groups nicknamed it the Mother of Satan after one or two of them accidently blew themselves up while making their devices.'

'Shame,' said Pullman. Crompton gave him a sideways glance.

'To be frank,' said Jamieson, 'it's unlikely we'll find much of the bomb to analyse; your forensic boys are collecting plenty of samples so if I can get those and mine back to the university I can carry out chromatography and spectrometry tests to see if TATP was the explosive used.'

'Tomorrow is Saturday professor any chance.....'

'No problem Chief Inspector it's ideal timing, I'll have the place to myself.'

'Thanks, much appreciated. Is there anything more we can do for you here?'

'Not really I've seen all I need to see at this stage so I'll collect the samples and head off.'

Pullman said, 'Nothing more for us to do here either ma'am. We'll collect the security tapes from the manager and then we might as well get back to the office, they'll have set the incident room up by now.'

He said a silent prayer that the Chief Constable wouldn't go back to the incident room with them. His prayer was answered.

Four

Saturday 8th November

Why indeed would a bomber want to blow up a fish tank? That was the big question to be answered. It was 7.30 am on Saturday; the Operation Alligator team was assembled with drinks and bacon sandwiches for those who wanted them. Pullman had personally footed the bill for the refreshments; the force would be footing the bill for the overtime. They had already brainstormed possible reasons for the previous night's bomb attack and had written a list of potential motives on the incident room wipe board.

'Right then,' said Pullman, 'Let's see if we can determine a possible motive and then we can decide on a course of action and allocate tasks as we go. First:

Did he just hate fish?

Sounds crazy I know but it never ceases to amaze me what cranks will take a dislike to but it's a hell of an elaborate method of taking revenge against the creatures whatever he thinks they did to him. We'll leave that aside for the moment.'

'Perhaps he suffered from ichthyophobia sir' said a uniformed PC with a look of embarrassment upon realising that he had interrupted the briefing.

Pullman looked at the young man. 'Itchy what? He asked.

'Ichthyophobia; the fear of fish sir' the PC replied sheepishly. As a lonely only child largely ignored by his parents he had amused himself by memorising phobias by heart; he also knew all the collective nouns for animals and people.

'I really don't think he was afraid of fish; he was sitting there watching the things swim past him; even sharks.'

'That's galeophobia sir.'

'What is?'

'The fear of sharks,' he replied

'As much as I appreciate the lesson on phobias young man we'll crack on; if that's okay with you.' The young PC looked down at his feet and nodded; right now he wished that a convocation of eagles would swoop down and carry him off.

Pauline Crompton and Iain Thwaite, the ACC, joined the meeting. They stood at the rear of the room to observe proceedings. Pullman acknowledged their arrival with a nod, he knew they wouldn't interfere. Crompton gestured to Pullman to ignore them and carry on. He was going to do so anyway.

'Was he an animal liberationist?

Could be; maybe he had some misguided thought that freeing them from captivity was a humane thing to do but all that did was succeed in killing thousands of fish – a form of liberation I suppose but anyone with any sense would have thought that through and would have seen the flaw. Mind you, the idiots that freed the wild minks a few years ago didn't think it through either.

Did he have a grudge against The Deep?

The most likely motive at this stage.'

Pullman looked at DC Ashley Sharpe. The fresh faced young man who had, until two weeks ago, been in uniform and looked five years younger than his twenty-fifth birthday would suggest. Olive toned skin gave him a Mediterranean look belying his mixed race Anglo-Caribbean parentage. He was keen to make an impression within the team. Pullman saw much of his younger self in the new recruit so wanted to do all he could to encourage Sharpe's raw enthusiasm.

'Ash as soon as we've finished here get a list of all staff who have left or been dismissed from the Deep. Go back as far as the opening, if they have the records. See if there are any obvious candidates amongst them.' It was an uncomplicated task that wouldn't present the novice detective with too many obstacles. 'Lynne first thing Monday morning you take a look at anyone involved in the development of the site for the same thing architects, construction firms, previous owners of the land you know the drill.'

He returned to addressing the entire gathering.

'We'll check back through the press at the time to see if there were any outspoken critics of the scheme amongst the public or anyone on the council opposed to the planning decision etcetera.'

Pullman glanced back at the wipe board to prompt him on the next point.

'Targeted murder?

Was the bombing carried out to cover the murder of one person? It's happened before so it's a possibility. The perpetrator could have carried out the attack to kill one specific person with everyone else being collateral, to cover the motive. What would be disguised as mass murder could in fact be a targeted killing. Steph do a background check on all the diners, deceased or not and see what it throws up.'

Detective Constable Stephanie Barnes nodded understanding. Unlike Lynne Sperring she was not so particular about her appearance; she had a hair style that needed little attention, wore no make-up but she didn't really need to; she had a natural, inherent beauty that didn't require embellishing and she dressed comfortably in ordinary chain store clothing. Pullman did not concern himself with her lack of cat-walk elegance only that she was dedicated to the job; so dedicated in fact that somehow, with

34

the support of her parents, she coped with caring for a recently disabled husband and being the mother of two young children. What Steph lacked in glamour Sperring more than made up for. It was a good balance and surprisingly the two women got on very well.

There was a knock on the meeting room door. Through the inset glass panel Pullman could see a uniformed officer standing outside. He gestured him to enter. The ACC had to stand aside to allow the door to open.

'Yes what is it?' asked Pullman.

'Sorry to interrupt you sir,' he noticed Crompton, 'Ma'am', he nodded towards her then looked at Pullman. 'There's a Corrine Browne outside says it's urgent.... to do with last night.'

Pullman looked at Sperring then at Crompton and Thwaite. Without speaking they all thought *shit it's Claude* or words to similar effect.

'Okay put her in my office I'll be right there. Right everyone, this could change everything so hang fire until I get back to you.'

He went to his office followed by Sperring and the CC and ACC. Corrine Browne was just being shown in.

'Hi Corrine,' said Pullman, 'this is the Chief Constable.' he gestured towards Crompton.

'Yes we've met,' said Browne.

'And this is the Assistant Chief Constable.'

Thwaite smile and said, 'We've met too. How are you Corrine?'

'Fine thanks. We've had a disc from Claude.' She said without further ado. She held up the CD. 'He's claiming responsibility for last night's bomb attack.'

This time Pullman said out loud, 'Shit. '

His laptop was already booted, he opened the CD tray, popped the disc into position closed the tray. He switched on the desk top speakers and turned up the volume.

Claude's voice was electronically disguised as if he was speaking in a reverberation chamber:

It's Claude here. I hope last night's demonstration will help to consolidate people's thoughts. Next time will be a lot more spectacular not that there need be a next time if my modest request is met. I've set up a Facebook page and I've sent you a friend request. I do hope you accept my request. Also I would like to invite Detective Chief Inspector Michael Pullman to be my friend too. I saw him doing the TV interview last night, didn't look as if he was enjoying himself, do assure him that a crime was committed. Also I've tagged him in a photo. I presume that everything is proceeding with the payment. Next Tuesday was just a guideline I'd like the one hundred million tomorrow. I'll let you know the details later today on my timeline. Chief Inspector I know you're busy so I have saved you time by recording this in a soundproof room – so no background noises to analyse. Also as you can tell my voice patterns are synthesised so no clues there either and naturally there are no residual fingerprints. But knowing the police that will not stop you wasting your time and resources trying. So Michael, do accept my friend request. I'll be in touch.

'Well we now know it wasn't a suicide bomber.' Pullman played the disc again. They mulled over the content in silence for a minute. 'I'll need to accept the friend request then and see what this photo is.'

Corrine Browne said, 'It's you outside The Deep talking to the media.'

36

'The bastard was there!' exclaimed Pullman.

'There was no way of knowing,' Crompton said as if excusing Pullman for not spotting Claude amongst the crowd. 'You will get the recording analysed won't you?'

'Of course ma'am if you're approving the budget,' said Pullman. 'But I'm sure we'll find nothing of use. He's been planning this for a long time.'

Crompton nodded approval and agreement to Pullman then said to Corrine Browne. 'Reporting restrictions still apply, has anyone else heard this?'

'My producer but she knows the situation; it won't go any further.'

That seemed to satisfy the Chief Constable. She turned to Pullman. 'Can we get a trace on his internet page?'

'Been there, done that. If he's half as clever as he seems to be then we haven't got a prayer not in the time scale anyway.' Pullman was dreading what was coming next.

'Iain we need to call another meeting straight away; could you organise it please and don't take no for an answer. I don't care if they're on the golf course, shopping or in the bath. We've got twenty-four hours to sort this or he might take more lives.'

Pullman raised his eyes to the ceiling. Yep another bloody meeting he'd have to try to get out of attending. He figured he could drum up a sufficiently logical argument for his omission from the think tank.

Back in the incident room Pullman played the disc to the team.

'So forget the animal lib route and the targeted murder line of enquiry. Now we know it was this bastard and the motive is extortion; should have known really. But I didn't expect any action from him until we failed to meet the deadline or told him where to shove his demand. Stupid.' He smiled inwardly *don't try to second guess me.*

DC Sharpe raised his hand. 'Could we listen to the disc again please sir?'

Pullman didn't see the purpose but agreed. Ashley Sharpe made notes as it played. When it had finished he said, 'I may be wrong sir but I'd say Claude is probably under forty.'

Pullman looked quizzical. 'Because he's using social media,' he said. 'Silver surfers use the net just as much as you younger....'

'No, it's not just that sir it's the way he talks about it. My folks are on Facebook but they never use words like post or timeline and tagging someone in a photo might as well be from Star Trek as far as they're concerned. Also sir, in his original note he used the term disrespect me or something similar, that's a younger person's word as well.'

Pullman understood what his young DC was saying but felt a little insulted that at the age of forty-five his colleague deemed him too old to be Facebook literate. He and Jane were avid users back in the day but he'd closed his account after her death because of too many sympathy messages; he didn't want anything intruding into the protective shell he'd built around himself. In reality he'd just lost interest in life in general.

'Interesting,' said Pullman. 'What do the rest of you think?'

The consensus was that, from their personal experience of family and friends of middle age and above, Ash could be right but that it shouldn't be prescriptive.

Pullman was more interested in why Claude had disguised his voice. Maybe there was something in his tone or accent that was distinguishable; otherwise why do it? It was highly unlikely that anyone would recognise him unless he was well known, perhaps on TV or radio. Just Claude being ultra-careful probably.

38

Pullman checked his watch it was 8.50am, ten minutes before the press conference was due. He looked out of the incident room window and saw the media gathering in the car park. There were three large vans with satellite dishes mounted on the rooves. Sky News had joined the pack along with BBC and ITV. Journalists were scurrying around like ants to a jam pot. Pullman was glad the Chief Constable was taking the chair or in this case, the steps, because the decision had been taken to hold the interview outside the main entrance rather than creating a makeshift press room. It was cold outside so the ladies and gentlemen of the media would not want to dally too long.

Between the CC, the ACC and Pullman, as the investigating officer, they had decided that at they would have preferred to claim that the blast was a gas explosion or that the exact cause was still being investigated; which in fact was true. Jamieson was hopefully at the Uni carrying out his tests on the explosive that very morning. Unfortunately it was too late to withhold all the truth; some of the more eager beavers amongst the national red tops had already invaded the privacy of the Royal Infirmary and harassed some of the injured into making comments. These journalists had already reached the conclusion that it was a bomb. Fortunately those same newshounds had not managed to interview Cheryl Baines, firstly because they had not yet identified her and secondly because even if they had done so Pullman had placed a uniformed officer outside the house. She was the only witness to the event and even though Claude had been heavily disguised he might still want to silence her. Pullman had now seen an image of Adrian Brody and agreed that he did indeed have a very distinct distinguishing feature.

Crompton had insisted that Pullman attend the conference with her and Iain Thwaite. Pullman hung back as she began her statement he was studying the gathering to see if Claude would

39

have the audacity to attend this time; not that he knew who he was looking for. He had also arranged for the gathering to be filmed.

'Good morning to you all. As you are aware there was an explosion at The Deep at 8.14 pm last night Friday the 7th of November in which there were seven fatalities, a further sixteen were injured of which three are critical. Naturally our thoughts and prayers go out to the family and friends of the victims. I can confirm that the cause of the explosion was not a gas leak. We are investigating the cause being an explosive device. We do not yet know the nature of the device used nor do we know the identity or the motive of the perpetrator; if indeed it was a deliberate act.'

Some facts, some fiction.

'We are conducting an ongoing investigation and would ask any member of the public who may have seen anything suspicious, in or around the Deep yesterday, to contact us. Thank you.'

The clamour to ask questions merged into a cacophony of indistinguishable wordage. Crompton raised her hands to shoulder height to quell the onslaught.

'Please one at a time.' She recognised Terry Grantham from BBC's Look North so isolated him to start the ball rolling. 'Terry you have a question?'

Thank you Chief Constable; was this a terrorist attack?'

'We really don't know yet but it is of course one of the lines of enquiry we are pursuing. Next.'

'Was any warning given?' asked a voice from the back row.

'No.' Crompton looked around the crowd inviting the next questioner.

'When will you be releasing the names of the dead and injured?' asked a female wielding a hand held recording device.

'Post mortems are taking place today. Some of the injuries made visual identification difficult. When we have formally identified each victim and informed the next of kin then names will be released.'

'When will that be?'

'We hope to complete that by the end of the day provided that the next of kin are contactable.'

'Is this an isolated incident or the start of a bombing campaign?'

'Naturally we hope that it is an isolated incident but until we have investigated the matter further I'm afraid I cannot rule anything in or rule anything out. I would however ask the public to be extra vigilant and report any unattended packages, bags etcetera or anyone acting suspiciously. The Press Officer will be issuing a dedicated number in due course. Thank you for your time. We will issue a further statement when we have something more to tell you. One final thing; three of my officers are waiting to collect your names, addresses and company details. Please co-operate fully with them. Thank you.' She turned and the three senior officers returned to the relative tranquillity of the police headquarters, leaving the throng frustrated. Smart of her to think about getting the attendees details thought Pullman, although he had not spotted anyone acting suspiciously or looking out of context.

There wasn't a great deal the team could constructively do until they had more to go on. It would be the best part of forty-eight hours before Sperring could speak to the people she needed to in order to access personnel records at the companies involved in the design and construction of the bombed attraction. Now that they had more or less eliminated the targeted murder motive, Pullman re-allocated Sperring's enquiries to DC Barnes which meant Steph could spend the rest of the weekend at home with her family.

Sharpe had managed to get the HR records of the Deep from the manager; neither he nor his staff had left the building since returning after the atrocity. Unfortunately he had only been employed there for seventeen months so could throw no light on the character of anyone who had ceased employment before that time, either voluntarily or otherwise.

The second shift of forensic scientists was still collecting and bagging evidence from the crime scene. So far the team had collected over two and a half thousand exhibits; fragments of the bomb, body parts, cloth fragments and particles of unidentified substances that might hold a clue. A team at the laboratories had commenced the intricate task of examining, analysing and cataloguing the collection. It was a mammoth task and would take days if not weeks to complete.

Pullman had declined the invitation to attend the post mortems. He detested the experience and, despite police procedural requirements, seldom attended the gory events. He admired pathologists for being able to do their job. He also admired brain surgeons but that didn't mean he wanted to observe operations. Not that there was a great deal of difference as far as he was concerned between pathologists and surgeons other than the neatness of their needlework.

He had set up the social media page and had his friend request accepted by Claude; they had now established a live communication channel. The profile picture Claude had used was a line drawing portrait of a man dressed in clothing from the late Middle Ages or early Elizabethan periods, according to Sperring's educated guess, her speciality being Ancient History. The man had a moustache and beard. It definitely wasn't Shakespeare or anyone else that they could recognise. The cover photo area had been left blank. Unsurprisingly he had not entered any personal profile details.

The photo in which Pullman had been tagged by Claude showed the DCI from around fifty metres visible through a sea of heads and hands, waving cameras and microphones. With all the flashes strobing and the television camera lights blinding him there was no way Pullman would have seen beyond the wall of reporters before him.

Pullman contacted Tom Nerbis at the National Crime Agency for advice on locating the source of Claude's Facebook page. He pretty much knew the answer before he asked the question. If Claude was half as proficient as the exponents had been on their previous case then it could take days, maybe weeks to locate him; if they succeeded at all. Chances were that the extortionist was that proficient; Pullman didn't have days or weeks to spare.

Forensics had checked the disc; no fingerprints were detected; they had also conducted an acoustic analysis but had been unable to detect any extraneous sound on the disc. Pullman was not surprised; he was convinced Claude would prove to be a very capable opponent.

The security tapes from The Deep proved pointless. The system was timed to automatically shut down each night when they closed the doors, after the final visitors had departed. The manager was unaware that this was the customary practice. He immediately issued instructions for the security CCTV to be operational twenty-four-seven.

Pullman made sure the tapes were checked from Friday lunchtime just in case the perpetrator had secreted himself earlier in the day. He hadn't.

The think tank was scheduled for 11.30am sharp at Priory Road. Crompton insisted that Pullman attend despite his counter arguments.

Pullman left the team to continue with the designated lines of enquiry and in addition set them two questions to ponder: apart from being a shed load of money could there be any significance in the demand being one hundred million dollars? Why target Hull?

Pullman had already reached his own hypothesis on the first question.

Five

Crompton called the third meeting of the whatif think tank to order. They discussed the terrible events of the previous night before playing the Claude disc.

Frank Delaney spoke. 'I am sure that I do not need to remind this meeting that we are in the delicate process of bidding to become the UK City of Culture for two thousand and seventeen. I cannot stress enough that we must keep this lunatic's actions under wraps. We're only six days away from the presentation in Derry; if word gets out that we have a maniac on the loose it would scupper our chances. It means millions to the City's economy.'

Crompton replied, 'We are all well aware of the bid Frank and what it means to the city. Perhaps the extortionist does too, which maybe the reason behind the timing of his actions and the enormity of his demand.'

'Well he's got that wrong for starters. We'll be lucky to boost the local economy by eighty-five million so a hundred is way over the top. Nevertheless we've got to stop him.'

'Mike what do you think?' Crompton asked Pullman.

Pullman sat up, leaned forward and rested his overlapping arms on the table. 'I think he's taking the piss,' he said. 'He's playing a game. He enjoys the killing and I don't think it will be the last, whatever this meeting decides to do about acceding to his demand. He booked the table at The Deep two weeks ago; the explosion was almost certainly planned a long time before that. He gave no

45

warning; did not wait to see if we were going to comply, just went ahead and killed seven people. For fun. The guy is a psychopath. I don't think he even wants the hundred mill. He knows we won't or can't pay, which is why he's set it so high. He just wants an excuse to kill more people. He wants someone to blame for his actions so in his twisted mind it wasn't his fault, it was our fault for not complying with the demand. In his mind we will be responsible not him; we gave him no choice.'

Crompton took a deep breath. 'So you think Claude expects us not to pay.'

'Yes ma'am.'

Delaney said. 'Well he's bloody well got that right.'

Iain Thwaite said, 'Do you think we should bring in a profiler?'

'I don't think it would do any harm sir,' replied Pullman. He didn't think it would do much good either but they had nothing to lose. He wasn't a trained profiler himself, just an experienced copper so maybe an expert would spot some character flaw that they could work on. 'A trained psychologist might be able to see some characteristic that we can use to negotiate with the guy, not that I necessarily believe he wants to negotiate,' he added

'You think he just wants to kill,' said Iain Thwaite.

'Yep.'

Crompton said, 'If you're right Mike then whatever we decide here isn't going to make any difference but if you're wrong and we haven't made a decision, we could provoke further bombings.' Pullman nodded. Crompton continued, 'So I think we should decide how we can meet the demand so that we're in a position to effectively stall any further action by being seen to be in a position to comply.'

Frank Delaney spoke up. 'With respect Chief Constable, There's no way on this earth that we can raise one hundred million pounds. As the leader of the council, I can assure you that we couldn't raise a hundred thousand let alone a hundred million.'

'I'm not saying we need to raise it, just to look as if we have or look as if we can raise it, given more time. The alternative is we tell him to go to hell in which case he will probably take a lot more innocent members of the public with him.'

The Police and Crime Commissioner said, 'Whatever happens, the people of Hull must be protected, that is our primary concern.'

'Perhaps the PCC would like to write a cheque out, payable to this Claude character, for a hundred million,' said Frank Delaney. 'That'll solve the problem and make sure the Commissioner gets re-elected next year.'

'All I'm saying is that the public have a right to expect protection from...'

Delaney slapped his palm down on the table. 'Oh get off your soap box you.....'

Crompton cut in. 'Gentlemen please,' she said firmly. 'This is getting us nowhere.' Pullman nodded agreement without thinking.

The Lady Mayoress joined in. 'Could we not contact the Home Secretary, explain the situation and ask the government for the money or at least access to it?'

'I'm afraid not Muriel. Our guidelines are quite clearly defined. We cannot, under any circumstances acquiesce to ransom demands at any time, home or abroad. There is no point in even asking the question and certainly no point in asking for financial assistance.'

'Then if you don't mind me asking, what the bloody hell are we discussing this for then,' said Frank Delaney. Pullman involuntarily shrugged. Delaney said. 'We haven't got, nor can we raise, the money so I suggest, with all due respect, that you concentrate your time and efforts on catching the bastard, scuse my French,' he added turning his head in Muriel's direction. He'd still

47

got the back nine to play and it got dark earlier since the clocks went back.

There was a knock on the meeting room door; Sperring entered without waiting for permission. She was carrying an open laptop which she placed down in front of Pullman. 'Excuse me but I thought you ought to see this immediately, it effects your discussions.'

The laptop was displaying Claude's Facebook page. There was a message for Mike. Crompton and Thwaite crowded around the device.

Mike I am bored. Transfer the 100 mil to this IBAN by 3pm
Zurich Nationale CH-ZX-77965-JKM-7410-VLP

'Jesus! exclaimed Pullman. 'That's less than an hour. This guy is seriously deranged. Like I said, he knows we can't meet this deadline even if we wanted to. Christ the bastard is going to explode another bomb for the fun of it. He's going to kill people cos he's bored.'

Pullman typed a comment in response:

Claude my friend you know we can't meet this timing. Be reasonable. We're working on it but it's the weekend. Banking system is shut down. We need until they open again on Monday morning. Work with us on this. Please. We're doing all we can.

Pullman was trying to put the ball back in Claude's court. If he didn't give them reasonable time he was taking responsibility for his actions and couldn't blame them. Pullman was hoping he'd correctly read the maniac's mind, if not he was in danger of pissing him off even more.

Within a minute Claude responded.

Oh Mike you don't understand do you – I no longer take orders, now I'm giving the orders. If I say jump you jump. You people have to learn to do as you are told.

48

Crompton said. 'We have to stop him.'

No shit Sherlock. Pullman closed the laptop. 'He's completely irrational. It's not easy to deal with insanity on this level, whatever we do or say he will kill again, almost certainly today; the money is a red herring. He's just pure evil.'

'Let's think where he might hit next,' said ACC Thwaite.

He walked to the white board and wrote KC Stadium. 'Let's make a quick list and look at the vulnerability of each one. Just call out anything you can think of.'

They all started shouting out potential targets at the same time.

'Whoa, one at a time please,' said Thwaite.

KC Stadium

Airport

Princess Quay Shopping Centre

Hull Truck Theatre

Hull New Theatre

St Stephens Centre

Hull University

Within a few minutes the list had grown to thirty-one possible venues; ranging from the twenty-five thousand seat capacity of the KC Stadium to the four hundred and fifty seats at the Hull Truck theatre.

ACC Thwaite commented. 'There's no way on earth we can cover that lot and that's assuming he'd target one of those anyway.'

Pauline Crompton said, 'There's not enough time to draft in extra officers from other forces.'

Peter Monkton said. 'All you can do is utilise the resources you have at your disposal to patrol the main possibilities and keep an eye out for him.'

Crompton had not missed the fact the PCC was clearly distancing himself from the operation by saying 'you' and not 'we' as he usually did when things were going well.

'How do you suggest we keep an eye out for a ghost Peter?' asked Pullman. 'We have no idea what this lunatic looks like. Besides if he intends to commit another atrocity I would venture to suggest that he has already set it in motion.'

'I agree,' said Crompton, 'He clearly intended to carry out another bombing regardless of whether or not we complied with his demand. I've come round to your way of thinking Chief Inspector; this is not about the money, he has an ulterior motive for this terror.'

'I would only add one thing to that ma'am and that is, it may be wrong to presume that because his first two attacks were bombings, assuming that the houses in Preston Road were his work, that explosives are his MO. Unfortunately we need another incident before we can be sure that bombing is his preferred method.'

'What are you suggesting?'

'I don't know ma'am; a shooting rampage, arson, mass poisoning.'

'Oh, wonderful,' said Crompton.

'Would you excuse me please?' asked Pullman.

'We really do need to focus on this.'

'Comfort break,' he said. The Chief Constable would not be able to argue with that. She didn't.

Nature wasn't calling but he desperately needed to shut his mind to the general debate going on in the conference room. How he would prefer to be in his own office where he could think in solitude. He went to the gents toilets and locked himself inside the first cubicle, lowered the oak laminated lid on the pan and sat down. It wasn't the most comfortable of chairs but it would suffice for this purpose. There was something important that he was missing. He covered his eyes and face with the palms of his hands to concentrate his cognitive power through the ensuing darkness. When he closed his eyes he could see. It was as if he could penetrate through his hands to a focal point beyond. It worked. The time was the key. Three pm. Claude had set the deadline for three pm and whatever the City's response to his demand he intended for something to happen then.

What would happen at three o'clock? The match between Hull City and Liverpool at the KC stadium wasn't being televised live, so would kick off at three pm sharp. Pullman could envisage the referee checking his watch before he blew his whistle as Claude simultaneously blew up the West Stand. Then the words *I will surprise you* scrolled across his mind. The KC was far too predictable; an obvious target that could definitely be anticipated.

It was the rugby league closed season so there was no game at Craven Park; that wouldn't be expected but what would be the point in demolishing an empty stadium. Not enough fun for Claude he suspected. Train; there was probably a three o'clock train leaving Hull station that would be up Claude's street or the airport – was there a flight due to depart then or the coach station or the Ferry port? He checked his watch 2.37pm just twenty-three minutes to the deadline.

He rushed back the conference room. The meeting had broken up into small conclaves.

'Ma'am,' called Pullman as he scurried across the room. 'We need to evacuate the rail station, coach terminal the airport the ferry docks everywhere that could have a three pm departure right now. Three is the key.'

Muriel Hudson said, 'It certainly is, I should be attending my niece's wedding at three. She's going to be very disappointed that I'm not there.'

Pullman and Crompton looked at each other; their eyes met in joint recognition. 'Why didn't you mention this earlier? asked Crompton.

'One's civic duties come before private interests.'

That was a debate for another day. 'Who would know about the wedding?' demanded Pullman.

'The family and friends of course, it was announced in the paper so I don't know who else.'

'Where's it taking place?' urged Pullman.

The penny dropped. Muriel rose to her feet 'You don't think,' she didn't finish the sentence. Her voice was silenced by panic.

'Where? Where's the wedding?' demanded Pullman again.

Muriel was hyperventilating 'Holy Trinity.'

Every sinew in Pullman's body was telling him the church was the target. 'Lynne get uniform over there right now clear the church, clear the area for two hundred metres in every direction and divert traffic. They've got nineteen minutes.'

It was a huge gamble on Pullman's part. If he was wrong then the consequences didn't bear thinking about. Realistically they would never have been able to deal with all the other possibilities in the time so the long shot was the best chance they had of averting disaster. Claude's grievance seemed to be against the City, so what better target than the Lady Mayoress. He couldn't have known that she would be in a meeting discussing him instead of being in the wedding party.

'Mrs Hudson do you have the mobile telephone number of your niece or one of her parents, or anyone else who might be in the congregation?'

'My husband should be there by now.'

'Call him and tell him to get everyone out of the church right now, no ifs or buts, now. Tell him that there's a suspected gas leak say the police are on the way.'

Muriel Hudson complied immediately. Her husband had just gone back to his car get his camera he had left in the glove compartment; fortunately he still had his mobile switched on. He took a little convincing but he could feel the tension in his wife's voice.

Crompton said, 'I'll alert the bomb squad and we'll try and evacuate other public places as best we can in the time'

'Okay ma'am but I don't think they've got a snowball's of getting there in time to disarm any device, even if we could find its location; zero casualties is the best outcome we can hope for now.'

She called them anyway; everything possible had to be seen to be done.

'Can you keep behind the uniforms sir,' he barked at Thwaite. 'Sperring and I will get over there,' he didn't wait for an answer.

Pullman and Sperring were still en route when the gilt minute hand of the clock on the Norman tower of Holy Trinity clicked to a vertical position; the bell struck the first of three chimes to signify the time. The second note was drowned out by the explosion that ripped through the seven hundred years old place of worship; arched columns supporting the vaulted ceiling collapsed like ten pins on an alley. Row upon row of oak pews disintegrated, obliterating Richard Thompson's mouse carvings and erasing irreplaceable medieval figures; stained glass windows shattered as they had done, a hundred years before, with the blast of bombs dropped from a First World War Zeppelin. Hundreds of the four thousand pipes on the country's biggest parish organ were tangled beyond repair and the priceless font that had carried christening water for seven centuries would carry no more. In a matter of seconds the stunning interior of the largest parish church in England had been reduced to rubble.

From two hundred metres away the evacuated congregation watched in horror as palls of smoke and dust rose into the air and billowed out of the open doors. They'd needed a lot more persuasive power than John Hudson possessed before they would abandon the special day and vacate the church. It took the police to finally persuade the groom and best man to leave; which eventually they did with less than two minutes to spare. The bride comforted by her husband-to-be, wept tears for what might have been; her mother wept for her daughter's sorrow. There had been no loss of life; no injuries.

Claude was going to be severely pissed off.

Six

The unofficial police line was that the blast had been caused by a gas leak. It had been a bad week for the corporate reputation of British Gas. Nevertheless they co-operated for a second time, arranging for their engineers to place signs and warning hurdles around the exterior of the church. All religious services were suspended.

Officially Pullman now knew they were dealing with a mass murderer and not a straight forward extortionist. They had thwarted him on this occasion but the repercussions could be catastrophic. The big question now was whether Claude would revert to his original pretence of the Armistice Day deadline or would he now extend his reign of terror beyond next Tuesday if he wasn't stopped.

When Pullman returned to the incident room he was greeted by DC Barnes, 'Professor Jamieson called; could you call him on his mobile.' She handed him the number on a scrap of paper. 'Also Mr Baines called on behalf of his daughter says he met you at the Deep.'

Pullman called Jamieson first. 'Hello Professor, it's Mike Pullman, you wanted me.'

Jamieson was on his Bluetooth hands free in the car, on his way home, he asked Pullman to hold while he pulled over.

'Sorry for the delay but safety first and all that. Right I've finished the analysis and it was Pentaerythritol tetranitrate known as PETN that was used. It can be made into a plastic explosive Like Semtex or C4 in fact it is actually used in the manufacture of Semtex. I found some trace of TATP which would explain the smell of bleach. My conclusion would be that it was used to detonate the PETN. Above and beyond that I'm afraid there's little I can tell you.'

'Does this explosive need to be kept in any special conditions?'

'Not really; as I said last night, TATP is notoriously unstable but it could be kept in a normal house or flat or anywhere. PETN on the other hand is much more stable. Although it starts life in powder form, it's easily converted if you know how.'

'What about storage, does it need a specific type of container?'

'Again not really. It should preferably be kept cool but it's okay at room temperature. Friction or an impact can explode TATP so it's best not kept close to the PETN.'

'How much would have been needed to cause last night's explosion?'

'A hundred grams or so would take out a car so last night was probably in the order of a kilo about the size of a bag of sugar or flour. Easily concealed in a rucksack.'

'He struck again this afternoon.'

'Where?'

'Holy Trinity church; tried to eliminate a wedding service, fortunately we got there in time to evacuate the place.'

'Christ you do have a problem on your hands.'

'Tell me about it.'

'Was there much damage?'

'Quite a bit. The structural engineers will go in on Monday to assess the situation.'

'Do you want me to take a look?'

'Don't think so professor,' said Pullman 'it's bound to be the same material. Now we know what we're looking for our boys should be able to identify the explosive.'

'Guess you're right. Well if there's anything else I can do for you Chief Inspector just let me know.'

'Will do. Thanks for your help.'

Pullman tasked Lynne Sperring with returning the call from Cheryl's dad.

'Mr Baines, hello this is DS Lynne Sperring how can I help?'

'Thanks for calling back Miss Sperring,' Baines had noticed that the DS had no ring on her left hand when he collected his daughter. 'Cheryl has remembered that the man she mentioned walked with a slight limp. Apparently she put it out of her mind because the staff are trained not to register physical disabilities, unless someone needs special access or specific help, otherwise their taught to focus on the customer's experience rather than their physical attributes.'

'Could I have a word with Cheryl?'

'She's asleep at the moment and I'd prefer not to disturb her if you don't mind. We've been at the RI most of the day. She's a bit battered and bruised. The A&E doctor reckons it was the buffeting from the blast.'

'That's fine please don't disturb her on my account. I can speak to her later. Did she say how noticeable the limp was and which leg?'

'Yes she demonstrated it to me. It was the right leg and it just sort of flicked from the knee as he walked as if it didn't quite bend properly.'

'Interesting. But it was definitely noticeable?'

'Oh yes. Hope it helps.'

57

'More than you might think. Thanks very much. One other thing, when she wakes could you ask Cheryl if the man had an accent.'

When she was off the telephone Pullman updated her on the results of the explosives analysis. She in turn briefed him on the conversation with Mr Baines. At least now they knew that if the situation arose they'd be looking out for a male with a limping gait.

Pullman logged on to his Facebook page. There was a post from Claude.

That was not very friendly. You spoiled my fun. Now I am going to have to find another way of amusing myself.

Pullman commented:

Claude, I'm curious, what do you find so amusing about killing innocent people?

Within seconds Claude responded:

Curiosity killed the cat.

Pullman replied:

No Claude, you killed the cat and seven innocent people.

Claude's response was instantaneous; his anger was almost palpable in the speed of reply:

No one is innocent my friend. We just do not always know what it is they are guilty of. Who can say, I have kept my heart pure; I am clean and without sin? Proverbs 20.9.

Now you will have to excuse me I have work to do thanks to your interference.

Pullman would have liked to respond with a religious retort but knew it would take too long to find an appropriate quote online. He certainly didn't know any off by heart.

Claude was beginning to show the signs of being a religious zealot or was this just another red herring. Would he really demolish a church – a house of god if he was a religious fanatic?

58

The problem was, Pullman knew from past experience that there is no reasoning with religious fanatics, they really do believe they are doing God's work and that he will forgive them their sins. Claude was quoting the King James Bible, not the Koran, so he wasn't an Islamic terrorist. That in fact made tracking him down more difficult. There was a register of known Islamic terrorist suspects he could consult but there was no such register of Christian zealots.

Pullman had no religious beliefs; quite the opposite. He found it quite irrational that people can put aside the irrefutable evidence of evolution yet believe a story written two thousand years ago that their ethereal God figure took a handful of clay and moulded man before breathing life into it. Yet there were those, like his parents, who accept evolution but nevertheless believe in a God. Such is their need to believe, that they can just choose the parts of the two concepts that suit them. Both he and Jane believed that religion was a crutch upon which leaned those needing a rationale for everything that happens to them. Nothing is their fault; it is God's will. It was not God's will that Jane died, nor that anyone else died for that matter; living beings die end of story. Some die too soon; some not soon enough. The dead do not go to an afterlife; there is no heaven, no hell. The dead no longer existed; the victims Claude killed were going nowhere, they simply ceased to exist. Pullman would have liked to think that Claude would spend eternity in Hell, if only there was such a place.

He needed to keep a line of communication open. He wrote:

Claude before you get too busy, tell me why you're really doing this. I won't judge you, I just want to know.

Claude was no doubt planning a demonstration of his anger. The good thing was that he himself could not have expected to be second guessed. He would not have conceived that the police would thwart his attack; spoil his surprise at the wedding, so clearly wouldn't have the next atrocity in place; he hadn't thought that he would need to retaliate which gave Operation Alligator time to make plans of its own.

Claude did not respond to Pullman's message.

All Humberside police service leave was cancelled for the Saturday night and all day Sunday. Patrols were increased, covering the most likely targets on the 'whatif' list but Pullman was not holding out a lot of hope that the additional cover would yield a sighting. Nevertheless, he understood the need to do so or at least the need to be seen to be doing so.

Pullman, Lynne Sperring and Ashley Sharpe were still at their desks late into the evening. They had independently decided to spend the night at Priory Road in case something went down. The fact that none of them had anything better to do on a Saturday night was a sad reflection on their social lives rather than a demonstration of commitment to the job. They were not expecting, nor would they get, overtime payment.

Lynne Sperring's split with live-in boyfriend, Gary, was as deep as the Mariana Trench. He had upped-sticks and moved to Newquay in Cornwall to fulfil his ambition to become a surf bum; she was certain it was a role to which he would be well suited. Since returning from the secondment to the NCA in London she had not had the opportunity to touch base with any of her friends. There would be time enough when Claude was behind bars. She busied herself with searching for information on 'Claudes' on the internet, in the hope that it might give an insight into why the pseudonym had been chosen. In doing so, she discovered that the illustration he had used on his Facebook page was one of Claude Garamond a sixteenth century French punch-cutter and printer who designed the typeface that bears his name. There was nothing she could see that linked the two men. On the other hand the basic derivation of the name Claude was limp or lame. He'd perhaps chosen the epithet as an ironic joke, given the additional information she'd now had from Cheryl Baines.

Ashley Sharpe was watching A Question of Sport on the BBC iPlayer, on his tablet whilst waiting for Match of the Day to begin. It was after all, his time he was expending.

Pullman was watching the inside of his eyelids. He had closed his eyes habitually to help him focus on trying to second guess Claude. What would the man do next? It had to be something significant; something that would make a big 'don't fuck with me' statement. Could he put together a device and a location in time to perpetrate a major incident so soon? Why not? Would it be a bomb? Yes, he seemed to have established his MO now. He was a bomber. But he'd warned them not to anticipate what he might do, so perhaps the shortage of time would force him to change his paradigm of mayhem. Whatever the madman was contemplating at least it had occupied Pullman's thoughts to the total exclusion of Jane; that made him feel both relieved and remorseful in equal amounts.

The CCTV control room in the council's state-of-the-art centre was buzzing. Saturday was their busiest night, marginally beating Friday; four hundred and seventy camera locations took a lot of monitoring. This Saturday extra staff had been brought in to cover the heightened alert of Operation Alligator. Vigilant eyes were glued to three banks of thirty screens as the operators switched views, panned around and zoomed in on potential incidents. Thousands of people were milling around the streets and wandering from bar to bar and club to club on the well-established pub crawling routes around the city centre. There was no way on earth they had any chance of spotting a lone man with a slight limp amongst the multitudes.

The high definition cameras could identify a face at one hundred and fifty metres and identify an offender's clothing at two hundred metres; a distance at which the offender would not even see the camera. The operators have direct radio links with most of the bars, clubs and shops in the city and can notify response units of incidents as they happen. Those same links enable the police to direct the CCTV operators to specific suspects and track their movements through the network, while police response units rush to attend the scene, if required.

This Saturday night was much the same as any other. Sporadic fights broke out in the usual trouble hot spots; men urinated off the quayside into the still waters of the artificial lake that fronted the Princes Quay Shopping Centre; drunks of both sexes and all persuasions staggered around like marionettes on elastic strings; it was just 10pm and the night was young.

A control room operator was keeping a watchful eye on two police officers who were doing their level best to quell a fracas involving a group of youths and young women on Princes Dock Street, between the shopping centre and the Water Mill nightspot. The affray was causing a crowd to gather and encourage the battle between the revellers and the police officers. It looked as if the situation might escalate; the operator made a judgement call and alerted the mobile riot unit to attend; back-up was only a few hundred metres away. It took just seconds for them to arrive on the scene and begin helping their colleagues to quieten the rumpus. Three young men were escorted to the mobile caged, prisoner escort van amidst jeering from the baying mob. Things were beginning to settle down when Sergeant Gilling, in charge of the back-up team caught sight of a flying object which appeared to be moving slowly in their direction.

'Why the hell's that flying so low,' he remarked to his nearest colleague.

'Looks like a spaceship,' said his colleague. 'Perhaps the Martians are invading,' he laughed.

The craft appeared to be some considerable distance away but visually was little more than roof height. The ambient street lighting combined with a slight November mist, that was beginning to descend, was making depth perception difficult, until Sergeant Gilling realised that the machine was actually not more than two hundred metres away.

'Jesus,' he shouted, 'that's one of those drone things; it's a big bugger though.'

The large gleaming white, metallic drone hovered fifty metres from them for a few seconds; it was cruciform in shape with a rotating blade on each of the arms. The machine rose vertically until it was higher than the three storey Water Mill. It banked gently to the right, flew over the neon sign on top of the red brick building and disappeared from view. Groups of people had followed the officers lead, they too were observing the aircraft, enthralled at the skill of the unseen remote control pilot.

'What sort of a nutter flies a toy at this time of...?'

Gilling's words were drowned out by the noise of the explosion. A ball of flame and debris erupted into the air above the roof of the nightclub. Initial shock turned to panic as the crowds dissipated in all directions to escape the raining masonry. The roof of the old building imploded, sending tons of rubble plummeting through the crowded level three bar area; crashing through the floor, down through the second level and descending further into the ground floor.

In the CCTV control room dumbstruck operators were stunned into momentary silence as the horror unfolded before their eyes. Debris flew through the windows on all three levels and cascaded on to the cobbled streets below; some masonry hailed down like a meteorite shower, falling into the shopping centre lake sending up fountains of murky water; some debris machine gunned the Princes Quay Centre, glass fronted building, shattering dozens of panes. Plumes of dust and smoke rose into the night sky. Not since the bombardment during World War Two had Hull experienced devastation on such a scale. Inside the club panic ensued; a mass surge of well-oiled young people stampeded towards the exits. Fire doors blocked by debris rendered egress impossible, funnelling the throng towards the alternative of the front entrance. The doors there were plenty wide enough for the normal crocodile file of customers, allowed in by the doormen, but were completely inadequate to cope with the hordes of would-be escapees; self-preservation took over as screaming people fought their way clear, pulling, pushing and trampling on fellow clubbers in a frenzied panic. People were being crushed underfoot. Hysteria reigned.

The bright neon sign on the top balustrade of the roof, having lost its mountings, came crashing down to the ground along with part of the outer wall, crushing an unfortunate girl and sending up a spray of glittering electric sparks.

Many of the walking wounded, outside in the proximity of Princes Quay and Posterngate, were fleeing the scene whilst crowds of onlookers were running towards the area, to see what had happened. From the top floor of the shopping centre security guards observed the chaos on the streets below which conjured up imagery of a termite nest having been kicked over. Police were trying to clear a pathway through the scurrying termites for the fire and ambulance service vehicles to attend the scene.

As the screaming died down, for a few seconds, an eerie stunned, silence fell on the scene. It was as if someone had hit the mute button on the remote; just as quickly, the hiatus burst back into life the commotion of sirens and loud hailers turned up the volume of the general hubbub. It was a scene that most had only seen on the television news bulletins or disaster movies. Devastation on a scale reminiscent of recent televised reports of war ravaged Middle Eastern uprisings.

No amount of fire drills or evacuation practice could prepare the emergency services for the level of destruction and loss of life before them. Firefighters and ambulance crews were scrambled from every available point around the city and beyond; police were doing their utmost to cope; directing operations as best they could amongst the chaos. For some it was going to be a long night for others the night and life itself, was already over.

The Hull Royal Infirmary could not cope with the sudden influx of casualties on top of their normal Saturday night emergencies; a violent mugging at the Humber Dock Marina, a knife fight in the Mariners bar, injuries following a football supporter's rampage after the match. The, already, over-burdened A&E department was completely overwhelmed. Ambulances were redirected; some of the less critical cases to Cottingham, some over the Humber Bridge to Grimsby, Scunthorpe and Goole. The most serious cases, needing specialist treatment, were air lifted by the Yorkshire Air ambulance service to York and Leeds. Teams of off duty volunteer nurses were applying medical attention at the scene to those with minor injuries. Florence Nightingale and her lamp would not have been incongruous.

Fatalities once declared dead at the scene, by a team of doctors accompanied by all available pathologists, were tagged with a number and moved to a make shift mortuary inside an empty unit in the shopping centre. Most would be identified by their belongings but several had nothing on them but cash and keys; no reveller expects the need for identification on a night out; unless they're male look under twenty-one years old.

Seven

Pullman, the supposed hard-nosed copper, stood amidst the devastation, tears filling his eyes. The cries of angst and pleas to deities, by friends and relatives, stripped away his resolve and rubbed raw the heartache of his own loss. There was nothing he could say to these grieving people; nothing that could, in any way, right the wrongs they had suffered. He was wrestling with an inner turmoil that was conniving to apportion blame to himself. A devil chiselling away at his senses, telling him he should be held responsible, even though logic said he was not. Perhaps he wanted to shoulder the responsibility but he had no way of anticipating the events of the night; so why torment himself. There was only one man to blame for all this pain and suffering. One sadistic son-of-a-bitch. One soulless sociopath. One man who had to be found and stopped before more innocent people perished; the maniac calling himself Claude.

Fire crews were actively engaged in digging through the collapsed building; twenty-three bodies had so far been recovered, more were certain to be found. Two black Labrador sniffer dogs were scampering amongst the debris. The dogs, Benny and Jed, were very experienced and well-travelled, both having recently been on duty in Mexico and India, helping to detect buried earthquake casualties; prior to that they and their handlers had been to the Haiti earthquake, helping the authorities there in the international rescue operation.

Crompton and Thwaite were on a walkabout supervising policing of the area and talking with some of the injured; three of whom were their own officers, including Sergeant Gilling who sat on the tail gate of a paramedic estate car, his crown and eyes completely bandaged.

The beleaguered Chief Fire Officer for the Humberside Fire Service was addressing the inevitable pack of hungry news hounds.

'There have been a number of casualties and my colleagues are doing all they can to locate any additional casualties remaining in the building. At this stage we do not know the cause of the explosion and our main priority is ensuring that the rescue operation is completed in the shortest possible time. This will be a painstaking operation due to the fragility of the structure and the need to protect the safety of those engaged in the rescue.'

A barrage of questions was fired at him.

'I know you have a lot of questions and they will be answered in due course but right now the rescue is paramount, so if you'll please excuse me, I'll return to the scene. Thank you.'

Pullman ambled over to Sperring standing as close to the main entrance as safety would allow. Through the gaping hole in the front elevation they watched the surreal scene as fire officers clambered over the rubble, removing bricks and beams with their bare hands. They began forming a human conveyor belt to remove the bricks and masonry. A mobile crane was en route but wouldn't be there for an hour or two; the people trapped beneath the wreckage of the nightclub could not wait that long.

They were under no illusion that Claude was responsible. Their action in thwarting the intended carnage at Holy Trinity had simply transferred the attack. The wedding party was alive; the revellers were dead. It was too much of a co-incidence to be anything else.

68

'Why?' was as much as Sperring could muster.

'Because he's a sick bastard,' said Pullman.

You spoiled my fun. Now I am going to have to find another way of amusing myself. That's what Claude had posted on his page.

'A total disregard for life,' said Sperring.

'On the contrary Lynne the sick bastard has a high regard for life, which is why I think he enjoys taking it. If it meant nothing to him, why bother. It's the ultimate thing he can take. It's irreplaceable.'

Pullman knew only too well how irreplaceable a life was.

Thirty one dead, sixty-four seriously injured – eight critically and dozens more suffering minor cuts and bruises. That was the official count three hours after the explosion; twenty seven fatalities at the disaster site with four more dying from their injuries while undergoing treatment.

The fire services were still at the scene, still digging, still hoping. The crane had arrived but was considered neither use nor ornament. It was unable to get high enough for the jib to be used over the partially collapsed outside walls.

Ironically three news reporting, eye in the sky, helicopters were hovering over the scene, transmitting aerial views of the devastation back to their twenty-four hour studio broadcasts. The Yorkshire Air Ambulance had returned from its last flight to Leeds Royal Infirmary and was on standby to transport any further casualties if need be.

The deflated Operation Alligator team were seated in a silent incident room at Priory Road headquarters waiting for Pullman and

69

Sperring to return from the crime scene. They watched the continuous online news coverage. The subsequent arrival of the senior officers did nothing to lift spirits. The first thing Pullman did was check Facebook to see if Claude had left a message. He hadn't.

'Right there's been no contact from anyone claiming responsibility for the bomb and yes we do believe it was a bomb. British Gas assure us that it could not have been a gas leak because the gas had been turned off for the whole block along Princes Dock Street from the corner with Posterngate along to Fish Street, and down to the A63. The gas had been off for over twenty-four hours. Now as surreal as this sounds, we have several eye witnesses who saw, what they describe as, a UFO hovering along Princes Dock Street from the direction of the main road, then fly over the roof of the Water Mill. None of them thought it could have been the cause of the explosion, so initially we might still try and play the gas leak card as far as the media is concerned. I haven't discussed that with the CC yet so there won't be any media contact until I do. Is that understood?'

It was understood.

'I am confident, as I'm sure you are, that this was perpetrated by Claude in retaliation for stopping his attack on the wedding this afternoon.' He glanced down at his watch it read 1.27am. 'Yesterday afternoon.' He corrected himself.

'Surely a small toy like that crashing on to a building couldn't possibly cause that much damage sir,' said Sharpe.

'It could if it had been modified to accommodate a PETN payload. At least I believe it could, given the information from Professor Jamieson, following the other two explosions. I'll confirm that with him first thing in the morning but in the meantime we will assume it was Claude and he used the remote controlled drone to deliver the explosive device.'

The Chief Constable entered the room and signalled with a slight movement of her head for Pullman to join her outside. He nodded in return.

'Refresh your coffee cups while I step outside for a minute.' He looked at Sharpe. 'I'll have mine black no sugar.'

Outside in the corridor the CC was looking anxious. 'What are we going to do Mike?' she asked when Pullman joined her; there was genuine concern and sorrow in her voice.

'Don't suppose we can blame this one on a gas leak?' he asked with little hope.

'No chance. As soon as the news broke I had British Gas lawyers on to me saying point blank that they would not cover up this time. Who can blame them? This is getting completely out of hand. I suppose it was Claude.'

'Who else?'

'Any word from him yet?'

'None.'

'What's your plan?'

'Not sure I've got one, ma'am,' he replied. 'If you'd care to listen in, we might come up with something.'

She thought for a moment. 'No, you do what you think best, Mike. I've every confidence in you and your team.' Whoops if he was a manager, getting the dreaded vote of confidence from the football club chairman, he'd be looking for another club tomorrow. 'I'll be with the press officers getting ready to meet the media barrage in a few hours.'

Pullman re-joined the team and collected his coffee. 'Well there's good news and bad news. The bad news is that British Gas won't take the rap this time. Wrecking a church is one thing but

71

obviously being the scape goat for multiple fatalities is another. So in a few hours' time the world and its mother will know for sure, that we have a bomber on our hands and all hell will break loose. The good news is that the Chief Constable has every confidence in us.' He resisted the impulse to accompany the line with a sarcastic smile. If morale needed boosting that didn't do it. 'Let's try and do something to justify that confidence.'

While they were talking in the incident room, three miles away at the Royal Infirmary two more victims on the critically injured list, transferred to the fatalities list. The death toll was rising steadily.

'If it was the drone that delivered the bomb then presumably the pilot would need to be fairly close by to maintain visual contact; so he could guide the thing on to the roof of the club. He could have concealed himself in a car or van parked close by; let's get all the CCTV footage we can and see if that throws up anything. Ash you get online and check what sort of distances these things can fly; if we know the average range, it will help us to determine where it might have taken off from. Lynne and I will get back out there and look for vantage points. We need to do that whilst it's still dark to have the same conditions as the perpetrator.'

'Nothing from forensics sir?' asked Ashley Sharpe.

'Can't go in there until the scene is declared safe; no idea when that will be; let's hope it doesn't rain in the meantime.'

The four mile journey to Princes Quay from police headquarters would normally take Sperring around twelve minutes at 2am but there were a lot more people and traffic around in the early hours of that atypical Sunday morning.

'How's that boyfriend of yours coping with you being out all hours?'

'He copes by not being home; we split a couple of weeks back. It was coming long before the secondment to the NCA.'

'I don't mean to pry,' said Pullman. 'I know only too well the strains the job can put on relationships.'

'I'll cope sir. What about you?' she asked.

'I guess I'll cope too,' he replied. 'Not that I've made a very good job it so far.'

'I'm sure it must be difficult.'

'Very.'

'The DCC couldn't handle it when his wife was murdered.'

'No and I'd have caved completely if Jane had been raped and stabbed by some drug crazed shithead.'

'Have you thought about it sir?'

'What being raped and murdered by a shithead?'

'Suicide.'

'It crossed my mind once or twice during the first few weeks after Jane died; you hit a real pit of despair; at least I did. Feel that there's no point in carrying on but I haven't got the bottle to top myself; with my bloody luck I'd end up doing myself irreparable damage instead and be worse off.'

'Doesn't seem fair when someone dies so young.'

'There's not a lot that is fair in this life Lynne. Think of all the grieving relatives we've got now; mothers, fathers, boyfriends, girlfriends, wives, husbands — none of them expected to lose a loved one when they woke up yesterday morning; I knew for over a year that Jane was going to die.'

'We're all going to die, I guess.'

'No guess about it. Taxes and death being the two certainties in this life, so they say. You just have to come to terms with it; one half of every couple will experience what I went through, am going through. It's not very often that both partners die simultaneously; maybe some did tonight.'

'But you will get through it.' It was more of a question than words of encouragement.

'It takes a certain kind of perverse courage to commit suicide. Bob Cole had that kind of misguided courage, but I don't.'

'Good to hear it sir, we'd miss you.' she meant it.

They sat in silence for the remainder of the journey. It was almost twenty minutes before she parked at the A63 end of Princes Dock Road. They remained seated for a minute or two surveying the scene through the windscreen. A cluster of TV cameras was positioned on the walkway between the road and the shopping centre entrance. Bright white camera flashes blended with the rotating blue lights of the emergency service vehicles. Two ambulances were still parked close by in anticipation of more survivors being extricated from the collapsed building. The vantage points giving clear visibility of the Water Mill were abundant. Maybe a reason Claude chose the location as the target.

They got out of the car and looked back towards the crime scene. The shopping centre was open twenty-four hours a day; which was more than could be said for many of the retail units inside the building. Many had been closed and shuttered permanently for months.

'He could have had a perfect view from any floor but there had to be a surface somewhere from which the model could have taken off,' said Pullman.

'Surely he wouldn't have left the device out in the open, unattended, while he sat in the retail outlet with the remote controller.'

'No he was too careful for that.'

'He could have parked on the upper level of the multi-storey car park, sir. That's open to the elements with a perfect line of sight and plenty of flat surface area for an effective take off,' said Sperring.

'A definite possibility,' said Pullman. 'There wouldn't have been too many vehicles parked up there at that time of night.'

Sperring had parked outside the Napoli Ristorante which had an ample sized car park for Claude's purposes. On the other side of the restaurant was a grassed area in the order of a third of an acre, surrounded by bushes – another possible launch site.

They started to walk back towards the devastation when Pullman's mobile rang. It was Ashley Sharpe.

'Right sir, not sure you're gonna like this.'

Pullman's heart sank. He switched the phone to speaker mode and held it out so that Sperring could listen.

'There are loads of different drones on the market some tiny and probably not up to the job and others that could almost go into combat in Syria. They have ranges from five minutes flying time up to twenty minutes for something called the long range models and can be operated from a distance of up to a mile away.'

Sharpe was right Pullman didn't like it.

'But here's the bit you're really not going to like; you don't have to have sight of the aircraft or the target. You can fit a tiny Wi-Fi camera which transmits its flight to your laptop. It gives you a view as if you are actually sitting in a real chopper.'

Pullman rubbed his brow wearily. 'Are you saying that Claude could have been a mile away sitting at home operating this thing from his sitting room?'

'Not sure about the sitting room sir but there's loads of clips on YouTube of guys sitting in cars with their remotes and laptops getting aerial flight pictures as if they were in the pilot's seat. Seriously sir the thing just flies around the countryside you wouldn't know it wasn't filmed from a normal helicopter.'

'Shit!'

Sperring joined the conversation. 'If he had a camera and a load of explosives on board wouldn't all that additional weight restrict the range by using extra power?'

'Yeah, maybe Lynne.' Pullman said. 'Ash is there anything you've got to cheer me up?'

'Not really sir. There's a model flying club at Thearne; they may be able to give us more insight, so I thought I'd give them a ring in the morning; also there's a model flying section at Hull History Museum so they might also be able to help.'

'Okay Ash, good stuff. Get behind it first thing. I suggest you go home now and grab a couple of hours sleep.'

'I thought I'd spend a couple more hours...'

Pullman interrupted his flow. 'Ash you'll soon learn that when I suggest something I mean do it. Clear?'

'Crystal sir. See you in the morning.' Pullman closed the call. 'Let's forget that for a moment and finish off here. I think our man likes to see the results of his work, so I reckon that he would have been around here somewhere. He wouldn't have had time to rent an empty office or shop.'

'Unless this was an attack he'd planned all along and he just brought it forward after the church failure.'

'Could be; quite a few of these offices look vacant. We'll need a team to cover them all, although we're probably wasting our time. I think we'll call it a day too Lynne; take me back please then I suggest you get some sleep as well.'

Sperring had worked with Pullman for several years she had long ago learned what a suggestion meant. 'Yes sir,' she said. 'But don't you think you should too?'

Eight

Sunday 9th November

Shortly before 10.30 am on Sunday morning, Pullman and DC Sharpe were standing in a field at Thearne. It was a crisp, bright morning with the sun lying low in the east; providing ideal flying conditions, if you were looking west, according to Steve Hawkins, secretary of the Thearne Model Aircraft Club. His scaled down replica Align Trex 700N helicopter sat on the grass, engine primed ready for take-off. The sleek red and green model looked immaculate yet, as far as Pullman could judge, it did not look capable of carrying a payload of a kilo or more.

'No, this one isn't,' said Steve Hawkins when Pullman asked the question. 'But there are plenty that are, if you know where to look. Quadcopters are used for all sorts of purposes now, but the principles are the same as my helicopter.'

'I'm talking about carrying something the size of a bag of sugar or even bigger,' said Pullman.

'At the Weston Park Air Show in Shropshire last year, they demonstrated models that could lift a week's groceries let alone a bag of sugar. Well that's perhaps a little bit of an exaggeration but two or three bags of sugar wouldn't have been a problem. There's talk in some of the magazines of one of the large online retail sites using drones to deliver parcels to customers. It's a bit far-fetched but the technology exists and if that's what they want to do I reckon they've got the financial clout to make it happen.'

'And you can fit a camera to these can you?' asked Sharpe.

'Of course; the military use drones in conflict zones to search abandoned buildings for booby traps and casualties. I've got a tiny digital FPV system on this one; let me show you.'

Hawkins picked up the remote controller from the boot of his aging Land Rover, fully flipped up the lid of his laptop, which he had previously booted up, then, pulling up the antennae on the remote controller, he flicked a switch and the blades on his Trex 700N started to rotate slowly; they gradually increased speed until they were a mere blur as the craft lifted expertly in to the air.

'Now you'll see I can manoeuvre it by looking at the screen. It takes a lot of practice but I've been flying these things since I was a boy so it was easy to adapt to using the latest gizmos.'

'What about night time flying though?' asked Pullman?

'There are models with lights but an enthusiast can modify a basic model any way he wants. I have done a few night flights but frankly, I don't see the point. In fact you don't see anything unless you are in a built up area of course and that's illegal.'

It hadn't stopped Claude but then legality was not a pressing concern of his. Hawkins' demonstration was more than enough to satisfy Pullman that the explosive could easily have been contained in a model aircraft. He and Sharpe left the latter day Biggles playing with his very expensive toy.

Claude's latest escalation of slaughter had now made his activities a national issue. The Home Secretary had been fully briefed, as too had the National Counter Terrorism Security Office and the Secret Intelligence Service (MI6). They had in turn informed the North East Counter Terrorism Unit which offered to

79

send two officers to advise on counter terrorism methods. During a conference call Pauline Crompton, and her ACC, explained the extortion threats behind the incident sufficiently to persuade the NECTU that this was not a political terrorist issue.

Of major concern to the Chief Constable was that her already stretched resources were about to be expanded to breaking point by a hastily planned visit of the Duke and Duchess of Cambridge. The royal couple would be flying up by helicopter from London, arriving at 3pm that afternoon.

That would pose a whole new batch of security issues. Officers from SO14, the Royal Protection Branch of the Metropolitan Police Protection Command would, of course, travel with the Royal party but there would be issues of crowd control and safety on the ground that her service would need to cover.

Thanks to government cut backs, her force was now down to less than two thousand officers covering an area of three and a half thousand square kilometres from Bridlington in the north to Cleethorpes in the south and across almost to Doncaster in the west. Currently twenty-seven officers were actively engaged in maintaining control at the road blocks around the blast site; curtailing traffic access along Princes Dock Road and feeder roads. Dozens more were involved in Operation Alligator monitoring potential targets for sightings of Claude. In addition to this her mind was occupied with allocating scores of officers involved in supervising numerous Remembrance Day parades right across Humberside. Those parades were all the more poignant given the previous day's events.

Pullman's mind was occupied with thoughts of Claude. Almost fourteen hours after the blast the maniac had not made contact. No mocking messages. No proclamation of responsibility for the incident. Nothing.

Back in his office Pullman went online to leave a message on Claude's wall:

Why Claude? What had all those innocent people done to deserve to die? What makes you think you have the right to take life? Just tell me why.

Pullman hoped that asking questions would stimulate a response. All he could do now was wait. Less than forty-eight hours now to the original deadline.

Although it was practical for the drone, or whatever it was, to have been manoeuvred by using a camera and laptop, Pullman was still of the opinion that Claude would have been within sight of the nightclub. He was too careful to leave it to chance, besides which he enjoyed seeing the results of his handiwork. That was the lunatic's fun.

Ashley Sharpe knocked on Pullman's office door and entered without being asked. 'Guv we've just had a call from the manager of the Holiday Inn; a guy booked in late yesterday, insisted on having a room looking east over the main part of the marina. He should have checked out by eleven but when he didn't they checked on him and his room was empty.'

'So what are we looking at a missing person or a fraudster not paying his bill?'

'No sir. The manager says that he left a case and all there was in it was a small bottle of engine oil, some batteries and bits of wrapping paper.'

'Your point is?' Pullman knew full well where the young DC was going with the conversation and was trying to encourage him to get to the crux of the matter.

'I've just looked at the location on Google maps and some of the rooms that face east, directly overlook the A63 and right across to Princes Dock Street; I reckon you might be able to see the Water Mill from that side of the hotel.'

Pullman was instantly up out of his seat and reaching for his overcoat. 'Right what are you waiting for? Let's get out there.' He took Sperring along with them; he wouldn't normally have taken three but he wanted Ash to get the credit for spotting the possible connection and the experience of the possible crime scene.

The traffic was horrendous. With several of the side roads closed, drivers were confused and bewildered as they tried to gain access to the high street and shopping centres. Even with the blues and twos going, it was a road hog journey; weaving in and out of the traffic, overtaking one or two vehicles at a time. Young Sharpe had all the makings of a Grand Prix driver.

The hotel was set back of the A63 behind a copse of skeletal, deciduous trees to the front and the marina to the rear. The manager took them to room 314 on the upper floor. As he was opening the door Pullman said. 'You haven't had the room cleaned have you?'

'No it's exactly as housekeeping found it.'

'Excellent. I don't suppose you could let me have a sheet or two to lay on the floor to protect the scene?'

'Can do but I'm afraid I've been in, my assistant manager's been in, the chambermaid and head of housekeeping have been in too, so...'

'Okay, but I still need to maintain the integrity of any remaining forensics; we can always segregate any contamination. It may not do any good but I'll get a slap from forensics if I don't.'

They waited outside the door while the manager fetched a roller towel from the linen store. He rolled it out across the room forming a narrow pathway. Pullman entered the room keeping to the towel path. The bed had not been slept in. 'When did he book in?'

'About seven o'clock last night. Fortunately for him, but unfortunately for us, we had several vacant rooms although he insisted on being up here, apparently he said it was something to do with Feng Sui and sleeping in magnetic lines or some such tosh; we get all sorts of requests so the receptionist didn't think it too far out of the ordinary.'

Pullman took one wide step off the towel to look into the case which was lying open on the bed. There were three packs of C2 batteries and a small bottle of model aircraft engine oil. Pullman bent down and sniffed the inside of the case; he got a faint but definite aroma of bleach.

'Air traffic control was here, then,' said Pullman. He went to the window which afforded a clear sight past the Italian restaurant, right across to the crumbling nightclub. He looked down to see a flat roofed extension jutting out one floor below. 'And there is the launch pad. He couldn't have had a chance to reccy this location so he must have just got lucky.'

Sperring said. 'Perhaps he'd already decided on this spot he might have been planning this all along, for Tuesday, just brought it forward because of the church failure.'

'Yes your right of course Lynne,' admitted Pullman. 'There's no way he could have acquired the drone, learnt to fly it and carried out the attack between finding out we'd thwarted the wedding massacre and booking in here at seven o'clock.'

The realisation hit Pullman that, by Claude bringing forward the bombing, many more night clubbers had died as a result. The venue would not have been anywhere near as busy on Tuesday. The fatalities at the church would, however, have been just as numerous if not greater than the club bomb, so it was probably the lesser of two evils. What a ridiculous thing to consider. He wasn't thinking straight. He should have taken his own advice and got some sleep.

'Ash, get forensics over here. I wouldn't have thought it was Claude's habit to leave residue lying around but let's hope the boys in white can find something.'

'And girls,' said Sperring.

'Boys and girls in white,' Pullman said apologetically.

'Yes guv,' said Sharpe. 'I wonder why he didn't come back and tidy up?

'Good point. In fact I wonder why he went out at all without tidying up and taking this stuff with him.' Pullman turned to the manager. 'Would you be able to give us a description?'

'Not personally; I never saw him check in, however Gail, one of our receptionists, will be able to, she's due back in about ten minutes.'

'What about a car did he register a car number? No question the home address he gave will be false.'

'What about a credit card did he.....' Sperring was asking.

'No car and he paid cash I'm afraid.' The manager anticipated the question.

What about CCTV security cameras? Do you have any?'

'Certainly, I'll get you the disc from yesterday.'

'Tell you what team; shall we grab a cup of coffee while we're waiting?' He felt the need for caffeine.

'If you go down to the bar lounge area I'll have the coffee brought over to you, with the hotel's compliments.'

The coffee was hot and so was Gail, the receptionist, according to Ashley Sharpe.

'You sit there tiger,' said Pullman. 'Lynne you talk to her I don't think Ash could speak without drooling.' Pullman smiled for the first time in twenty-four hours, probably months.

The guest in room 314 was described as white, somewhere between five-ten and six foot in height, neatly trimmed light grey hair and beard, small scar below his left eye, spoke with a refined Scots accent; left handed– he'd had to turn the registration card sideways to accommodate the slope of his handwriting – wore a black or very dark blue, padded, front zip jacket. She had not noticed if he walked with a limp but she hadn't noticed him walk in or walk to the lifts. He'd registered in the name of Roger Endout, which caused Sperring to give an ironic smile, with a home address that would undoubtedly prove to be non-existent. No vehicle registration number had been provided.

Pullman checked his Facebook account on his smart phone; still no message or comment from Claude.

'I must admit I'm concerned that Claude hasn't rubbed our noses in it yet or responded to my post.'

'Maybe he's ill,' said Sharpe. 'There's that winter vomiting bug going around again.'

'Hope it's nothing trivial, if he has caught something,' said Sperring.

'How are we getting on with the other CCTV viewing?' asked Pullman.

'We've got five Researchers on it, as we speak but if he launched the device from here, then I don't suppose he'll figure on the tapes that we've got, he might be on the hotel's though.'

'He still had to get here from base camp so we might pick him up outside somewhere.'

'Might help if we knew who we were looking for and what transport he used.'

'Well, the picture is building,' said Pullman, draining the coffee pot into his cup. 'If we ignore the things he can disguise or change, then we know he's around five-eleven tall, left handed and probably does have a limp. At some point in his life he had a sense of humour which surfaces now and again.

'Difficult to spot a sense of humour on CCTV,' remarked Sperring.

'Our friendly neighbourhood profiler should be here in the morning; we'll see what he makes of Claude. Maybe he can figure out what his motives are.'

Surgeons at the Hull Royal Infirmary were working as if they were in a M.A.S.H battle zone; allowing just enough time for scrubbing up and down before the next casualty was wheeled in. All that was missing was the cry *incoming wounded* as the choppers landed. The Intensive Care Unit was filled to capacity.

Several unfortunate victims, at the epicentre of the blast, required metal rods and plates inserted to support smashed limbs; where those limbs could be saved. Where they were beyond salvation, victims were undergoing amputations. Neurosurgeons were operating on head traumas. Blood stocks were being raced across the country to meet the huge demand for transfusions.

One of the victims involved in the unrelated knife fight required eight pints, yet was, regrettably, unable to be saved; another was still on life support. The mugger's victim had not regained consciousness and was scheduled for a CT scan on his head wound the following day. All of the football supporters had been patched up, shut up, sobered up and sent on their way; two of them had been detained by police for causing an affray in A&E.

Those victims deemed, by triage, to be less severely injured were still on gurneys in overflowing corridors, radiating from the

A&E department. Waiting areas were crowded with anxious relatives seeking news of injured family members. Agency nurses had been drafted in to augment the overworked nursing staff, many of whom had worked through the night administering to the needs of the casualties. The WVRS canteen was hitting record sales figures.

The last thing on anyone's mind was the Royal walkabout planned for that afternoon.

Four more bodies and the last badly injured survivor had been pulled from the carnage during Sunday. The Fire Service was now certain that no more victims were buried under what remained of the rubble and issued a statement to that effect.

Total fatalities were now confirmed at thirty-seven.

With the exception of Doctor Harold Shipman, who it is alleged may have killed some two hundred and fifty patients, the anonymous Claude was officially pronounced the worst mass murderer in British history; meaning that he had killed the highest number of victims not that he wasn't very good at what he did; on the contrary Claude was very proficient.

The visiting Royal party came and went. Prince William and the Duchess of Cambridge toured the scene of the tragedy, speaking to rescue workers and the top brass of both the police and fire services. Their visit was televised and captured by dozens of DSLRs, mobile phones and tablets but they did not speak to the media. At the hospital, which was opened by his Grandmother in 1967, the Prince spoke cheerily with those victims capable of coherent speech and praised the work being done. The royal couple captured the hearts of patients and staff alike; the latter getting the clear impression that the Duchess in particular, had she been permitted, would have rolled up her sleeves and helped in any way she could.

Nine

Monday 10th November

As the team filed into the incident room, just before 8am, on Monday morning, there were just twenty-seven hours before the original extortion payment deadline. Ominously there was still no word from Claude.

The bombing made the front pages of the nationals, copies of which were spread around the room. Headlines ranged from the sedate Daily Telegraph proclaiming *37 DIE IN BOMB BLAST* to that of a red top which read *JAGER BOMB MASSACRE*. No doubt the sub-editor thought it clever but the German makers of Jagermeister probably wouldn't agree. The Hull Daily Mail ran a black border around its front page, with the headline *CITY IN MOURNING*. It listed the names of the dead, that had so far been released by the police amidst a four page, centre pull-out of images from the blast site; likewise the Yorkshire Post.

The briefing was short. Pullman informed the group of the hotel find and hoped that the forensic lab would throw more light on the identity of the occupant within a day or two; they were currently swamped by the amount of evidence being examined from all three crime scenes.

The researchers had not finished examining the CCTV footage available but had so far drawn a blank in their quest to identify a five foot ten man with a limp. Much to the viewers' relief they were not required to go back through the tapes looking for the same man with a grey beard and grey hair.

Cheryl Baines had telephoned and left a message for Sperring that the man she served at the Deep had a local accent. They knew he could change his accent so maybe he could update his knowledge of internet language to inject an element of misinformation into the investigation. Claude could not only morph into different identities and adopt different accents he might also adopt a range of writing styles. During the Reign of Terror, the French probably knew more about the Scarlet Pimpernel, than Pullman currently knew about Claude. The significant difference between the two being, that Pullman's mysterious foe was not, unfortunately, fictitious.

Dr Robert Allwood arrived on the stroke of ten o'clock. He was in his mid-fifties, six one tall with a shock of blonde hair covering his ears and resting on his jacket collar. A neatly groomed Van Dyke beard completed his Richard Branson doppelganger appearance. Pullman welcomed the distinguished Criminal Profiler into his office. Sperring had been tasked with getting stuck into the Wethersby enquiry, so Pullman asked DC Steph Barnes to sit in on the meeting with Allwood. After introductions, the serving of coffee and a minute or two of pleasantries, the conversation focussed on the matter in hand.

Allwood opened the conversation. 'I've read the notes and listened to the disc that Iain Thwaite sent to me and of course I've read the press reports of the tragic events of the past few days. So tell me what do you think about Claude?'

89

Pullman remembered something an ex-colleague of Jane's had once said at a dinner party. He'd left a senior marketing job at the company at which he, and Jane, worked and joined a major marketing consultancy; his role was to analyse the marketing plans of Blue Chip companies and advise them on what action they should take to achieve their objectives. When Pullman had asked him if that wasn't just a bit daunting their friend said *'it's a piece of piss. All clients really want to hear is that they're doing the right thing. They want you to re-affirm their intelligence. So you simply ask them what it is they're doing, re-phrase it and quote it back with a couple of bells and whistles that you know they won't ring or blow, then submit the bill'.* Jane had asked him what happened if it all went pear shaped. It wasn't a problem. Catch 23 came into force. *You simply blame it on them for not ringing the bells or blowing the whistles.* Was the illustrious profiler about to do the same? Was he going to repeat back, his client's own views?

Pullman played along. He told Allwood exactly what he had told the whatif meeting. 'The guy is not really an extortionist. He's a psychopath; a cold blooded killer with no remorse and no respect for human life. The extortion demand is so that he can blame us for the deaths because he knows that, under no circumstances, will we submit to the demands. Therefore we are forcing him to carry out his threats. We, society as a whole, is the murderer not him.'

'You're absolutely right of course. We know that from his actions but what do you know about his make-up his personality.'

'Nothing.'

'Really?'

'Well we have a hypothesis that he may be under forty from his use of social media terms; he seems to have a pretty good local knowledge which, combined with his accent, would mean he's local but we know he can disguise his voice. He walks with a slight

90

limp, is left handed, and likes the theatricality of using disguises. Oh yes, he's a cold hearted, murdering bastard but, I don't know what makes him tick; which is why you're here.'

Allwood remained silent for a few moments to allow the venomous frustration to leech from Pullman.

'It's a proven fact that most psychopaths and sociopaths have it in their genetic make-up— they are born with the traits. Usually those traits are combined with some form of abuse in childhood whether physical, mental or sexual, which determines the degree of psychopathy they develop in later life. There is no doubt that, from his communications and violent acts, this Claude meets many of the factors in Hare's Psychopathy Checklist, by which we gauge the level of propensity to commit sociopathic acts. He has shown a complete lack of remorse or empathy in carrying out his persistent violation of normality. His emotions are shallow, if not non-existent. I would agree with you that he has clearly lied in making the extortion demand and that he has a low frustration tolerance; his need to speed up his activities demonstrates an identified need for stimulation. So, on this level alone he meets six of the twelve keystones of a psychopath. Normally meeting three traits on the PCL would ring alarm bells but qualifying for six traits, makes our man very dangerous indeed. What we need to do is figure out why he's doing it and what could have triggered these violent crimes.'

You think! Pullman hoped that his snort of derision hadn't been audible. The fact the Allwood continued his dialogue suggested that he hadn't picked up on Pullman's involuntary comment.

'I also agree with you that he is almost certainly from the local area. Since ACC Thwaite called me, I have been doing some research, I can't find any record of any public incident that would logically tip the balance of the perpetrators mind; unless you can think of any major occurrence'. Nothing sprang to mind. 'So it's probably something personal; something in his family or workplace or social life that initiated this terrible chain of events.'

Pullman was fighting his instincts to say *I know all that.* Yet somehow having someone else telling him what he already knew was helping to clarify the issues. It was how he thought bereavement counselling would have been. Allwood's presence also made him realise that he had stopped discussing things with his team the way he used to. These days he assigned tasks, issued instructions and barked orders but he couldn't remember the last time he'd actually talked a case through with any member of his team, outside of the incident room; he'd put that right as a matter of priority. He returned his attention back to the profiler's continuing diatribe.

'..... possibly the death of a loved one, redundancy — although if he is under forty it's unlikely that it would have been a big enough blow to his ego to be the cause. It could be a divorce or the old elbow, from the great love of his life, which has caused him to vent his spleen on the world.'

'We all go through events like that in our lives; I have myself but it didn't turn me into a psychopath,' said Pullman.

'I'm pleased to hear it,' said Allwood with a smile. 'But then presumably you don't have the genetic traits to go with it.'

Steph Barnes cut in, 'I can see that Doctor, but how does it help us find him. If it is something private how would we discover that? We can't interview every Hullensian.'

'Of course you can't.' He didn't mean it to sound quite as condescending as it came across. 'Given the high level of impatience the perpetrator has shown, I would think that, whatever the trigger was, it occurred within the last three months, at the outside. So a study of death registrations during the period could be a starting point. You'd be looking for something slightly out of the ordinary not just a simple death by natural causes; the extortionist's initial pretence of the claim against the City could mean local authority were implicated in some way'

'Likewise for divorce petitions and decree nisi completions,' said Barnes.

'Yes and cancelled weddings,' said Pullman. 'The bomb at the church may not have had anything to do with the mayor, perhaps his own wedding had been cancelled and that was a case of *I can't have mine so you're not having yours.*'

'There have been less trivial reasons for homicidal revenge,' said Allwood. 'Now this is a long shot, but by all accounts the way the quadcopter was piloted demonstrated an immense amount of skill. It's possible that the controller was a member of a model flying club but it's a skill that can also be picked up in the military. Model drones fitted with spy cams are used in war zones for reconnaissance, searching through empty or demolished buildings looking for booby traps or wounded personnel. Maybe Claude is one of the thousands in the armed forces being made redundant. That might also explain his proficiency with explosives.'

'Maybe that's not such a long shot,' said Pullman. 'In one of the communications I received on Facebook, the man said *I no longer take orders, now I give the orders* or words to that effect. *No longer take orders* could indicate he was in the armed forces.'

'Or he was a waiter.' Allwood smiled.

'A disgruntled squaddie, mmmh, that would make sense.'

'We should be able to get a list of redundant soldiers from the MoD.' Barnes said, 'I'll get on to it.'

Pullman sat forward and leaned on his desk. 'Claude hasn't contacted us since the bomb went off on Saturday night. Our thinking is that he's been taken ill or had an accident but can you think of any psychological reasons that might explain why he hasn't made contact?'

'Well it certainly isn't shyness or modesty,' said Allwood. 'Your reasoning would be the simple answer.'

'I'm nothing if not simple,' said Pullman.

'I didn't mean it like....'

'It's alright Doctor, I'm just kidding.'

'What I meant was, there's no logical reason other than those; he said it would escalate so I don't think the extent of the death toll has rocked him into some transient state of shock. Could he have been close enough to the nightclub to have sustained injuries?'

'We don't think so; we think he piloted the chopper from a nearby hotel, although he did leave the room without taking his paraphernalia with him.'

'Careless. Doesn't sound like the usual meticulous person.'

'Our thinking too; Steph add hospitals to the list let's see if he's amongst the injured or walking wounded.'

'How would we know?'

'If we get all the names and cross check them against the deaths, marriages etcetera we may find a match or at least a link of some sort.'

Wow some task and some long shot. 'Yes sir.'

'Doctor Allwood can you think of anything else at the moment?'

Not right now but I'd like to take a look over the crime scenes.' He noticed Pullman raise his eyebrows. 'Don't worry I'm not clairvoyant or a mystic; I don't bend spoons or see dead people, I just like to get a feel for the locations. It usually helps. I don't know why.'

'Okay, no problem. So will you be staying over?'

94

'Sure, I'm all yours for three days initially, longer if you want me.' His usual day rate would apply.

'In that case could I discuss another matter with you?'

'Tempus est mihi tempus.'

Pullman guessed *my time is your time*, in which case he intended to make the most of it.

Ten

Pullman introduced Lynne Sperring to Robert Allwood then sat back while she gave the profiler a potted history of the Wethersby case.

'So as you can see we have no idea who killed him except that we believe it to be a woman or women. Unless they commit another murder we frankly have little hope of catching them but I'm hoping that you might be able to throw some light on Wethersby personality traits; enabling us to understand him better. If we can do that maybe, just maybe, we can get a handle on what he was doing in Bridlington; as well as who his friends and acquaintances might be.

'I'd need to study the files in more depth to make any real assessment, but I have come across similar cases. The critical thing with this victim is that he would appear not to have been a paedophile; their interest lies in children of all ages – literally from new born babies to sixteen year olds and usually of both sexes. Your man appears to only have been fixated with young girls who had reached puberty. He was, as you say, a Hebephile. Now these people see themselves as being quite normal compared to paedophiles; perversely they consider paedophiles to be depraved. Hebephiles simply believe that when a girl reaches her reproductive stage, nature has made her receptive for sex; all they are doing is enjoying the fresh fruit, to put it crudely. The prize is of course being first; taking a girl's virginity. I've heard this called cherry picking. Some victims are known to their cherry picker for many years prior to being sexually abused. He, although it's not always a he, there are female Hebephiles, could be a family member or close family friend, who cultivates a relationship with a girl through her formative years, building up a trust over a period of time, which is then exploited when the fruit is ripe, so to say.'

Pullman wondered how his colleagues, in Child Exploitation and Online Protection commands across the UK, could deal with this day in day out. He knew he didn't have the stomach for it yet was glad someone did. The world would be a sadder place if no one cared.

'These people are still predators and, like most predatory creatures, they prefer to hunt in packs or at least with a fellow predator or two.'

Sperring said. 'So we are right in thinking that Wethersby would have belonged to a Hebephile ring.'

'An orchard. Witches have covens, masons have lodges, paedophiles have rings and Hebephiles have orchards. I know it sounds odd but they don't refer to themselves as being in a ring but an orchard. Don't know what Anton Chekhov would have made of them plucking their ripe fruit from the cherry orchard.'

'How does an orchard grow? Asked Sperring, inadvertently continuing the theme. 'Can't exactly advertise in the local paper for new members can they.'

'Not the local rag but, these days, there are plenty of specialist web sites where you can locate fellow deviants of all persuasions, with little problem.'

'In the wild you'd recognise a predator but how do you recognise a fellow human being as having shared interests?' Pullman asked.

'They normally recognise one another by displaying some form of recognisable symbol; could be a small lapel badge or a specific

97

design of tie, something innocuous like that. It would mean nothing to anyone but a fellow orchard member, and would have a rational alternative meaning if questioned.'

'How about a tattoo?'

'Possibly.'

Pullman said. 'Lynne, show Doctor Allwood the tattoo that the victim had on his arm.'

'Please call me Robert, Detective Inspector,' said Allwood.

'Okay, I'm Mike.'

Sperring pulled a print from the file and passed it to the doctor.

'Could that be an orchard symbol, Robert?' asked Pullman.

'I'm not an expert symbologist; however I could easily interpret this as being the identification of an orchard. The circular snake's body could be the O for orchard; the H could stand for Hebephilia. Where did you say this Wethersby came from?'

'Howden.'

'Yes this could be a double H not a drop shadow, as I first thought; this could be Howden Hebephilia Orchard, if we wanted it to be. On the other hand it could stand for Herpetology which is the study and keeping of reptiles including snakes; or that could be the cover story, if the meaning was ever brought into question. Alternatively the diamond pattern on the snake image could be that of a harlequin snake and stand for Howden Harlequins, perhaps a rugby or sports club. The problem with interpreting symbols is that generally they can be made to fit whatever meaning you want them to represent; as we know from recent popular literature.'

Pullman said. 'I sent a copy of the symbol to a DS at Howden, it meant nothing to him. He asked around some of his team down there and so far nobody recognises it.'

'If it is a symbol of Hebephilia then it's not surprising that no one has identified it, is it? There's only one reason they would.'

'Let's assume he was a member of one of these orchards; isn't it likely that he would have had regular contact with other members, yet by all accounts he never went anywhere, apart from the college and church, had no friends and was a bit of a loner,' explained Pullman.

'Don't think he would be a solitary predator, it's not the usual paradigm. As a teacher he would have had some influence over the young female students but probably not continuous enough to groom them. More likely the activities revolved around an orchard centred on the college; you might certainly consider taking a look at the church congregation,' said Allwood.

'Robert, I've met three of the other six members of the congregation, they're certainly odd but believe me they're stuck in a time warp; they couldn't groom a horse.'

'The head teacher did say there were one or two other members of the teaching staff at the college who didn't join in social activities and kept themselves to themselves,' said Sperring. 'Perhaps I ought to pay the place another visit and interview the staff, sir,' she suggested.

'Yes do that Lynne. Prioritise the women teachers; maybe there was a female Hebephile teacher or two, who didn't like Wethersby picking the ripe fruit; and obviously keep a look out for pit bulls,' he added with a smile and an uncharacteristic wink.

'I'd include ancillary staff in your enquiries too,' said Allwood. 'Maintenance, catering, office, whoever; perversion isn't just the preserve of the academics as we know only too well from the Soham tragedy.'

'Right Lynne over to you; forget about Claude and concentrate on this. I'll get DS Peak at Howden to assist; if you need any additional resources just shout.'

PC Simon Sinpul had lived with his parent's insensitivity throughout his twenty-two years of life. He was determined that one day he would either change his surname by deed poll or his forename. It wasn't quite so urgent now but in his school days he was ribbed mercilessly especially when the teacher called the register — Sinpul, Simon – it never ceased to raise a chuckle with his classmates and unsurprisingly school disco parties were a nightmare.

Even now, introducing himself as PC Sinpul was embarrassing so he always spelled it out, to leave the recipient in no doubt. Today was no exception, not that the overworked ward sister was paying any attention.

'Follow me constable,' she said ushering him into a side room. 'This is the man,' she said in dulcet tones, pointing to a patient lying unconscious on the bed. He had drips attached to a cannula on his right hand; a pulse monitor clipped to the index finger of the same hand and a heart monitor was blipping rhythmically by the side of the bed. 'He was brought in on Saturday night but not from the nightclub bombing. He was attacked and robbed close to the Humber Dock Marina. We have no idea who he is and he's been unconscious since he arrived.'

'He had nothing on him to identify who he is?' asked the young constable.

'Nothing at all.'

The fact that the patient's entire head was swathed in bandage wasn't going to aid identification. PC Sinpul was bewildered. 'Will he regain consciousness?' he asked.

'I do hope so constable. He's had surgery on the wound to remove bone fragments. He's still heavily sedated but the consultant expects him to be sitting up within the next twenty-four hours. There's no long term damage.'

'Well I can check the missing persons file to see if anyone of his description.....' He stopped and thought about the futility of that. He doubted that anyone had reported an Egyptian mummy missing, so until the bandages came off, who exactly would he be looking for. 'Can you give me any clues as to what he looks like under there?'

'He might be an actor or something like that, because he was wearing a false beard and his hair, what little there is, had been whitened. His natural colour is mousey brown. We think he's aged somewhere between thirty and forty.'

'Any distinguishing marks— tattoos or scars?'

'Yes, he's got two deep scars; one on his left thigh almost the entire length of the femur, the other is above his right clavicle. The consultant thinks it's most likely the result of a gunshot wound. There is also a tattoo on the bicep of his right arm.'

'Of?'

'Some words in Latin so the consultant says. I'll have to check his records; we've written them down but I can't remember what they are.'

'I don't think there's a lot we can do until we can get a shot of his face or talk to him. I'll have to leave it for a day or two until he regains consciousness.

'Yes, I can see that but we are required to report it, so we have.'

'Of course. Perhaps you'd give us a ring when he can be questioned. And could you get those words on the tattoo for me?'

'Please come with me to the nurse's station.'

101

As soon as they turned their backs the patient opened one eye; watching them leave the room. The Sister led the way to the central hub of the ward; the area was buzzing with nurses and consultants discussing patients and viewing notes. Orderlies with wheelchairs were waiting for paperwork, to move two patients to the radiography department and a third to the operating theatre. Sinpul was eyeing up the nurses as he followed in the wake of the Sister. She went to an overflowing wire basket and extracted the Invisible Man's case notes. She opened the slim folder and flipped through several pages.

'Here we are,' she said showing the PC Sinpul the open page.

He noted down the three words of the tattoo *Fortes Fortuna Adiuvat*. He had no idea what they meant.

Eleven

DC Steph Barnes was supervising the researchers in cross matching the list of dead and injured in the bomb blast with the list of people otherwise deceased in Hull, during the previous three months. Their efforts had so far produced no connection between the two files.

The forensic tests on the blast at the Deep had been put on hold. By the time the forensic scientists had finished collecting samples there were more than three thousand. Pullman had agreed with Crompton that, as they now knew that Claude was behind the blast and what explosive had been used, there was little point in wasting their scant budget resources on testing all those exhibits; especially now that they had Holy Trinity, the nightclub crime scene and the hotel room to examine.

Pullman had re-assigned Lynne Sperring to progress with the Wethersby murder case so he called Ashley Sharpe and Steph Barnes into his office for a brainstorming session, along with Robert Allwood.

'Right guys.' In the context of police brainstorming gals were guys too. 'We have little if any factual evidence that will help us identify, let alone catch, Claude,' said Pullman. 'So I want us to develop a profile of the sort of man we could be looking for. Doctor Allwood has given us some pointers which I'd now like us to flesh out so that, like Mary Shelley, we create our own monster. Now before you clever people say it, I know it was Frankenstein who created the monster but she created the fictitious doctor first, before he could do his bit.' He could see they all understood the basis of what he was saying. 'Now we have our own Doctor Frankenstein here,' he pointed to Allwood, 'so let's start with the skeleton. Over to you Robert.'

Allwood wasn't sure he liked the analogy with Frankenstein but let it ride. 'Well,' he stood up and moved to the flip chart stand, 'we know for sure that he is between thirty and forty years old.' He wrote down the key points as he spoke. 'That he's approximately five ten tall, walks with a limp; is left handed; was born locally or has lived in the area for a number of years.'

'Certainly lives locally,' said Sharpe. 'He had to be able to find out that we had aborted the church bombing, then react by creating the flying bomb and delivering it, all within about three hours, because we know he booked into the hotel at around seven pm.'

Allwood nodded agreement. 'We also know that he is an explosives expert; I think it's fair to say expert because he is certainly very good at what he does. And also he knows how to fly a model aircraft with extreme precision. That's why I think that he is connected with the military.'

'Let's take that as a profile of Claude, we know who he is but not what he looks like.'

'You asked me to check with the MoD which I am doing; I also recalled that, in the recently announced cut backs, the government is going to disband the second battalion of the first Yorkshire Regiment; so I've also been in touch with the barracks direct and they're getting together a list of all personnel being made redundant; from the top brass down.'

Pullman smiled. 'Good thinking, Steph. Nothing pisses somebody off more than being discarded; especially after they've put their life on the line serving Queen and country.'

'Yes sir, even more so when they've just come back from their fourth tour in Helmand Province.'

Not to be outdone Sharpe said. 'It occurred to me that as well as possibly having had an accident, the reason Claude hasn't been back in touch could be that he has been arrested on an unrelated charge. So I've checked with all the local nicks in a thirty mile radius and four have come back to me with a possible candidate. One was arrested in Cottingham, one in Beverley, another in Howden and another one in Goole. Should I speak to them sir or would you like to?'

'I think the local boys can do that Ash. All they need do is establish if the candidates have an alibi for Saturday night and last Friday night. If there is a firm favourite, then we can both go along to have a word if necessary.'

'Okay sir. One other thing sir; I was thinking that we ought to check out the Swiss bank account number that Claude gave us...'

'Bloody right we should Ash; I knew there was something gnawing away in the back of my head.' A possible prime lead and he'd overlooked it. 'Get on to it as soon as we've finished here,' he instructed Sharpe.

So now they knew who they were looking for; they just didn't know what he looked like or his location. Minor details.

The big issue on Pullman's mind was that the original deadline, set by Claude in his first extortion note, was rapidly approaching; now just twenty hours away. The hope that he might be apprehended before 11 am the following morning was not even in the mix. Patrols had already been assigned to guarding the Hull War memorial between Ferensway and Paragon Street.

Although a parade had taken place the previous day there was another planned for Tuesday morning. No cars were being allowed to park within a hundred metres of the sculpture for twenty four hours. Everyone wishing to pay their respects, at the memorial, would be allowed to do so but all bags would be searched prior to allowing access. Not that Claude was a suicide bomber but it was better to be over cautious than regretful.

'Ah young man you're awake. We were beginning to worry about you. How are you feeling?' asked staff nurse, Sara Collins.

'Where am I?' asked the mugging victim.

'Hospital, Hull Royal Infirmary you've had a bump on the head.' Something of an understatement. 'You were attacked by a mugger.'

'What day is it?'

'Monday. You've been unconscious for about thirty-six hours; you're lucky to be alive'

'Terry couldn't do it so it'll take more than some scumbag to finish me off.'

SN Collins didn't answer; confusion was commonplace after a cranial injury; the patient might still be concussed. She said, 'I'll inform the consultant that you're awake. I expect he'll pay you a visit a bit later. Are you comfortable? Anything I can get you?'

'I can look after myself; don't need you to do anything.'

'Sure, no problem,' said nurse Collins with a placatory tone 'But if you think of anything, just press your buzzer.'

'Where are my clothes?'

'The police took them away for checking, I think. You were attacked, pretty viciously; I guess they'll be looking for evidence of the attacker.' SN Collins didn't notice the patients pupils dilate. 'I expect they'll want to ask you a few questions when you're up to it; tomorrow perhaps.' She didn't explain that his jacket was covered in his own blood and that he had defecated when he was struck on the head and knocked unconscious. His clothes were unwearable but it wasn't important — he wasn't going anywhere for a few days yet.

'When can I have these bandages off?'

'I'll check with Mr Robertson.'

'Who's he?'

'The consultant surgeon who removed the bone fragments from your wound. It really was quite nasty.'

'It feels it.'

'What's your name?' She asked. The patient was silent. 'We'll need to get some particulars from you, Mr?' she asked but was ignored. 'Unfortunately the attacker took all your belongings; you had nothing on you to show your identity.'

'I don't know my name. I can't remember anything.' He lied.

'Where do you live?'

'I said I don't remember anything. I have no memory at all.'

'Are you married?'

The patient did not respond.

'Are you an actor?' she asked in reference to the false beard he was wearing on arrival. 'Do you have amnesia?'

He had to think quickly; would a patient suffering from amnesia know what amnesia was? Would he know what bandages were? Does loss of memory mean that you don't know the meaning of words? Bit late to be worrying about that now. 'For Christ sake stop asking questions, I don't remember anything!' he yelled in feigned frustration.

'I see; not to worry I'll let doctor know.'

The nurse left the room. The patient raised his head in an attempt to sit upright but the pain was too great for comfort and he

107

gently laid it back on the pillow. He didn't want to be in the hospital, he had things to do; that much he could remember.

Twelve

Tuesday morning was bright and sunny. The extra police presence, in the area around the war memorial, was self-evident, as was the traffic chaos caused by the stop and search procedure. The jams were further exacerbated by the parking restrictions in the immediate vicinity. Local businesses were much quieter than usual; complaints were made, by owners, to uniformed patrols, that such a heavy presence was somewhat excessive for what would, inevitably, be a small parade. The retailers were unaware of the reason for the heightened precautions.

In the CCTV control centre, staff were studiously monitoring pictures transmitted from cameras that had been refocused along Ferensway and numerous other approaches. Nothing seemed out of the norm. Pullman looked at the clock on his office wall; one and three quarter hours to go before the eleventh hour and still no contact from Claude. There was a surreal hush of expectancy around the building. Everything had been set in place; it was now just a question of waiting.

DS Sperring and DS Peak sat in a spare office at Howden College carefully sifting through forty-nine CRB and DBS certificates. Thirty-eight were for teaching staff and the remainder covered ancillary staff, including part-time workers. Nothing jumped off the pages to cause the pair any alarm or cause them to be suspicious of anyone in particular but then they weren't expecting to find that anybody on List 99 had been employed. Despite being renamed *Section 142 of the Education Act 2002* the list of people barred from working with children and vulnerable adults was still colloquially referred to as List 99. Habits developed over a ninety year period are hard to change. The list was maintained by the Department for Education in its various guises over that period but not every known sex offender was on the list — only those who worked with children or vulnerable adults whilst employed in a direct capacity. A sex offender who worked in a non-educational field may well find themselves on ViSOR, the Violent and Sex Offenders Register but would not appear on List 99 even if they switched careers into one where they had access to children. Only persons proven to be a sex offender whilst employed in an educational position were listed.

Having had specialist child protection training, Sperring was aware of the difficulty in identifying child abusers. Eleven members of the teaching staff, including Trevor Johnston, the headteacher, had been employed prior to the introduction of the Criminal Records Bureau in 2002, which meant that they had been checked out by the local police and, presumably, given a clean bill of health. Peak had been responsible for carrying out many of the checks himself, so he was familiar with the contents.

Although of equal rank, Peak fully understood that Sperring was leading the enquiry. She decided that they would split the interviews between the two of them rather than sitting through all forty odd together. The teaching staff had to be interviewed, as and when, classroom commitments would allow, so she was more than prepared to stay late into the evening and attend early in the morning, if necessary, to complete the sessions.

110

There were three key areas to be determined. How well did they know Wethersby? Did they have an alibi for Sunday October 6^{th,} when he was murdered, and did they know what the tattooed symbol meant? The division of the interviews was completely random; Sperring quite literally made two matching height piles of reports and handed one set to Peak who would conduct his interviews in a separate vacant room. The headteacher's PA was tasked with arranging the interview timings, which she did in no particular order; so neither Peak nor Sperring knew who amongst their allocated list would be next through their respective doors.

Sperring's first was Barbara Maldon. She looked little older than the students to whom she taught Media Studies, which seems to be the latter day catchall for students with no idea what they want to do for a career — apart from being famous which appears to be classed as a career in this era of instant celebrity.

'Hello I'm Barbara Maldon; I teach Media Studies.'

'DS Lynne Sperring,' she introduced herself gesturing to the teacher to take a seat. 'Thanks for sparing the time. As you know we are investigating the death of Thomas Wethersby.' The young teacher nodded demurely. 'How well did you know your colleague?'

'Not very,' she replied. 'I've been here about eighteen months now; we've exchanged a few words in the staff room but not really had a conversation.'

'Did you like him?'

'I didn't know him well enough to form an opinion. He seemed harmless enough.'

'What did you think of the allegations of rape made against him?'

'None of us thought they were true but I suppose there's always a little doubt in those situations.'

111

The police had not revealed the contents of Wethersby's hardrive to the public or media, whilst it was being investigated by the NCA, as part of Operation Yewtree. There was nothing to be gained from fanning the flames at this stage of the investigation.

'You've no idea why anyone would want to murder him?'

'Absolutely not!' Maldon exclaimed, surprised that she should even be asked the question.

'You've not seen any arguments or heated discussions he may have had with anyone since the allegations were made, or even before.'

'No.'

'Where were you on the night he was murdered, Sunday 6th October?'

Maldon's eyes widen to popping point. 'Me?'

'We have to ask everybody.'

'I was at my parents in Gainsborough for the weekend; it was my mother's sixtieth birthday; we had a family gathering before they went off on a cruise.'

'You were there Sunday night?'

'Not all night. The party was Saturday but my parents, my sister and my brother and his family and I, all went out for Sunday lunch. I left there about seven that evening, dropped my sister off in Louth, then drove home.'

'What time did you get home?'

'Nine o'clock just in time to watch the start of Homeland.'

Sperring showed her a picture of the tattoo. 'Have you seen this symbol before?'

Maldon studied it then turned her head to the right and looked down at the floor in deep in thought. 'Yes, I think I have.'

'Where?'

112

'I can't remember but I think I have seen it, or something very similar somewhere, but it's just not coming to me.'

'Think hard.'

'Is it important?' asked Maldon.

'It could be.'

'There's something in the back of my mind but....'

'Okay, please do think about it and if you can recall where you've seen it, I'll be here for the rest of the day or give me a call.' Sperring handed her interviewee a contact card. The young teacher did not look as though she had the strength to decapitate a male colleague but there was always the possibility that she knew someone who was capable.

The next three interviews went pretty much the same way. Ambivalent feelings towards Wethersby as a human being, a teacher and a possible rapist but they had no knowledge of the symbol.

The final interview before lunch was Bob Jenkins, the college caretaker. He wore a dark blue boiler suit and looked ten years older than the sixty-three years shown on his CRB report.

'Hello Mr Jenkins, I'm DS Lynne Sperring. Please take a seat. I understand that you knew Thomas Wethersby quite well.'

'I wouldn't say well but yeah I knew Tom,' said Jenkins as he sat down gingerly. 'I've done me back in,' he explained.

'If I remember rightly, you looked after his house and cat when he was on holiday earlier this year.'

'Yeah, true enough. I live in the next village to Tom; I pass his cottage on the way home so it was no problem to stop off and feed the cat.'

'Did you talk much with Tom?'

'Tom wasn't a great conversationalist. We just exchanged the time of day at college and odd words now and then, when we'd

113

cross paths in the post office in Clipton – we don't have one in our village anymore.'

'What interests did he have?'

'I know he was interested in photography, he had a good classical music collection and he had a thing about Julia Roberts.'

Sperring didn't think Wethersby's interest in the actress was something he would openly talk about so she guessed that Jenkins had wandered around the deceased's house in his absence.

'I understand that Mr Wethersby went to Thailand for his holiday.'

'Yeah they both did.'

'Both?'

'Him and the head — not together I don't mean; Mr Johnston's wife is Thai, so they go there twice a year I think.'

'But the head and Mr Wethersby were out there at the same time?'

'They overlapped certainly but Tom went out about a week or so before Mr Johnston and came back a week later than him I think. Yeah, I remember, Tom was only just back in time for the start of term. But I don't know if they go to the same place.'

Sperring raised her eyebrows in a gesture of both interest and surprise. She showed the image of the tattoo to Jenkins. 'Does this mean anything to you?'

He undid the pop stud on his breast pocket, pulled out a pair of spectacles and put them on, to study the image. He nodded 'Yes. Tom had this tattooed on his arm.'

Sperring didn't ask him how he'd come to see it but made a mental note that it might be something to bear in mind in the future. Have you any idea what it stands for?'

'It could stand for Heinrich Himmler or Hoorah Henry for all I know,' said Jenkins.

Sperring pulled back the photograph. 'Can you recall where you were on Sunday 6th October?'

'Yep, where I always am on a Sunday night; the Flying Horse quiz night; haven't missed one in over twelve years.'

'Did anyone see you there?'

'Everybody; I'm the quizmaster.'

'What time did the quiz end?'

'I try to make it last as close to last orders as I can so around ten thirty.'

'What did you do then?'

'I usually help Jed and Gwen tidy up and have another pint.'

'Did you on that night?'

'I expect so; no reason why I wouldn't have.'

It was a long shot to think that the old boy had finished his quiz and driven to the coast in the time scale; judging by his nose, which resembled a piece of cod roe, he liked a drink or two. Chances were that he'd had a few during the quiz and wouldn't have been capable of driving. Sperring thanked the caretaker and bade him farewell as he left the office. She flipped through the remaining CRB records on her pile and was disappointed that the headteacher was not amongst them. She'd check with Peak over lunch to see if he'd already seen Johnston; if not she would wrest the interview from him.

The eleventh hour of the eleventh day of the eleventh month came and went without incident. The planned parade march by ex-servicemen and several groups of Scouts proceeded without a hitch. Not so much as an inflated crisp packet had exploded. The

115

excessive police presence would not have deterred Claude; he would have anticipated the likelihood of that happening and, would certainly, have planned accordingly. Nevertheless the relief amongst the Operation Alligator team was palpable. The question as to whether or not it had been an idle threat was answered when DS Sharpe received an email from the bank in Zurich, to confirm that the account number given by Claude was fictitious. It was not a sequence of letters and numbers that was applicable to any financial institution in the country.

So now they knew for sure that the extortion demands were nothing more than part of a sick game being played by the seriously warped mind of a mass murderer.

DS Barnes had received the list of redundancies from the Yorkshire Regiment; she was busy checking them against the list of deaths and divorces in the area, over the previous six months. There were some five hundred and fifty soldiers in the 2nd Battalion of which half were being merged into the 1st and 3rd Battalions and half being told they were surplus to requirements. The check revealed nothing. Four of the surnames appeared on both lists, drilling down showed that they were all unrelated.

So it would appear that Claude wasn't a disgruntled soldier of the Yorkshire Regiment.

Sperring met Peak in the canteen. He'd opted for the chicken curry, she for the vegetable lasagne. Not that Lynne Sperring was a vegetarian, rather she was not a great fan of curry; the third choice of poached haddock looked singularly unappetising, having dried out under the display lights, in the warming cabinet.

'Any joy?' she asked Peak.

'Nothing so far; they've all got watertight alibis. Everyone thinks Wethersby was Mr Wonderful and no one knows what the tattoo symbolises. You?'

'Alibis seem okay. Same situation with Wethersby's character; one woman did think she'd seen the snake tattoo before but couldn't remember where or when. Could you pass the salt please?'

Peak passed both the salt and pepper.

'Did you manage to see Johnston?' asked Sperring.

'He's got a rock solid alibi; you already know what he thought about our man and he didn't know what the symbol was. Let's hope we have more joy this afternoon.'

'I'm not holding out a lot of hope.'

They ate in silence for a few minutes. Sperring pushed aside her lasagne. It was fine but she simply didn't feel like eating. 'How long have you been at Howden nick?' she asked Peak.

'About twelve years now.'

'Not thought about moving on?'

'Once or twice but it's an easy... ish life. Not too much hassle, I'm not overly ambitious; do me until retirement.'

'Does your wife like it here?'

'No wife. Got close to it once but it didn't work out. You?'

'A partner but we split a few weeks back. He's down in Cornwall now being a beach bum.'

'Upset?'

'No, not at all. It had run its course,' explained Sperring. 'You know how difficult it can be in the job. Hours aren't exactly conducive to playing happy families.'

'Difficult but not impossible. I know plenty of coppers who make it work well. It's down to individual personalities in the end I guess.'

'CID's worse of course.'

'I don't have any problem. It's all about work life balance.'

'And the cases you're on.'

'Yeah, I must admit this is the first murder case we've had locally for over ten years, and that was a domestic – over and done within a couple of days. He actually walked into the nick and admitted killing his partner. What's the situation with your bomber?'

'No joy identifying him yet. Supposed to be a big bang today but I'm sure the boss would have let me know if anything had happened. Our man Claude seems to have disappeared pro tem.'

'Just as well really. Nasty bastard.'

'And then some. Right I suppose we'd better get back to it. I was thinking that unless one of us has a breakthrough, we might as well call it a day when we've each finished. No need to hang around waiting for whichever one of us is last to finish; if there's anything that needs discussing call me, otherwise I'll give you a call tomorrow to wrap things up.'

'Suits me,' said Peak.

Sperring finished conducting her interviews half an hour later than Peak, who was long gone by the time she made her way through the reception atrium. Sperring left her visitor's badge on the reception counter and almost collided with Johnston as she turned towards the door.

'Whoops. Sorry about that,' said the headteacher. 'Have you finished what you came for?'

'Yes thanks.'

'Any outcome?'

118

'Not so far but it's early days.'

'Okay, if there's anything else you need just let me know.' He turned away and then turned back to face Sperring. 'You'll need an umbrella out there, it's raining heavily.'

Sperring nodded and walked to the door. Something made her stop and think – the female intuition for which she was famed; she turned and went back to the reception desk.

'Could you tell me what time Mr Johnston went out please?'

'He didn't go out, because he hasn't been in, until just now,' replied the receptionist.

'Are you sure?'

'Yes.' She checked her computer screen. 'Yes he's only swiped in once today, just a couple of minutes ago.'

'Might he not have forgotten to swipe in earlier on?'

'Mr Johnston! You must be kidding. He designed this system; they say he's a genius with computers besides which he's an absolute stickler for time keeping. Never forgets to swipe in and woe betide anyone who does.'

Sperring nodded. 'Thanks.'

Thirteen

The Chief Constable Pauline Crompton, her ACC, all the team on Operation Alligator and the good burghers of Hull had spent an anxious Tuesday on tenterhooks. No word from Claude. No explosion. No incidents. In fact it had been a quieter day than usual.

The CC, Iain Thwaite and Pullman sat in her office. It was pre-breakfast and they sat in silence, as if waiting for something, anything, to happen. Pullman sat opposite Crompton and noticed how agitated she looked – far from her normal ice maiden exterior. Her lips were pursed and she was moving them noticeably from side to side. Finally they parted and she said. 'What do you think Mike?'

Pullman thought it very unlikely that his boss would ever have a copy of Harry S Truman's sign on her desk. The bucks stops here was not a sentiment that he readily associated with his Chief Constable, not that he'd ever had occasion to test the validity of his viewpoint. Perhaps he was being unkind. Perhaps she genuinely had regard for his input. That's the way he chose to take her question.

'I've not heard the fat lady sing, so I'm guessing that it's not over yet. There will be a very good reason why he didn't carry-out his threat. We're looking into the possibility that he has been laid low with an illness or was seriously injured in his own blast, which would be poetic justice. We're still checking out the identities of

120

the injured in the hospitals. Some are still on the critical list. Most have been identified but there's half a dozen, or so, who don't seem to have anyone who's noticed they're missing. At the moment that's our best hope. If he's injured and gone to ground then all we can do is wait until he recovers and resurfaces. We're also checking to see if he's been arrested on some other charge.'

Compton said 'Be nice if we already had him in custody.'

'Sure would,' said Pullman, 'but I'm not holding my breath.'

'Wait and see is not a very proactive strategy,' said Thwaite.

'What choice do we have?' said Crompton. 'All we can do is maintain a high alert; keep the whole force on its toes and pray that we've heard the last of him. Keep me informed Mike.'

That was Pullman's cue to leave the office. 'Of course ma'am.' He said on his way out.

When he had gone Crompton took a light blue folder from her top drawer and placed it in front of her. 'The PSD have finished their investigation into Bob Cole's suicide. Nothing conclusive but the long and the short of it is that they believe the probability is that he did kill himself, over grief at Meg's murder.'

'So they couldn't find any other reason either,' said Thwaite.

'No.'

'Good. Well, not good; you know my view; I don't believe Bob had any other reason to hang himself. The loss of her son could have tipped her over the edge, could have tipped them both over in fact but they both knew Barry was doing what he loved best.'

'But even so not having a body to bury must have been very difficult.'

'Yes, Bob said that obviously seeing the video of Barry being executed by his captors was horrific and destroyed Meg; she couldn't obliterate the image from her mind; her son's body lying, rotting in some Afghanistan cave. He understood why the army

121

couldn't give in to the kidnapper's demands but Meg couldn't accept it. She couldn't understand why they wouldn't exchange her only son for the release of four Taliban prisoners. She never wanted him to join the army in the first place.'

'Like this Claude situation, you just can't give in to terrorist demands or there's no end to it.' Easy words for Crompton to say but not such an easy principle to accept by anyone personally involved in such an event.

'Losing a step son shattered his world too but then to have his wife murdered within a few months, unbelievable.' He shook his head in a display of disbelief. 'It's no wonder he became unbalanced; how could anyone cope with that.'

Crompton didn't know what to say now, any more than she had done at the time. She took a deep breath and exhaled forcefully. 'I want to recommend that you to be made up to DCC; would you have any problem with that?'

Thwaite was taken aback by the change of subject. 'Of course not. Thanks for the confidence.'

'I'll talk to Monkton; don't think he'll raise any objections.'

'Morning.' Pullman greeted Lynne Sperring as he walked through the outer office.

'Morning sir. Could I have a word?'

'Sure come in.' He walked into his office and booted his laptop. Sperring followed him in. 'How'd it go yesterday?'

'That's what I wanted to have a word about,' she said.

'Something interesting crop up?' He gestured for her to take a seat; she did.

'Not sure,'

'Okay what's on your mind?'

'Peak and I split the interviews and neither of us had any joy.'

'No confessions then?'

'Everyone seemed to like Wethersby and they all had pretty good alibis. I'll check out some of them but I don't think it will lead anywhere. One teacher said she recognised the H symbol but couldn't remember where from – she's thinking about it.'

'Good. So why the uncertainty?'

'The caretaker,' she referred to her notes, 'Bob Jenkins, told me that the Headteacher...'

'Trevor Johnston.'

'Yes, has a Thai wife and that they were both in Thailand at the same time as Wethersby this year.'

'Coincidence?' queried Pullman.

'Could be, but don't you think it strange that Johnston never mentioned it when we interviewed him.' Pullman moved his head from side to side in a maybe, maybe not, gesture. 'Well I think it's odd; what's even odder is that Johnston was on Peak's list and when I asked him if he'd questioned him, he said he had and that Johnston had a cast iron alibi for the night in question.'

'What's odd about that?'

'I don't think Peak actually interviewed him. When I was leaving last night, Johnston was just coming into the college. The receptionist said he'd been out all day and showed me the attendance record on the computer to prove it. So Peak couldn't have interviewed him.'

'Did you talk to DS Peak about it?'

'No, he'd left the college before me so I thought I'd discuss it with you first. See what your thoughts were.'

'My thoughts are that there's probably a perfectly reasonable explanation. Have a word with him and see.'

'Yes sir. I gather nothing happened on the Claude front yesterday.'

'Not a bloody thing.'

PC Sinpul stood in the hospital side room staring, wide eyed, at the empty bed.

He's not well enough to be out of hospital on his own,' said the staff nurse.

'When did he go?' asked the young constable.

'Sometime between 4am, when he was last checked and 7.30 am when the day shift took over.'

'How did he get out?'

'Can't answer that I'm afraid. No one saw him go.'

'Did he take his clothes?'

'Didn't have any. They were taken away by your lot, to examine I guess.'

'So what's he wearing?'

'He had one of our gowns on, as far as I know he still has.'

'So you're telling me that a patient, with his head in bandages, dressed in an operating gown, can get out of bed and leave the hospital without anybody noticing?'

'They had a cardiac arrest to deal with in the early hours. All the nurses had their hands full. We have got a hospital full of critical patients you know.' She snapped 'We're severely understaffed, particularly at night. It must have happened then. We found his bandages in the bathroom.'

'What about CCTV. Do you have any?'

'Not in the wards but we do in the main corridors and public areas.'

'Have you had a look?'

The nurse threw him a visual dagger. 'Of course, we've got plenty of time to sit around watching videos; the patients can just look after themselves while we look at films to see if we can spot an idiot.'

'Sorry, I wasn't thinking.'

'Now there'll be an inquiry, and that's more time and paper work; as if we don't have enough to do.'

'Will the guy survive out there without proper care?'

'He'll have a sore head for weeks but providing he doesn't get it bashed again, he'll live I suppose.'

'Did you get any information from him, name or anything?'

'No, he said he was suffering from amnesia and couldn't remember his name or any details of his past.'

'You don't sound convinced.'

'I'm not and nor was the consultant. It's very rare to get someone with full amnesia and we didn't get the chance to assess him properly.'

'I think I'd better report this one straight away. Sorry to be a pain, but do you think you could have a word with whoever and get me the CCTV recordings for the period he went missing?'

The nurse was not happy about it judging by the glower on her face, nevertheless she went off to sort it out.

Sinpul radioed in to the station. The situation rang sufficient alarm bells with Sergeant Carter, on the desk, for him to send the details up to the Operation Alligator incident room. DC Sharpe spotted the possibility immediately. He knocked on Pullman's open door and went in.

'Guv, think we may have Claude or rather had Claude.'

'What?'

'A mugging victim discharged himself from the RI in the early hours of this morning and disappeared.'

'So what makes you think there's a connection to Claude?'

'According to the initial report on Monday the hospital called in to report him as a missing person....'

'I thought you said he disappeared this morning?'

'Right let me start again guv.'

'Yes, please do.'

'Last Saturday the victim of a severe mugging at the marina – a stone's throw from the Holiday Inn' he said with a knowing look, 'was taken into the RI. He was unconscious and had no ID. He underwent some minor surgery and, on the Monday morning, the hospital reported the matter to us. We sent along a young officer who, according to his report, was told that the victim was probably an actor because he was wearing a false beard, a white goatee beard.'

Pullman's eyes widened. 'Go on.'

'The guy was wrapped in bandages and attached to various drips and machines, so our young friend decides to log the bare details and go back this morning, by which time the nursing staff said, he should be in a fit state to be questioned.'

'Sounds reasonable; pity they didn't let us know.'

'Uniform didn't think there was anything worth informing us about, it was just a case of identification against the missing persons register. Can't blame them it was only yesterday that we started to look at the possibility that Claude may have had an accident or be ill.'

Pullman begrudgingly accepted the explanation. 'So what have we got?'

'An unknown male, IC one, mid-thirties, short cropped hair grade one by all accounts.'

'Army?'

'Half the male population look like squaddies these day guv. Hang on a minute though.' Sharpe turned to the second page of the report. 'He did have a tattoo on his upper right bicep saying Fortes Fortuna Adiuvat.'

'Fortune Favours the Brave,' translated Pullman. 'It's the motto of the Yorkshire Regiment – my uncle was an officer, captain I think. Make sure Steph knows that.'

'What? That your uncle was a captain.'

If looks could kill Sharpe was a goner. 'Save the comedy Ash. Time and place and all that.'

'Sorry guv.'

'Any other distinguishing features?'

'He was admitted along with dozens of others on Saturday night, covered in blood. They eventually cleaned him up to operate but no one was paying that much attention to his appearance. A and E was just a conveyor belt for twenty-four hours.'

'Did he have a limp?'

Sharpe raised his eyebrows in surprise.

'Okay, forget I asked that.'

'Actually he did have a scar on his right leg and his shoulder so he may well have been injured at some time; a limp is a definite possibility.'

'This is sounding better and better. Don't suppose they took any photos?'

'There'll no doubt be an x-ray of his head but that's not much good for an e-fit.'

Pullman let the joke pass this time. 'What about CCTV?'

'That's being brought in now. We'll get straight on to it when it arrives.'

'This could be the breakthrough we need. It's sounding hopeful. Whoever he is, he obviously didn't want to be questioned.'

'Apparently not guv or else he had some very urgent business to attend to.'

'It's him Ash. I know it is. I can feel it. Bollocks, we had him.'

Lynne Sperring rang DS Peak at Howden Police Station four times before she got to speak to him. He was either out, interviewing suspects or just not at his desk. When she eventually got through to him, he was his usual ebullient self.

'Hi Lynne how's it going? Any more on the Claude front?'

'Fine thanks; no, nothing further yet.'

'What can I do for you?'

'Just following up on the interviews; when you saw Trevor Johnston yesterday was he co-operative?'

'He's always his normal self, generally a placid character.'

'You say he had a cast iron alibi. What was it?'

'Have you got a problem with him then?'

'No, no, just wondering.'

'Well actually if you must know, I'm his alibi.'

'Sorry?'

'We were together that night; he was with me.'

'You. Together with the headteacher. Why?'

'Don't sound so surprised. I may not be brain of Britain but I happen to be very good at chess and we meet once a month for a game or two.'

'I didn't know. So you were together that night playing chess; your place or his?'

'Mine. What is this? Do you doubt him or me if it comes to that?'

'No, it's just that I've been checking through the staff attendance system and according to them Johnston wasn't in the college until gone five last evening.' It was an acceptable white lie to expose another.

There was a silence before Peak said. 'Alright, I didn't actually speak to him yesterday. But I knew where he was that night; we already knew what he thought of Tom and I'd previously questioned him about the tattoo, so there didn't seem to be any point in seeing him face to face.'

'Tom? Did you know Wethersby on a personal level as well?'

'No, of course not; never met the guy except for questioning him about the allegations. I know Trevor because we used to both belong to the Howden team that played in South Yorkshire Chess League. Look where are you going with this? Okay so I used a bit of poetic licence, don't tell me you've never done it.'

'Okay, I won't tell you; but I haven't. Anyway that clears up the discrepancy on the attendance system. Thanks. One other thing any comeback on the DBS checks?'

'Not so far.'

'Looks like we're drawing blanks all round then. Ah well back to the grindstone. Thanks. You'll let me know if you come up with anything.'

'Of course. See you.'

Sperring replaced the receiver and sat back in her chair. Perfectly plausible excuse she thought; hardly a disciplinary matter. But it was the fact that he had referred to Wethersby as

129

Tom that concerned her more. On an intuitive whim she rang Dorothy Grimshaw the college secretary.

'Hello it's DS Sperring, we met briefly on my visits.....'

'Yes of course Detective Sergeant how can I help you?'

'Are you responsible for doing the DBS checks on staff?'

'Well yes, I suppose I am. When it was the CRB, I just gave the details to our local police station and they ran the checks.'

'Anybody in particular.'

'Detective Sergeant Peak.'

'What about now with DBS checks?'

'Mr Johnston said to keep doing it through DS Peak to save me any additional work.'

'Despite the fact that you can easily do it direct online.'

'Yes Mr Peak, DS Peak,' she corrected herself, 'vets them for us and acts as an unofficial advisor.'

'I see.'

'I hope I haven't got him into trouble. It's very kind of him.'

'Isn't it just.' Lynne Sperring mulled over the situation. Being friends with Johnston wasn't illegal and doing the checks didn't constitute a breach of procedure. Nothing untoward that warranted the involvement of the Professional Standards Department, although that wasn't her decision to make. She decided to dig a little deeper before she took it to Pullman.

Ashley Sharpe and Steph Barnes were watching the hospital CCTV recordings. The cameras recorded one still frame every three seconds and, being in black and white, had the stuttering visual appeal of watching an old silent movie; all that was missing was the occasional caption frame and piano music. The nurse's report clearly showed that the patient was still in bed at 4 am. Access and egress, via the main entrance, after 10 pm at night, required a security pass to be inspected by a security guard. It was not a perfect system, so, as a precautionary measure, the recording for that entrance had to be viewed, as well as the busier entrance to the A &E department. They saw nothing of interest. No one that looked like their suspect went in either direction.

'Nothing guv,' said Sharpe.

'He must have got out of the building somewhere,' said Pullman.

'Maybe a fire door that wasn't covered by the cameras,' suggested the young DC. 'Possibly a window?'

'He didn't have the time or opportunity to reccy the place so I reckon he would probably have had the balls to just walk out of the front door, as bold as brass. If he did that, then he would have been dressed so as not to arouse suspicion. He could hardly have strolled past everyone with his arse hanging out of a hospital gown. Let's have another look. Set it up, I'll join you.'

Watching three thousand six hundred frames, at the rate of twenty frames a minute over three hours, is enough to ensure a visit to Specsavers. Pullman rubbed his eyes wearily, he yawned deeply and sent a Mexican wave of stretched arms and contorted faces sweeping around the office. According to the tape at 6.32 am a patient in a wheelchair was manoeuvring himself towards the door when he was stopped by a security guard, who appeared to be questioning him, before helping the incapacitated man to turn around and return to whence he came.

'That's him,' said Pullman with excitement rippling through his voice. 'Gotcha.'

131

Sharpe looked perplexed. 'Guv? He's too old surely. He must be eighty if he's a day and suffering from dementia, if he's wheeling himself around at that time of the morning.'

'Not the patient Ash. The guard; look closely. That uniform is just a bit too tight for him and the cap doesn't fit properly but the big giveaway is the feet.'

'Christ he's wearing black trainers! But hang on guv he's not limping.'

'With these jerky pictures it's difficult to tell. Rewind a couple of frames.' Sharpe complied. 'There look, just a hint of a limp. Let's face it we don't know how severe the limp is.'

'Yeah could be guv,' said DC Sharpe.

'Look, he's just flashed a pack of cigarettes at the Triage nurse to indicate that he's going outside for a smoke,' said Pullman.

'But she'd know that smoking isn't allowed anywhere on the hospital grounds.'

'Yeah, like she's going to argue about it at six-thirty in the morning, after a night shift in A and E. You've noticed the bastard is making sure the cameras don't pick up on his face though. Where are the tapes from the external cameras? There must be cameras outside.'

'We haven't got them. I thought we'd see him from the inside on the internal system.'

'Well get them here pronto.'

'Sorry guv I....'

Steph Barnes interrupted the apology. 'Boss, the collator thought this might be of interest; a nurse reported her Mini Cooper stolen from outside A and E at 7.30 am this morning when she finished her shift.'

'Bingo,' said Pullman. 'Too much of a coincidence not to be our man. Right, get a description of the car out there. I want it found. Get the CCTV checked for that time, on all roads leading from the hospital. It's bound to have been caught on at least one. Then, when you get the direction, see how far we can follow his route on cameras. Wherever it's abandoned won't be too far from his base. He'll be too weak to travel far on foot.'

Pullman made a mental note to get the team to agree how to address him; sir, guv, boss he was never too sure if they were talking to him or not. He thought that perhaps guv was the best, less formal option although he knew, from past experience, that getting Lynne Sperring to call him anything other than sir, would be an uphill battle.

Pullman went back to his office to check his Facebook. There was still no message from Claude. He hoped it was a good omen but experience told him otherwise. If the anonymous patient was Claude then surely it was just a matter of time before he resurrected his plans; unless of course he really was suffering from amnesia and had forgotten what his plans were.

Hope springs eternal.

Fourteen

Thursday 13th November

Operation Alligator was building momentum. Pullman called the team together for an update briefing.

'Right ladies and gentlemen it seems that our man Claude was mugged at the Humber Dock Marina last Saturday; presumably as he was leaving the hotel, having detonated the club bomb. That explains why he never went back to clean up and why we've not heard from him since. It makes finding him all the more urgent, before he has time to pick up where he left off. As well as the profilers description, we are pretty confident that he is ex-military and almost certainly in a battalion of the Yorkshire Regiment, given that he bore a tattoo of their motto on his upper arm. Steph.'

Steph Barnes stood up and addressed the gathering. 'We've checked the records of the proposed regimental redundancies against the list of possible trauma victims over the past six months; so far we haven't come up with a match. We now know that our prime suspect has a deep scar on his right leg, possibly indicating that he has been injured in service so I've arranged an interview with a...,' she consulted her note book, '...Lieutenant Colonel Richard Allenby, to check out any member of the regiment who has been discharged through injury or has been dismissed the service in the last two years.'

Pullman took back the floor. 'Although the profile puts him as a local man he could have served with the first battalion which is

134

stationed down in Warminster. They're equipped with armoured vehicles and are also experts at close arm combat. Alternatively he could have served his time on Cyprus, at Episkopi, with the second battalion. They're a highly trained infantry unit capable of sorties anywhere they're needed. Whichever battalion our suspect was in, you can be sure he knows how to look after himself so when we do find him, I don't want any heroics okay; he's a cold blooded killer, so it's team handed with armed back-up. Do I make myself clear?'

Judging by the enthusiastic nods of agreement, Pullman had made himself abundantly clear, much to the relief of most of the team. They all accepted that putting themselves at risk was sometimes a necessary part of the job but being ordered not to do so made the decision process a little easier. Pullman knew however that, if push came to shove, they'd disregard his words and do what their instincts told them.

'We believe that our man stole a red and black Mini Cooper from the hospital car park.' Pullman stepped to his right and pointed to a street map. 'From the CCTV footage we know that the mini turned left on to Anlaby Road when it left the hospital.' He indicated the route. 'It then turned left again onto Ferensway, left again onto Spring Bank before turning right on to Princes Avenue; a residential road leading towards Pearson Park. Then it disappeared. Our man may have hidden it somewhere; we're prioritising locating the stolen mini with the beat bobbies including PCSOs. I'm convinced that he will have abandoned it within a maximum of two or three miles of his base, which will allow us to concentrate resources. Any questions?'

Barnes said, 'Not exactly a question sir but if he is in pain from the head wound he may need to visit a pharmacy for painkillers so perhaps we ought to alert all the local chemists to keep an eye out.'

135

'OK Steph good point. Ash can you get that sorted? And get them to double check their security. Our man isn't beyond breaking in to get what he wants.' Pullman was annoyed with himself for not thinking of it but at the same time pleased that Steph had. Sharpe nodded affirmatively. 'Anything else?' asked Pullman.

'Couldn't we issue details of the car to the media; a member of the public might know where it is.'

'Maybe in a couple of days, if we don't find it. I don't want to let Claude know we have connected him with the hospital. He's probably figured out that we have but I'd rather leave him unsure.'

Sharpe said, 'Should I go along with Steph guv?'

'I'm going to tag along for that. I need the fresh air.' Pullman said with a smile. In actual fact he had decided that his rank might help to get more joy from the army and he wanted to have a private chat with DC Barnes, to make sure she was coping with her problems at home. 'Anything else?'

There were no more questions or suggestions.

'Okay then before you disperse I'd like to say a couple of things. Firstly thanks to you all for your thoughts over the past few months it's been a difficult time but the spell in London and chasing Claude has helped a lot.' Pullman thought it was best to raise the issue and clear the air. It would hopefully allow them to concentrate fully on the job in hand rather than keep watching him to see how he was coping. 'I'm sure I will get down from time to time but right now I am completely focussed on the job.'

'Yeah we know guv,' said Sharpe assuming responsibility as the team spokesperson.

'And that's the other thing,' said Pullman, 'I don't know if I'm guv, boss, sir, twat or even something worse, so could you please decide what I am. If it's any help I'm not so fond of boss, sorry Steph.'

'I call you guv, guv,' said Sharpe, 'but I don't mind what I call you.'

'I prefer sir to guv, sir,' said Sperring but I'll go along...'

'I don't care what it is; just agree amongst yourselves but don't waste time discussing it. Okay?'

'Right guv.'

'Yes sir.'

Not even the Women's Institute can make a jam like the traffic in York; certainly not when road works on the inner ring road reduce the flow to a single lane, controlled by temporary three way traffic signals. Pullman lowered the window on Steph Barnes' Citroen and took a deep breath of, not very fresh, air. They had moved little more than one hundred metres in ten minutes. They were on their way for the interview with Lieutenant Colonel Richard Allenby at the headquarters of the Yorkshire Regiment.

'How's Jack doing?' Pullman asked his driver.

'So so,' Steph said looking out of the driver's side window at nothing in particular. 'Has his good days. Unfortunately I'm rarely there when they occur. But we manage.'

Steph's husband, Jack, had been a paramedic with the RAF Search and Rescue Service. Highly skilled, incredibly fit and dedicated to his job, he had dealt with hundreds of call outs to rescue sailors from capsized craft, irresponsible members of the public cut off by incoming tides and even on remote hilltop locations, which the Yorkshire Air Ambulance couldn't access. But that was all in the past. Eighteen months previously he had been part of the crew called out to Bempton Cliffs, to rescue an errant birdwatcher who, having ignored the RSPB's cliff top warning signs, jumped over a fence, ventured too close to the cliff edge and slid down seventy feet to a rocky outcrop inhabited by nesting gannets, puffins and guillemots. The man had a serious head injury along with a broken leg, requiring urgent hospitalisation.

The crew of the Sea King helicopter consisted of two pilots, the radar operator who also acted as the winch operator during the rescue and Jack the winchman, a fully trained paramedic. His role was to be lowered on the winch line to supply medical assistance and comfort to the victim, before hauling him up to safety.

Bempton Cliffs are amongst the highest and most rugged on mainland Britain. They look spectacular but the ravages of the North Sea make them extremely inhospitable to all but the most fearless of seabirds.

On that particularly blustery afternoon Jack Barnes was being lowered very carefully. Every correct procedure and precaution was being rigidly implemented. He had descended about fifty feet and was establishing verbal communication with the conscious man when a freak updraft, of almost gale force wind, caught hold of Jack and sent him crashing uncontrollably into the cliff face. He hit the Limestone rock with such force that he broke his back in several places along with an arm and his clavicle. It was all over in a few seconds. Jack was dangling unconscious on the end of the winch cable like a broken, one string puppet. There was nothing for the crew to do but winch him delicately into the helicopter and fly him straight to hospital. The captain radioed RAF Leconsfield and another rescue team was scrambled to complete the rescue of the stricken amateur ornithologist.

138

'I don't suppose he'll....'

'No.' said Steph anticipating the question. 'There's nothing more they can do. He'll be in a wheelchair for ever.' Jack was paralysed from the waist down. His upper body and all normal senses had been unaffected. 'He's not finding it easy to come to terms with being paraplegic, nor are the kids.'

'Must be difficult for you too.'

'Very.'

'Look Steph, once we've got this case under wraps, I'll see if I can arrange some leave for you. Spend some time at home.'

'To be honest, I'd rather be at work. It's a terrible thing to say, I know, but while he's still in a prolonged self-pity stage, all we do is argue, so the less we see of each other the easier it is.' She moved the car forward a few yards.

'It might seem tough now but at least he's still around.'

'It's terrible I know but once or twice I've thought it would have been easier for both of us if he wasn't.'

'Don't even think it, not for one minute. The torment you're feeling now is nothing compared to the pain and emptiness you'd feel if he hadn't survived. Trust me I know.'

'You're right boss, sorry.' She realised it was a selfish comment to make, given what he'd been through.

Equally he couldn't think of anything appropriate to say to Steph on the issue that wouldn't rekindle his own feelings so he changed the subject. 'How are you getting on with young Sharpe then?'

'He's alright. A bit over enthusiastic but weren't we all to start with.'

'Seems a bright lad, very willing. I've got high hopes for him.'

'We should get through the next signal change. I was thinking we could park in St George's and walk from there.'

'Yeah, good idea. I could do with stretching my legs.' He glanced sideways at Steph to see if she had any reaction to that comment given the subject of the previous conversation. She showed no reaction.

Steph paid and displayed. They walked along Tower Street past the grassy mounds, where York castle had once stood, to Clifford's Tower, which is just about all that remains of the castle built by William the Conqueror. At the far end of the ancient monument, Tower Street ceases to be designated the B1229 and becomes a side road on the corner of which, stands the Georgian terrace that houses the Yorkshire Regiment headquarters and the museum.

They were greeted by Lieutenant Colonel Allenby; a tall man in his mid to late forties with salt and pepper hair and piercing blue eyes. The officer welcomed them and took them through to his tastefully decorated office. Aged oil paintings of distinguished soldiers adorned the oak panelled walls. Pullman assessed that they were surrounded by antiques of sufficient auction value to have generated funds for enough pairs of boots to shoe all three battalions or keep the Ark Royal from being decommissioned. It occurred to him, in that moment, that there were probably enough valuable antiques, in similar government buildings around the country, to halve the national debt, if sold off.

'What exactly can I do for you?' asked the officer.

Steph spoke first. 'As I told your Captain Morrison on the telephone, we believe that the person we are looking for in connection with a series of bombings in Hull is, or rather was, a member of the Yorkshire Regiment.'

'On what do you base that belief?' said the affronted officer.

'The man we're looking for has a tattoo of Fortes Fortuna Adiuvat on his bicep.'

140

'And because that is the regiment's motto you think he's a soldier?'

'Well it's the obvious line of enquiry sir.' said Steph.

'I wouldn't disagree but, although it is our motto, it is not exclusive to the regiment. Those words have been in general use for hundreds, if not thousands, of years...'

Pullman interrupted. 'As DC Barnes said sir, the regiment is the most likely starting point and there are other indications that our man was in the military.'

'Such as?'

Pullman ignored Allenby. He came here to ask questions not answer them. 'We have a list of all those who are being made or are likely to be made redundant but we need a list of all soldiers over the last, say two years, who have been discharged due to injuries or dismissed on disciplinary grounds.'

'That will probably take some time.' said the Lieutenant Colonel.

'Captain Morrison told me that the information was all on computer here and could be pulled off in a matter of minutes,' said Steph.

Pullman added. 'I'm sure you want to fully co-operate with us, don't you sir.'

The officer smiled and leaned forward, stretching his arm across the desk. 'Of course Chief Inspector, I apologise if it sounded as if I was being obstructive.' He pressed a button on his intercom and said, 'Captain Morrison would you come to my office please.'

Morrison must have been waiting outside the door because it seemed to open almost immediately. 'Sir,' he said as he entered the office.

'Nigel would you get together a list of everyone who has left the regiment in the last two years for any reason whatsoever.'

141

'Sir.' Morrison left the room.

'Thought it best to cover all possibilities while we were at it.'

'Thanks.'

'Tell me Lieutenant Colonel, are any of your men trained to fly remote controlled reconnaissance drones.'

'We leave the ones that carry weaponry to our American cousins but we do use low level spy drones for surveillance; safer than sending one of our chaps into tricky areas.'

'One particular battalion?'

'No. All four, well three now. Even our reservists undergo training, although none of them has yet been required to use their skills, as far as I am aware.'

'Are they trained down in Warminster?' asked Pullman.

'No; that's the armoured divisions. Our infantry is trained over at Catterick Garrison; it's the largest training centre in the UK. I was stationed there myself for a while.'

'Oh yes. I've seen the shooting ranges on Grinton Moor. My wife and I used to walk over there quite often.'

'Yes I love the Dales too, especially that stretch from Leyburn across to Grinton; once you get past our ranges the views are quite spectacular. You don't walk there now?'

'My wife died a few months back...'

'I'm terribly sorry I didn't mean to...'

'Don't worry.' Pullman knew he was going to have to get used to that happening. 'Friends tell me that bereavement is not as torturous as a divorce that you weren't expecting. Knowing that someone you love is with someone else and doesn't want to be with you.'

'It's certainly not something I'd want to go through again that's for sure,' said Allenby.

Now it was Pullman's turn to apologise. 'I'm sorry I didn't mean...'

Allenby smiled. 'Touché,' he said. 'Let's quit this before we both get depressed.'

The efficient Morrison entered the office and handed his commanding officer a slim sheath of paper. 'These are the misconduct discharges and the honourable discharges for injury and incapacity sir. The 'all others' category will be off the printer in a few moments sir.' He left the room.

'Doesn't look too big a list,' said Pullman.

'Deceptive I'm afraid,' replied Allenby. 'There are two hundred and seventy three on the sick and injured list and,' he turned over to the final sheet, 'thirty eight on the list for disciplinary reasons.'

'Really,' sighed Steph.

'As you can tell we weren't expecting that many,' explained Pullman.

'It's a sad fact of life that literally thousands of our armed forces personnel are discharged each year on medical grounds. That sounds as though we discard anyone who isn't fit, without a second thought, but I assure you we don't. All soldiers leaving us go through a resettlement process, which includes re-employment courses, how to apply for positions, CV preparation that kind of thing, some do work placements, training and further education. If a soldier is being medically discharged with an injury or illness which means they require additional support, in finding suitable employment, a Personnel Recovery Officer will put his or her name to the Defence Transition Assessment Board for them to access the Recovery Career Services.'

'Don't suppose you would have retrained our man to be a mass murderer.'

'As far as I'm aware that isn't one of the courses we offer.' Allenby placed the lists on the desk close to, and facing, Pullman. 'As you will see there's the name, last known address details, army number and reason for discharge.' He pointed at the first name on the list. This one had an arm amputated; the next one had severely impaired eyesight...'

'Right we can rule out those then. Our boy has both arms and good enough eyesight to fly a quadcopter drone, loaded with explosives, into a crowded night club.'

'In that case you'll be able to rule out a lot more for similar reasons.'

'Our guy has a damaged leg, big scar walks with a limp.'

'Well you see the ones with leg injuries so that will whittle it down for you. But do watch out because the person may have a leg injury but been discharged for psychological problems, which may or may not have been related to the injury; in which case only the mental issue would be listed as the reason for discharge.'

Nothing is ever straight forward, complained Pullman inwardly. Ah well he was sure that Steph and Ash between them would sort the wheat from the chaff. In this case of course it was, unusually, the chaff that they wanted.

'Guess we'd better start sifting,' said Pullman. Steph knew she was the one who would be handed the sieve.

Captain Morrison re-entered the office clutching an additional list. Allenby motioned to him to give the papers directly to Pullman. 'These were discharged for miscellaneous reasons ranging from natural causes, cancers, heart problems that sort of thing to dishonourable discharges for a sudden attack of pacifism or cowardice in the face of the enemy etcetera.'

144

Allenby said. You'll forgive me, if I hope the man you're looking for was never with the regiment; it's the sort of thing with which the media would have a field day.'

'Thanks for all your help,' said Pullman.

'You're welcome. I'm going to be out and about a lot over the next few weeks so, if there's anything further we can do, please speak directly with Captain Morrison.'

They exchanged farewell handshakes. Pullman and Barnes walked back to the car. The traffic was now even more congested, however they had no option but to take their chances because, as rush hour approached, the situation would worsen. Pullman was very tempted to instruct Steph to switch on the blues but being the fine upstanding copper he was, he resisted the temptation.

Fifteen

The man they suspected of being Claude had now been out of hospital for over twenty-four hours but still no word. Pullman sat in his office, pondering the lack of contact, when his mobile phone chimed to indicate a text message. It was in fact a picture message from Richard Pointer at the National Crime Agency in London. It was a picture of the same tattoo that had been found on Thomas Wethersby's arm.

The accompanying message simply read – *Call me. Richard*

Pullman did so. Pointer answered immediately.

'Hello Mike, how's things?'

'They'll be a lot better when we find our bomber,' said Pullman.

'I was wondering if you'd had any joy on that front. Still, just a matter of time, I'm sure.'

'So what's with the picture?' asked Pullman.

'I thought you'd be interested. I was in a meeting yesterday, with colleagues in the Child Exploitation and Online Protection Command, discussing the latest Operation Endeavour success.'

Pullman cut in, 'Yes nasty business, bloody sick world we live in.'

'Yes, sure is. Anyway, as you know they just made some arrests in the Philippines; they're closing in on a paedophile ring in Thailand and one or two of the suspects have been seen to have a tattoo of that symbol. If I remember rightly the murder victim in

Bridlington case you were working on also had that symbol tattooed on his arm.'

'Absolutely right he did. Any idea what it means?'

'According to CEOP it's used as an identification mark by the Thai syndicate they've uncovered in Hua Hin.'

'Ah, so it is a double aitch. So this Hua Hin is in Thailand?'

'Yes.'

'How do you spell that?' As Pointer spelled it out Pullman entered it into a search engine. 'I see; it's on the long thin bit that leads down to Malaysia.' The geography wasn't important but Pullman wanted to have a clear picture in his mind of the region, which he now realised was close to Singapore as well as the Philippines.

'That's right but that isn't the important bit. They believe that the gang are being orchestrated from somewhere else.'

'The Philippines?'

'They're not sure yet but according to my colleague DI Sue Proctor they believe the trail may lead back to the UK as it did with the current case.'

'Interesting,' said Pullman. 'So you're thinking Wethersby could be connected.' It was a statement rather than a question.

'The thing is, Sue reckons it's too much of a coincidence and she doesn't believe in coincidences. Very pragmatic is our Sue, so she wants to talk to you about the case.'

'No problem. I'd obviously want Lynne involved. She's been working on enquiries whilst our bomber has been quiet.'

'So is it alright if I get Sue to give you a call to set something up?'

'Absolutely.'

'Okay might be tomorrow now but she'll call. Whilst I'm on you might like to know that we're still tracking the SOC situation.

147

Things are quietening down on that front but we're keeping an eye out for splinters.'

'Thanks for that Richard. I expect I'm going to be down in London when the trial starts in January, any chance we could meet up for a beer.'

'No problem. Be nice to see you again.'

'Thanks. I'll wait for Sue ...?'

'Proctor.'

'I'll wait for Sue Proctor's call then. See you.'

'Cheers.'

Pullman called Lynne Sperring into his office and updated her on his conversation with Pointer.

'This is warming up nicely,' she said. 'Right I'll find out where Wethersby's holiday destination was – I just know it's going to be this Hua Hin place.'

Pullman nodded agreement. 'While you're at it find out where Johnston's wife comes from. Five will get you ten that it's....'

'Hua Hin,' Sperring completed the sentence. She was way ahead of him.

Steph Barnes and Ashley Sharpe were ploughing through the lists collected from regimental headquarters. Descriptions of the injuries sustained by the soldiers were horrific to read, as were the psychological assessments of the consequences of post traumatic syndrome.

'These guys are real heroes,' said Sharpe.

'Why are they?'

'They're putting their lives on the line every day for Queen and country.'

'Some are, but that's what they're paid to do, doesn't make them heroes,' said Steph, 'it makes them serving soldiers.'

'Your Jack was a hero risking his life the way he did.'

'He was doing his job. Why does that make him a hero? He knew the risks. It's what he wanted to do. I'm very proud of what he did but doing his job doesn't automatically make him a hero.'

'Yeah but fighting in a war is....'

'Dangerous, sure but they're not forced to sign up. I've got a cousin who has wanted to be a soldier since he was a child. It's all he ever dreamt of doing, now he's in Afghanistan living that dream. Why does that make him a hero? Same goes for thousands of others.'

'More of a nightmare than a dream. I bloody well wouldn't want to do it,' said Ash.

'Nor would I, and don't get me wrong, I like living in a free country, well relatively free country; and I'm very glad that there are men and women who fight so that I can, but they're not conscripts, they're not press ganged into doing it; it's their job they apply to do it. Of course there are some heroes, some soldiers that go beyond the call of duty, you know, rescue their wounded mates from burning buildings whilst being shot at by the enemy or whatever, but they're few and far between. They're heroes and they deserve all the praise they get but you'll never convince me that someone, doing what they're paid to do, should be lauded as a hero. I think we're debasing the meaning of the word.'

'Alright then what about this guy – had both his legs blown off by a land mine he's a real...'

'Don't tell me that he's a real hero, cos in my book he's not. I'm sorry it's a horrible, horrible thing to have happened and I feel

149

very sorry for him and his family, I know what they'll be going through, been there, bought the tee shirt but he was out there doing his job.'

'So to you it's no more than a work place accident?'

'Sort of....more or less.'

'Jesus,' said Ash.

'Okay tell me is a fireman who goes into a burning building to rescue someone, doing his job. Doing what he picks up his wages for?'

'I suppose so.'

'Does that make him a hero?' Sharpe was pondering his answer. 'Alright then,' said Steph, 'You're on a shout to an armed robbery in progress; the perp pulls out a firearm and shoots you. Does that make you a hero?'

'No,' said Ash reluctantly, 'I suppose I'm just doing my job.'

'I rest my case m'lord,' said Steph.

She could see that Ash wasn't convinced. 'Okay then, an accountant is walking through the park and sees an old lady about to be stabbed; he goes to her rescue, saves her but in the process gets stabbed himself. In my book that chap's a hero. He selflessly put his life at risk; didn't have to but, nevertheless, put his life at risk, to save someone else. Not a copper, an accountant. Not his job. Not getting paid to protect the public. In my book that's the definition of a hero.' Steph wanted to conclude the topic. 'Look our job, firefighting, air sea rescue, the services, whatever, all carry risk of injury, even death; we all try to minimise those risks, take precautions, but in the end if we do get injured in the line of duty it doesn't automatically make any of us heroes; it makes us employees doing the jobs for which we get paid.' Steph took a deep breath and put her soapbox away. 'We're also getting paid to find Claude, so let's get on with it shall we.'

150

Sharpe shrugged and returned his attention to the task in hand. He'd think of some cogent counter arguments another day.

Pullman received notification that Claude had written on his timeline. He logged on to his Facebook account immediately, with a rush of anxiety.

You've no doubt woken up to the fact that some bastard split my head open last Saturday. Had to discharge myself before that juvenile cop you sent round, smelt the coffee.

Now you will understand why I'm a bit behind schedule but don't worry I'll catch up. I've checked the account in Zurich and was pissed off to find that you haven't deposited my money. I had time to think while I was in hospital and I've decided that I'll settle for £10 million but I will have to teach you a lesson for not meeting my demands on time. The size of that lesson will depend on whether you do as you're told this time.

I'm giving you a full week to get the money into the account. Don't let me down you know how it upsets me and forces me to punish you.

Claude

So it definitely was Claude in the hospital. At last, something concrete to work on. Pullman was guessing Claude's injury was causing him to take his foot off the gas, to more fully recover from the mugging, before he was in a position to implement his next atrocity. The mugger had probably saved a lot of lives in the short term. Claude was still clinging to the nonsense claim of having a

Swiss bank account; he must know that the police would have checked it out. Whether it was £10m or £100m made no difference; no amount could be deposited into a fictitious account. Either Claude was still suffering from concussion or he was completely delusional; maybe both.

Pullman convened a team meeting.

'Okay settle down. We know that Claude was the mugging victim in the hospital. So we were that close to getting him.' He indicated with his index finger and thumb to demonstrate the small gap. 'Close but no cigar. He says he's giving us a week to meet his new demands; he knows that's an impossibility, so he intends to kill again, come what may; which makes it all the more urgent that we find him asap. Steph tell us what you've got?'

'Ash and I have gone through the list we got from regimental headquarters; we've whittled it down to seventeen possibilities, the most likely possibilities at any rate. We've also prioritised them.'

Pullman sucked his teeth. 'That means we could be looking at seventeen armed raids which could blow the budget but that's not something we need concern ourselves with, the CC has authorised me to spare no effort or expense to catch our man. Steph do any of the names live in the Pearson Park area?'

Steph reacquainted herself with the list. 'Most of them come from outside the city but there's one actually in Pearson Park Road itself and one further north on Beverley Road.'

Sharpe said, 'You can get to Beverley Road from Pearson Park sir, so both are possibilities.'

'Yes Ash they are. I don't suppose either of them goes by the name of Claude?'

'That would be handy boss but no, I'm afraid not.' Steph smiled.

'What do we know about them?'

152

'Andrew Milner, he's the one in Beverley Road. Twenty-nine years old, Sergeant, First Battalion Yorkshire regiment. Leg was partially crushed in a logistics accident whilst serving in Helmand Province eighteen months ago; a forklift truck toppled over and fell on him. Dismissed six months ago, at his own request.'

'Crushed leg, could he walk?'

'These reports don't go into that much detail boss, just basic stuff. We've requested more info on the prime seventeen.' Pullman nodded. Steph continued. 'The second one is Barry Smith, same regiment but he was court marshalled on psychological grounds – mental instability – he was captured for a short period, escaped and burnt his captor alive in revenge, also threatened to barbeque the MPs who picked him up.'

'And he's back in the community?' said Pullman sarcastically.

'Apparently so.'

'Good of the army to dump their problem on us. Right then we'll hit them both at 6 am in the morning. Lynne you take Milner with Ash, Steph and I will take Smith. I'll organise the armed support. We'll liaise later.' Pullman decided that he would take the greater of the two evils.

'What if it's not either of them guv,' said Ash having reverted from the agreed 'sir' epithet.

'Coming to that Ash. Let's say that our man will be at neither location, which means, that if he is one of the other soldiers on the list, he could be commuting to his place of work.' Pullman made quote marks in the air despite his personal loathing for the gesture. 'So we need to visit every industrial estate, workshop and similar business premises in the area; the sort of location in which he could be concealing the mini cooper, as there hasn't been a single sighting yet. If he's renting a place then we need to find it.'

'There's a lot of them sir.'

153

'There's nothing else for it but a lot of leg work I'm afraid. It'll be a slog but we're talking about saving lives here, so we'll leave no turn un-stoned.' He was thinking so far ahead that he didn't even hear himself make the Spoonerism. 'Sergeant Carter, as co-ordinator, split the area up into a grid pattern and assign a team of mobile officers to systematically check each location but no heroics; they just ask questions. They can say we're looking into a spate of burglaries whilst keeping their eyes open for anything suspicious. If we can uncover anything before the morning it will save us paying for a lot of front door repairs.'

'Aye sir.'

'We've not had any response from the public on the whereabouts of the mini I presume?' asked Pullman.

Carter checked his notes needlessly he knew that there had not been any reported sightings. 'No sir, nothing as yet. But the nurse who reported it stolen mentioned that it only had a teaspoonful of petrol because she was going to fill it up on her way home. Doesn't reckon it had more than ten miles or so in the tank, tops. I've already got a couple of lads picking up CCTV tapes from all the petrol stations within a ten mile radius of the hospital, starting with a forty-five degree segment north of the RI.'

'Good man. If he's not on them, then the chances are he hid the car somewhere close by.'

'I've also checked that no other vehicles have been reported stolen from anywhere near where our man could have been.'

'You after my job Sarge?' Pullman smiled. 'Good thinking, well done.'

Lynne Sperring's mobile rang, she answered. 'Hello,' she said on her way to the door. 'What, you're kidding?' she stopped in her tracks. 'When? She turned back towards Pullman. 'Where? Can you text me the post code?'

Pullman was looking at her, intrigued. Sperring closed the call and took a deep breath. 'Trevor Johnston, the headteacher at the college, has been killed in a hit and run outside his home.'

'Poor sod. Any witnesses?'

'Don't know any details. Peak's at the scene now with the traffic boys. The pathologist is on the way. I think I'd better go over there, if that's okay sir.'

'Sure. We're about wrapped up here so I'll come with you.' said Pullman. 'Give me five minutes to sort the firearms for tomorrow with the ACC.' Pullman knew that the Chief Constable was in Leeds at a policy meeting.

Sixteen

The light was failing fast and the rain was falling even faster when Pullman and Sperring arrived at the entrance to Woodlands Farm, on Wood Lane, a mile outside Howden. It was the only dwelling along that stretch of lane, edged with a narrow grass verge and screened with sparse autumnal hedgerows. The single track road had been cordoned off at both ends, with traffic diversions set in place. Screens had been placed around the body with lighting rigs mounted at each corner. DS Peak was talking to a Tyvek clothed female when the new arrivals approached.

'Not moved the body yet?' said Pullman. 'What's the problem?'

'Hi sir,' said Peak. 'This is Maxine Davies.'

'I know. How are you Max?'

'Fine Mike, and you?'

'I'm good. How come you drew the short straw?'

'I'm heading up the forensic department these days but I was free so...'

'Congratulations. I missed that.'

'Well you've been away for a while.' Maxine didn't want to dwell on the reason for his absence. 'I don't want the victim moved until a full forensic examination has been carried out.'

'Is there an issue?'

'I'm afraid so.'

'I thought it was a hit and run.'

'That's what it looked like at first glance but the victim was run over twice.'

'Twice!' said both Pullman and Sperring in disbelief.

'Well three times really.' She stepped into the road. 'The first impact was about here,' she indicated an area of the road. 'The victim would have been thrown into the air and landed where you can see him now.'

Pullman studied the scene. 'Yes I see.'

'But as you will also see,' Maxine Davies walked six paces along the tarmac, 'there are skid marks here.' She indicated black rubber tyre pattern on the tarmac.

'So the driver braked hard but too late. Must have been travelling at a hell of a lick; these conditions wouldn't have helped.' Pullman looked back at Johnston's body. 'Dressed in black on an unlit road, failing light and heavy rain, perfect scenario for a collision I'd have thought.'

'Ordinarily I would agree, but after braking you can see...,' she walked back again to her original position close to the body, 'that the vehicle then reversed back completely over the body and then forward again before leaving the scene. Now whether or not the first collision was an accident I can't say but the second and third most certainly were not. They were deliberate acts intended to make sure that the victim was dead. In my book that looks like murder.'

Sperring looked at Pullman. 'That's murder in anyone's book.'

Pullman asked, 'Any tyre prints?'

'Oh yes,' replied Davies. 'We're pulling those off now. Some footprints too; I think most of them are from the traffic cops and the DS here.' She pointed to Peak, 'but we'll eliminate those and hopefully, we'll be left with something identifiable.'

157

Sperring asked, 'You think the driver may have got out of the car then?'

'Yes, it looks like the victim has been turned on to his back after the third time he was driven over, possibly to feel the neck pulse, to determine death.'

'You didn't do that Sergeant?' asked Pullman.

Peak shook his head. 'No sir. The traffic boys had already established death before they called me.'

'What was he doing out here?'

'He lives down there sir,' Peak indicated an unmade mud track. 'Woodlands Farm, although it's not farmed these days.'

Pullman peered down the rough track; deep ruts caused by heavy vehicles led to a large, stone built residence set amongst a small copse of mixed deciduous trees; pools of water filled the ruts at intervals. 'You say this place is not farmed anymore.'

'Not for several years.'

'Okay, said Pullman with an *if you say so* tone. The house looked unkempt; a plume of smoke was rising from the chimney. To the left of the house was a large barn with a long open fronted, lean-to construction attached, housing a dilapidated antique tractor, covered in dust webs. 'Have you spoken to Mrs Johnston?'

'Yes sir. You can imagine she's very upset; there's a WPO with her. She was inside the house and didn't hear a thing. The first she knew was when I told her.'

'What did she say?'

'That Trevor got a phone call.'

'From whom?'

'She doesn't know. After the call, Trevor said he was just popping out for a few minutes for some fresh air.'

'Whoever did this, possibly made the call.'

158

DS Peak nodded. 'Seems most likely. Got him out of the house on the pretext of meeting him, and then ran him over.'

'Who found the body?'

'A couple of walkers. They thought it was a bundle of rags at first then realised it was a body and called the ambulance... and us.'

'Where are they now,' asked Sperring?'

'Inside the house. I've spoken to them. They were doing a circular walk along the lanes because the rain has made the cross country route impassable in places.'

'We'll have to eliminate their boot prints too,' Maxine Davies pointed out.

'I'm guessing they didn't see a car,' said Pullman.

'You're guessing right,' said Peak. 'They did see a cyclist but I don't think this was done with a bike,' he added facetiously.

'There's no fooling you, is there.' Pullman shook his rain sodden head to disperse the water. 'Right let's get out of this rain and allow Max to get on with her job. I'd like a word with Mrs Johnston.'

Peak said. 'You'll be the SIO on this will you sir?'

'I don't believe in coincidences Sergeant and I have a gut feeling that our unfortunate headteacher's death will turn out to be linked to Wethersby's, so I guess I will be the SIO.'

'Yes sir.'

The three detectives walked along the track to the house. 'How long had they been married?' he asked Peak.

'About seven years. Caused quite a stir when he returned from one of his trips to Thailand with a wife in tow, I can tell you. Most people wouldn't believe she wasn't a mail order Philipino bride. You can imagine what those kids at the college would have made of that, if social media was as popular then.'

'Do you think it was a genuine marriage?'

159

'Oh yes sir. As you're no doubt aware from Lynne, I know them on a personal level and I'd say that it was perfectly genuine.'

'Well you've lost your chess partner now,' said Pullman to let Peak know that he had indeed spoken with Lynne.

Peak knocked on the front door of the farmhouse and entered. 'Only Ray, DS Peak,' he called out. 'Okay if we come in?' All three of them entered and went through to the large kitchen. Mrs Johnston was sitting at a large battered pine, refractory style table, both her hands clamped around a mug of tea. In the corner of the room was what looked like a mini temple with a statue of a squatting golden idol in the centre.

The ramblers were sitting on one of the two shabby-chic floral patterned, two seater settees positioned either side of the wood burning stove, blazing in the inglenook fireplace. They stood up as the police officers entered. Pullman smiled in their direction, motioning them to retake their seats, which they did. The WPO, sitting alongside the new widow, stood upright and stepped back from the table allowing Pullman to take her place. As he did so, Pullman glanced around the kitchen. Apart from the spirit-house with the golden Buddha the room was cluttered with all the paraphernalia he would have expected to find in a country house kitchen, including the obligatory oil fired range cooker.

He smiled reassuringly at Mrs Johnston who was staring blankly at the mug she was cradling. She was not the most beautiful of women. Not exactly full of eastern promise. Her face was featureless with a flat nose typical of much of the Thai population. Her skin was quite dark indicating that she was from a working class background. Many younger, class conscious Thais cover their faces when outside in direct sunlight to help keep their skin as pale as possible. 'Hello, I'm Detective Chief Inspector Mike Pullman, the Senior Investigating Officer; this is Detective

Sergeant Lynne Sperring and DS Peak you know already.' Mrs Johnston made no movement or acknowledgement of having heard the introduction. 'I know this is a very difficult time for you but I need to ask you a couple of questions about the phone call your husband received. Is that alright?'

Her face showed no sign of emotion. She gave an almost indiscernible nod of the head, enough to dislodge a tear that had been balancing precariously on her cheek, it trickled down and fell from her chin.

'Did your husband say who the call was from?'

She shook her head.

'Did he mention a name?'

She shook her head.

'Do you remember any of the conversation at all?'

She shook her head once more then said, slowly in hushed tones, 'I assumed it was from someone at the college. Almost all his friends worked at the college. Whoever called did most of the talking Trevor just said *yes* a couple of times and *I understand.* Then when he'd finished he put on his coat; said he was popping out for a few minutes and wouldn't be long. I told him to take an umbrella but he said he wouldn't need one. That's the last I saw of him.'

'Did you get the impression from the conversation that he had arranged to meet someone?'

'Yes, but I don't know who.'

'I'm sorry to have to ask you this but did your husband seem to be his normal self. Did he appear worried or concerned?'

'No everything was normal.'

'Why wasn't he at college today?'

'It was Thomas Wethersby's funeral service this morning. He took the day off.'

161

Fuck, screamed Pullman's brain. Fuck, fuck, fuck. It had completely gone out of his mind. He looked at Sperring who grimaced. They'd both forgotten. He'd wanted to be there to study the mourners. To see who turned up that hadn't, so far, figured in their investigation. 'I'd forgotten.' He looked at Peak.

'Yes, I went sir. All pretty straightforward, nothing unusual; just the church congregation from Clipton, Trevor and two other colleagues from the college. No family or other friends, and the vicar of course. No strangers lurking in the background.' He added with a smile, knowing why Pullman would have wanted to be there.

'Thank you for your time Mrs Johnston. Is there someone we can call for you? Someone who could come and stay with you? asked Pullman.

DS Peak said, 'If it's okay sir I'll stay with Anchali, Mrs Johnston, for a while until we can sort things out. She has a sister and a cousin or two in London so I'll establish contact and make sure she's all right.'

'Sure, good idea.'

Pullman interviewed the ramblers. They confirmed what they had already told DS Peak and could add nothing further to their statement. Outside, night was falling rapidly so Pullman offered them a lift in a response car back to Howden, they gratefully accepted. He thought that one pedestrian road accident was enough for the day.

Pullman and Sperring left the house. As they walked back to their car, the senior road traffic accident officer, carrying a clip board and a tape measure, approached them. 'Excuse me sir can I have a word?'

'Of course.'

'If you wouldn't mind coming up here please sir,' he shone his flashlight towards the cross roads about one hundred and fifty metres away. A patrol car was parked close by with its headlights switched on, illuminating the stretch of road.

'What have you found?'

The officer shone his torch onto the verge. 'There are tyre tracks on the verge here. Looks like a car was parked with its nearside wheels on the grass.' He shone his torch to illuminate the two indentations where the vehicle's wheels had rested. 'I'm certain that they are the same tread pattern that we found at the scene of the accident.'

'Meaning?' asked Pullman

'Meaning that the vehicle involved was parked here prior to the accident.'

Sperring said. 'So you're saying that the driver was waiting for the victim to appear on the road before deliberately driving at him?'

'That would be my assessment.'

'Excuse me a minute sir,' said Sperring; she turned and sprinted back to the house.

The two men looked at each other nonplussed. Pullman shrugged, as if to say, I've no idea what she's doing either. He turned his attention back to the tracks. 'So the driver could have called the victim from a mobile; enticed him out of the house on some pretext or other, then deliberately run him over.'

'Seems a reasonable assumption to me. If he was parked here, then decided to pull away normally, just as our victim emerged from the driveway, he wouldn't have been travelling at much more than thirty miles an hour tops. Even without lights, in these murky conditions, and with the rain falling there would have been sufficient light at the time for the collision to be avoidable. I think the depth of these tracks show clear signs of wheel spin, which would indicate that the driver gunned the engine and took off at speed.'

They turned and began walking back to the main crime scene. 'If you're right then we're not looking at the callous act of a hit and run driver, eliminating the only witness, but at premeditated murder.'

'That would be my belief sir.'

'Thank you officer...'said Pullman in a tone to solicit his name.

'Craig sir; Sergeant Daniel Craig; and no, I'm not that one, unfortunately.' He was well accustomed to pre-empting the inevitable comments he'd heard time and time again since the release of Quantum of Solace.

'Thank you Sergeant Craig. When do you think I could have the report?'

'I'll have a pre-lim emailed over first thing in the morning and a full report within forty-eight hours.' That satisfied Pullman.

Sperring trotted up to them. 'It suddenly occurred to me that we might get lucky with one-four-seven-one on the house phone.'

'Did we?'

'No, caller withheld the number.'

'Can you do that on a mobile?'

'Yes sir, with calls but not texts.'

'Shit. Nice try though.'

'Could I have a word sir,' she asked with a slight sideways jerk of her head, indicating the need for privacy.

'Thank you Sergeant Craig. I'll expect your email.' Craig nodded and walked away. 'What is it Lynne?' asked Pullman when the traffic cop was out of earshot.

'When I went back in, Mrs Johnston was kneeling bare footed in front of that little temple arrangement you probably noticed in the corner.'

'Yes I saw it. Presumably she was saying a prayer for her husband.'

'I guess so,' said Sperring with a hint of impatience. 'The thing is, I couldn't help noticing a little tattoo on the heel of her left foot...'

'THE tattoo,' emphasised Pullman.

'Yes sir THE tattoo.'

Pullman thought for a moment. 'Hang on Lynne; let's not jump to conclusions here. Maybe it just means Hua Hin which is where she's from and this alleged gang have adopted it.'

'Maybe sir. Could be perfectly innocent but that's not my point.'

'What is your point then?'

'DS Peak was standing right behind her, the tattoo was clearly visible. If I noticed it, so should he. He knows the significance but didn't say anything. Why?'

'Why indeed?'

Seventeen

Friday 14th November

Pullman and Sperring were back at the coal face by 5.15 am the following morning, along with Barnes, Sharpe and sixteen Authorised Firearms Officers, clad in their Kevlar body armour and ballistics helmets. The AFOs had been assigned into two teams of eight; one under the command of Sperring and the other under Pullman.

Pullman was standing in front of maps and identification photographs of the two suspects and the houses the teams were about to raid. 'Okay we all know what we're doing but let me repeat, we don't know for sure that either of the targets is the man we're after so we don't know if he'll be armed or not. Neither do we know if either house will be booby trapped – let's not forget our man is an explosives expert. No gung-ho attitudes and no heroes.' Sharpe gave Steph Barnes a sideways glance. Pullman wagged his index finger. 'So utmost diligence and caution and if we do encounter any armed resistance ... well I wouldn't presume to tell you your job. Any questions?' There were none. 'Right let's get to it. Good luck everyone.'

The raids did not need to be coordinated. This was not a network of criminals who might sound alarm bells. In fact Pullman knew for sure that at least one of the men was completely innocent; he just didn't know which one. He hoped that one of them would be their man but had a distinct feeling of foreboding that neither man would be Claude.

In Pearson Park Road, The Willows was an impressive Georgian mansion converted into four, one bedroomed flats, although the landlord referred to them as luxury apartments. Barry Smith was known to occupy the ground floor flat, No1, to the left side of the house, looking from the street. The house had been under surveillance for twenty-four hours so they knew the suspect was at home.

The imposing main front door was activated by a push button security system allowing access to the house. Each flat then had its own private security door. CCTV was operating above the main door and in the stairwells on both floors. Pullman had previously acquired the front door pass key from the landlord, who was more than pleased to co-operate rather than have the inconvenience of waiting for the police to replace the door, after they smashed it down.

The road was deserted save for the stream of AFOs snaking out of the transit carrier and the two detectives emerging from Pullman's Volvo S40. Despite the gravelled driveway the team made very little noise approaching the front of the house. Pullman made his way through the vanguard of armoured officers to open the front door. He then stood aside while the officers swarmed in to the lobby, surrounding the door to flat No 1. Pullman nodded to the commanding AFO who gave the order to bust the lock, using the portable battering ram. It took three rapid hits with the Enforcer to beak the high tensile lock, allowing the men to funnel into the flat;

they fanned left and right into the room with their Heckler & Koch MP5s sub machine guns ready for action.

'Armed police officers,' they repeatedly shouted to the empty room as adrenalin pumped through their veins. In less than five seconds they had ensured that the sitting room and kitchen were clear before they burst through to the bedroom. Barry Smith was sitting up in bed with a look of abject fear and horror across his unshaven face.

'Armed police officers,' they shouted again. 'Don't move, don't move. Not a muscle.' Instinctively Smith raised his hands to the surrender position. 'I said don't move,' screamed a very agitated officer.

Pullman entered behind the shield of armed officers. 'Barry Smith?'

'Yes,' said Smith his raised hands trembling. He was a war veteran; he'd been captured and tortured by the Taliban but he had never been more frightened in his life, than he was in those few moments. 'What's happening?'

'I have a warrant to search the premises.'

'What for? I'm not a user. I don't do drugs.'

Pullman knew instinctively that Smith was not their man. Certainly they hadn't just invaded a bomb factory. Everything looked normal; a thorough search of the compact flat proved it to be so. He may have been dismissed from the service on medical grounds but he looked perfectly normal to Pullman. He wasn't angry; no hint of aggression; nothing to suggest a psychological disorder. In fact, books and paperwork, on the only table in the flat, showed that he was studying for a degree in Sociology with the Open University. The conclusive proof was spotted by Pullman within seconds of entering the room; the ex-soldier did not have a head trauma, meaning that he had not just spent a few days in the hospital.

A similar scenario had unfolded at the raid lead by DS Sperring, on the second target. It was a long time since so much egg had been on so many faces.

'So a complete waste of time, resources and budget,' said Pauline Crompton with controlled anger. 'In fact an unmitigated disaster.'

Pullman had no room for manoeuvre. The Chief Constable was absolutely right on all three counts.

'Did you deliberately wait until I was unavailable before you got Iain to sign off on the operation?'

'No ma'am speed was of the essence, I thought.....'

'If you'd have thought Mike you wouldn't have needed to organise armed raids. Why didn't you just pick them up while they were away from their homes? No need to endanger lives then, Christ you've had them under surveillance.'

'The ACC agreed....'

'Never mind what Iain agreed, I'll talk to him later. You're the SIO Mike; you didn't think it through properly. There was no need for such heavy handed tactics; none whatsoever. I've already had the press on. I told them, that they were drug raids, the last thing we need is for them to link this with the bombings. This way the raids will hopefully just blow over, instead of being headlined as another police failure to catch Claude; and I'll have Monkton on my back. He'll seize the opportunity as another excuse to have a go at my leadership. Bloody PCCs.' She took a deep breath, looked at

169

Pullman and shook her head in resigned disbelief. 'So we're back at square one, are we?'

'Not quite ma'am, we're following up several more leads and I'm confident that we'll have some positive developments in the next forty-eight hours.' Why did he say that? He was no closer to a breakthrough than before the raids. Now he'd just put pressure on the team and set himself up for another confrontation in a couple of days; always assuming of course that Claude had not struck again by then.

'We don't need developments Mike, we need results, fast.'

'Yes ma'am.' He was fleetingly tempted to bring her up to-date on the Wethersby/Johnston case but decided against it until he had something positive to impart. 'If that's all ma'am, I'll get behind it.'

'That's the problem Mike; you've been behind it all the way, now it's time to get ahead of it.'

The bollocking from Pauline Crompton was still ringing in his ears when Pullman sat down at his desk. An 'unmitigated disaster' was what she'd called the events of the morning and he couldn't disagree. A complete fiasco was, no doubt, what Peter Monkton the PCC, would call it when he heard the news. Pullman was still licking his wounds when, an equally wounded, Lynne Sperring put her head around his office door.

'I don't suppose her ladyship was very happy.'

'That would be the understatement of the year. Trouble is she's every right to be pissed off with me; I'm not on my game.'

'Let fly did she?'

'And some. I don't envy Thwaite when she sees him.'

'Anyway sir, DS Peak just called to say they've found a freshly burnt out car on a small, disused industrial estate, north of

Howden. Forensics are on to it but the likelihood is that it's the hit and run vehicle.'

'That reminds me I was expecting an email from Sergeant Craig.'

'And DS Peak also said that he's taking Mrs Johnston down to London...'

'He's what?' exclaimed Pullman angrily.

Lynne Sperring held up her hands. 'Don't shoot the messenger. He's taking her down there to stay with her relatives apparently.'

'Well stop him. He's got a murder to investigate.'

'He was already on the way when he called me sir. His inspector at Howden nick cleared it.'

'For fu...' Pullman capped off the sentence and took a deep breath to compose himself, allowing his anger to subside. 'I'll have something to say about that when he gets back.' Pullman was also controlling a growing apprehension at Peak's involvement with the Johnstons. He wasn't sure that the DS was treating his friends with impartiality. He was unaware that Sperring was harbouring the same doubts about her counterpart at Howden.

Pullman logged on to his email. Amongst the dozen or so waiting for his attention was the one from Craig. 'Ah, here it is.' He read it through. 'Nothing we didn't already know; it confirms that only one set of tyre treads made all the marks left behind at the scene, proving our driver parked up prior to the murder.'

'So we're definitely treating it as murder then?'

'Definitely. Ah, here's one from Max.' He skipped through it, and then opened the attachment. 'Bloody hell!' he exclaimed.

'What's up sir?'

'Max has completed the post mortem. Guess what Johnston had on his upper bicep.'

'I'm guessing a tattoo,' she said. Pullman nodded. 'Possibly a double aitch in a round snake,' she mocked.

'No wonder Johnston was so vehement in protesting Wethersby's innocence; they were both members of this Hua Hin club or paedophile ring, if our colleagues in London are right.'

'And presumably Mrs Johnston was as well,' added Sperring.

'Looks that way. If DI Proctor doesn't call me in the next hour I'll call her. In the meantime we'd better concentrate on getting Claude, and getting the CC of my back.'

He went into the main office. A quick glance showed him that the entire team was present, bar one of the civilian staff. 'Right listen up everyone.' All heads turned towards him. 'After this morning's non-event we need to step things up a gear. I made the wrong call so let's review everything we've got; there must be something there we've overlooked; something that will ignite this enquiry. Find it. I need a spark in the next twenty-four hours.'

Steph Barnes spoke. 'Sir, Ash and I have been back over all the records from the regiment and we can't see that any of the other names fit the profile, our man might not be on the list of those that have been dismissed, made redundant or have left the service of their own volition.'

'You're thinking that he's not military after all then?' said Pullman.

'He still could be sir, but he may not have been dismissed. He could be injured, on rehabilitation leave or just on leave for some other reason; compassionate grounds maybe, in which case he won't be on any list we've drawn up so far.'

'Maybe he's just gone AWOL,' ventured Sperring.

'Okay Steph get on to it.'

Sergeant Carter's uniformed team had been assigned the task of studying the CCTV recordings from all the filling stations in the

172

locale of the hospital. He stood up, 'Sir we been through as much CCTV footage as we've been able to obtain so far; there's no sign of the mini being refuelled. There is one garage whose system is down but it's on the fringe of the area, we'd be unlucky if that's the one he used.'

'So far, sergeant, luck hasn't been going our way but I agree that the odds are he abandoned the vehicle or he lives within the fuel range of the tank which was enough to get him home. Let's step up the search and the door to door enquiries; someone must know where it is.'

'On to it sir.'

'Any DNA results back on the bandages from the hospital?' asked Pullman, looking at Ashley Sharpe.

'Not that I'm aware of sir,'

'Then make yourself aware,' snapped Pullman.

It was 11.15 am when Pullman took the call from DI Sue Proctor. 'Hi, Richard Pointer warned me you might be calling.'

'Yes; I meant to call yesterday sir, sorry, I got side-tracked.'

'Do you mind if I put the call on speaker so my DS, Lynne Sperring, can listen in, only she's running the case?' Sperring raised her eyebrows and nodded her head in a *yeah right* gesture.

'Fine by me sir,' answered Proctor.

'Thanks, save me relaying it afterwards; actually it's just as well you didn't call yesterday, we would have had a partially wasted conversation.'

'Why's that?'

'The headteacher of Wethersby's college was killed in a hit and run yesterday, we're pretty sure was deliberate.'

'Murder?'

'Looks like it.'

'Any suspects?'

'No, but you might be interested to learn that the pathologist found the double aitch tattoo on his arm.'

'Interesting,' said Proctor.

'Even more interesting is that his Thai born wife had the same tattoo on her heel.'

'If it's alright with you sir, I'd like to come up there and speak to the lady.'

'She's actually on her way down to you, well to London. The DS working on the case is also a family friend; he's taking her down to stay with relatives.'

'No children then?'

'No.'

'You might find this a bit unorthodox sir but I'd like to come up there with a colleague and take a look around while she's not there.'

'I don't have a problem. I'll get a warrant organised.' He nodded at Sperring, she nodded back. 'Grounds being a suspected paedophile ring, yes?' he said to Proctor.

'Sure. That symbol keeps turning up in our investigations so there has to be a connection to your case' she said.

'We've identified Wethersby as a Hebephile which could mean that the others are too.'

'We don't differentiate between the two; we classify all child abusers as paedophiles sir. Hebephile isn't used, besides it would only confuse the great British public; especially those on a jury. Everyone understands what a paedophile is.'

'More's the pity. Okay, we'll bear that in mind.' Pullman shrugged towards Sperring as if to say tomatoes, tomaytoes. 'When can we expect you?'

'Sometime in the morning hopefully; we'll get a train up to Hull.'

'Saturday' queried Pullman.

'Is that a problem sir?

'No, no; tell you what, get the train to Doncaster and we'll pick you up from there. It's about the same distance from here to Howden as it is from Donny by car; it'll save you over an hour on the train. There's probably a fast train from Kings Cross.

'Sounds like a plan.'

Although the number plates were destroyed by the fire, Howden police traced the registered owner of the burnt out car, through the Vehicle Identification Number. The owner, who claimed to actually be the previous owner, told the officers that he had sold the car, a 52 registration Ford Focus on Ebay, for seven hundred and fifty pounds. The man who bought it paid cash and said that he would send off the V5C to the DVLA.

The vendor was only able to provide a vague description of the purchaser, with whom he had tried not make eye contact. He was a bit nervous about the price being almost three times the value he'd been offered, as a part exchange, by the local dealer; he was also selling the car knowing it needed a new exhaust and, that it had a sick clutch. The guy who bought it however, didn't seem concerned about the price or condition, other than wanting to know the engine was okay. He seemed in a bit of a hurry considering his claim that he was buying it for his student daughter. The buyer was probably mid-forties about five feet ten, maybe eleven, brownish hair mainly concealed under a plain blue baseball cap with the image of a upright, brown bear on the front; wore jeans and trainers. When asked if he would be able to recognise the man again he thought that he probably wouldn't. Not that he gave it much thought.

Eighteen

The train arrived on time at Doncaster station. Pullman and Sperring were waiting on the concourse along with a uniformed officer they had temporarily seconded from British Rail police. Pullman thought that having the uniform alongside them would immediately flag them up to their visitors. Much simpler than a carnation in the button hole or holding up a board displaying their names. The ploy worked.

'DCI Pullman, I presume,' said Sue Proctor.

'Indeed.'

'Proctor, Sue Proctor,' she introduced herself. The DI was early thirties with flawless skin the colour of latte; her head crowned with silky black hair, cut short and wild. 'And this is Ben Cartright.' He was more like a cross between Little Joe and Adam which fortunately for him meant he did not resemble Hoss.

'Welcome to Yorkshire. This is DS Lynne Sperring.'

The detectives all shook hands.

'The car's just outside.' Pullman motioned towards the side exit. 'Thank you,' he said to the uniformed officer, who, being duly dismissed, nodded and went about his duties. Pullman guided his visitors to Sperring's car.

The journey to Woodlands Farm lasted a little over thirty minutes, during which time the four occupants of the Mondeo discussed the Wethersby case, interspersed with small talk and sound bites, befitting the Yorkshire Tourist Board.

Diversions had been set in place around the area of the accident, to preserve the integrity of the scene; a single patrol car was positioned to ensure no interlopers trespassed on the area. Sperring gave a short burst of the blues, concealed in the grill of the Mondeo, to signal to the lone occupant that they were police. The uniformed WPO stepped out of her car to acknowledge their arrival.

Pullman got out of the passenger door and called out. 'Anybody been around?'

'Not while I've been here sir,' she called back.

'Okay, we're going inside.'

The other three detectives disembarked from the car, on the outside of the taped off area, and made their way, on foot, down the dirt track to the farmhouse; donning latex gloves as they did so.

'Let's see if we can find a door key, before we break any windows,' said Pullman.

He felt along the top of the door frame, while the others lifted various pots and stones; eventually they found a key, under a highly decorated, reproduction milk churn. Surprisingly the kitchen struck warm as they entered, thanks to an electric convector fire having been left on. 'Good job we turned up or their electricity bill would have been phenomenal; that's if the fire hadn't melted in the meantime.' Pullman looked around the room and sucked his teeth. 'Right Sue, you're the expert; what should we be looking for?'

'Difficult to say really sir; anything that might throw light on their trips to Thailand; travel documents; personal documents. Probably best to start with any computer kit they may have. Ben is one of our IT specialists so we'll leave that stuff to him. It's unlikely that they will have left anything on display, always assuming of course that they are involved in illegal activity.'

'Finding that out is the object of the exercise,' said Pullman. 'So shall we take a room apiece and hope we find something?'

'It's a big house,' said Sperring. 'We could do with a few more hands or we'll be here all night.'

'No can have, Lynne; the CC made it quite clear that we don't have the resources or the budget to waste on *another one of my theories,* as she put it.'

'Well at least we didn't break down any doors here sir.'

'Yeah, that would have made me flavour of the month. If we find something that warrants SOCO taking a look, I'm sure she'll concede but it would have to be pretty good. How about you concentrate on the kitchen and dining room; Sue, you and DS Cartright take the sitting room and any other rooms that are down here; he's bound to have a study with a PC for Ben to play around with; I'll wander upstairs. We can only do a cursory glance so let's hope they've been careless. We'll cover the outbuildings when we've finished in here.'

Sue Proctor gave a thumbs up sign. 'Sounds like a plan.' It was obviously her pet phrase.

They found nothing that in any way suggested criminal activities were taking place at the farmhouse. In the study DS Cartright had interrogated the PC and a laptop but found nothing of interest on either. One Excel document folder contained details of their numerous trips to Thailand; the spreadsheets   seemed to indicate pretty normal arrangements. It would require further forensic work back at the office to determine if anything had been erased from the hard drive.

The team re-grouped in the kitchen.

179

'Right then it's almost one o'clock,' said Pullman, checking his watch. 'We can carry-on with the outbuildings or we can get some lunch.'

Proctor shrugged. 'I'm good sir; we had breakfast on the train. Well, microwaved bacon rolls and coffee.'

Much to Pullman's chagrin the others agreed. Right then you and me, Sue, will take the main barn and you two check the other sheds.' He indicated Sperring and Cartright.

The barn was constructed from pre-cast concrete panels surmounted with aluminium cladding. A single side entry meant that they didn't have to open the huge main doors. Roof lights gave sufficient illumination for Pullman to locate a power box on the wall, to the right of the door; he pulled the handle down. A fusillade of fluorescent lights came to life in sequence along the entire length of the barn. Milking stalls lined both sides of the construction. The metal rails were tarnished and draped with dust webs; all the electric milking equipment had long since been removed.

'Not been a working dairy farm for quite some time,' said Pullman.

'Must have been an enormous herd, looking at the size of this place,' remarked Proctor, her voice echoing in the cavernous interior.

They strode down the centre isle towards the rear doors, glancing from side to side as they went; their footsteps softened by a layer of decaying straw and hardened cow pats; the odour of damp cattle and sour milk had long since dissipated.

'Doesn't look used at all, does it,' said Pullman. Proctor shook her head. 'Makes you wonder why people buy a place this size if they're not going to make use of it; shame really but that's the way of the world I guess.'

180

They reached the far end; there were several discarded milk churns scattered on the floor; a hand pulled cart with several more churns together with some rotting hay bales and half empty sacks of cattle cake. They glanced around, turned and strode back. 'Nothing here,' said Pullman.

'Not that I can see,' Proctor said with a shrug of both shoulders. 'Perhaps it's been a wasted trip after all.'

'Looking like it; let's see if the others have had any joy.'

They hadn't. 'You haven't been watching TV in there have you sir? Sperring asked Pullman.

'Yes fifty inch plasma thought we'd catch Bargain Hunt,' joked Pullman; then added. 'Why would you ask that?' It was a strange thing to say he thought.

'Because there's a satellite dish on the back of the building,' she answered.

They walked around to the back of the barn and looked up at the small satellite dish which had been partially camouflaged, with an adhesive vinyl cover, displaying a leaf pattern.

'That's odd,' said Pullman. 'I didn't notice anything inside; did you Sue?'

'Nothing but it seems a bit far away from the house to place the dish, wouldn't you say.'

Pullman nodded and puckered his lips. 'Mmmh, strange; let's have another peek inside and see if it has ever been connected to a receiver.'

Cartright quipped, 'Perhaps the cows liked to watch Countryfile while they were being milked.'

Back inside they made their way to the far end of the barn and stood side by side, studying the wall and floor.

'Did you move that trolley when you were in here sir? Cartright asked.

'Nope.'

'Someone has, in the not too distant past by the look of it. See those tracks; they run through the dust; so probably not more than a week or two ago.'

They all studied the tracks. He was right. 'Let's move it,' said Pullman. He, and the young DS, grabbed the handle and pulled it into the centre of the isle; not that it needed two men, it was surprisingly light to manoeuvre. Having done so, the outline of a trap door was revealed. 'Well what have got here,' wondered Pullman. Lifting the trap door revealed a set of steps leading down. Pullman switched on the light on his mobile and shone it down into the space below. He ventured down the steps, flicking on a light switch as he went and turned off his phone torch. At the bottom of the stairs were two closed doors. He opened the one on the right hand. The others followed him down 'Jesus H Christ,' exclaimed Pullman as he entered. The others followed him into a space that left them astounded; suddenly their lungs were filled with an overpowering stench; Sperring retched.

'Oh my god,' cried DI Proctor.

Sperring retched again.

The horrendous scene shocked them all into momentary immobility. Around thirty Orientals, mainly women it seemed, were locked into a row of five, filthy barred cages. Some were unconscious; maybe dead. All were weak and emaciated, lying on bare concrete floors, in their own waste.

Pullman regained movement. 'Lynne get out of here; call in and get a fleet of ambulances, medics... erm SOCOs... erm and see if the fire brigade have some kit that can pump air down here also call for back up to lock this place down for a mile around.' He moved towards the cages. 'Anyone here speak English,' he looked despairingly along the row. 'English, anyone speak English?' There was more than a hint of panic in his voice.

A faint voice croaked a reply. 'I speak little,' the voice emanated from a skeletal figure of a woman, hunched against the rear wall of the middle cell. Her desolate, sunken eyes looked towards Pullman. 'Can you help us?'

'Help is on the way,' he explained gently. 'We are the police. You are safe now. We don't want to move you without expert medical advice. We call doctors. But, I say again, you are safe now; we will get you out of here, soon.' Pullman was speaking slowly together with unnecessary hand gestures, in a style that Brits use when talking to 'foreigners'. The woman may not have understood all the words but she appeared to understand the tone; her head turned wearily; her lips curled slightly to form a semblance of a smile. She uttered something in a language that meant nothing to Pullman.'

'That's Thai,' said DI Proctor. 'I've heard plenty of it during my time in this job.'

The woman's words were repeated by others, as the word spread among the captives that they were being freed. Pullman moved closer to the cage holding the woman. 'Are you from Thailand,' he asked. The woman closed her eyes and nodded her head slowly, exhaling a shallow sigh in the process. Pullman turned to his colleagues. 'Let's see if there are any keys so we can get these cages open; might give them a little relief and hope.' He walked along the row of cages counting the occupants; there were thirty-one; five or six of whom were showing no signs of life. He took photos on his mobile as he passed each section; the flash did little to settle their nerves. Cartright found a bunch of keys in a drawer and began opening the cage doors.

'We've got to get some air down here,' said Pullman. 'I'll see if I can get the big barn doors open, I'll call the Chief while I'm at it.'

He was very relieved to get out of the dungeon. Before he climbed the stairs he checked the room to the left. It was kitted out as an office; there were no more prisoners there. Once up stairs, he opened the main rear doors and drew in a lungful of crisp, fresh air; stepping out into the open he called Pauline Crompton.

'It's Pullman ma'am. I'm at the Johnston's place in Howden with DI Proctor and DS Cartright; it's horrific. We've discovered a dungeon under the barn with over thirty prisoners confined in airless cages.'

'Prisoners? What do you mean prisoners?'

'Prisoners, captives; they're Asian, oriental; Thais we believe. I'll send over some pics ma'am. Sperring has called for ambulances, paramedics, fire brigade and back up, to keep the area clear.'

Ambulances? Are they injured?'

'They're mainly women and most of them are barely alive; could be some casualties; the pictures will tell you more but I've never seen anything like it, not even in the movies.'

'How did they get there?'

'Don't know ma'am, I haven't questioned anyone yet; to be frank, I don't think they're up to it. I think the medics should treat them first; there'll be plenty of time for questions; they're not going anywhere, anytime soon.'

'So are they connected with this suspected paedophile ring?'

'These aren't kids ma'am, they're adults, but it's difficult to determine ages at the moment because of the condition they're in; I suspect we're looking at trafficking'

'My god can things get any worse.'

'Not for these poor sods it can't.'

184

'I think I should come over; visit the scene?'

'Might be a good idea ma'am; the press will eventually be all over this, it might be prudent for you to have been on the scene when you face the inevitable media barrage.' He was preparing the ground for her to deal with the media. Once she knew as much as he did, there would be no reason for her to stick him in the limelight.

'Agreed, I'll leave straight away.'

Margaret Goodenough was hanging her brand new curtains in the upstairs front bedroom when she first noticed, what looked like, flames in the house opposite. Normally all she could see from her windows was the high box hedge that screened the house from view and the police incident tape that had been guarding the drive since her neighbour's suicide; but given her lofty, temporary vantage point, she had a clear view over the hedge. She held on to the bar at the top of the lightweight aluminium steps she was balancing on and leaned forward towards the window for a second take. Her first instinct was correct; they were flames. 'My god,' she uttered. 'Jerry,' she shouted. 'Jerry,' she shouted again, louder.

'What?' her husband called up the stairs from the hallway.

'Jerry, come here quickly.'

'What for?'

'Come here, now.'

Jerry knew an order when he heard one. He rushed into the room. 'Where's the fire,' he said prophetically.

'There,' she said pointing across the road. 'The Cole's place; look, it's on fire.'

185

Jerry looked across. ''I can't see anything.'

'You can from up here.' They changed places on the step ladder.

'Bloody hell,' he uttered before rushing down stairs to the hall. He picked up the phone and dialled 999.

'Which service do you require?'

'The Fire Brigade'

'Connecting you to the Fire Service.'

'Fire Service'

'There's a fire in the house opposite me'

'Could I have the address, please?'

'Seventy-eight Park Crescent I think, yes we're eighty-three so yeah, that's seventy- eight.'

'Could I have your postcode, please?'

'What you gonna bloody well do, send me some water.'

'No sir, it's just to help us locate the property; it's alright sir you've come up on the system. An appliance has been despatched and should be at the scene in less than four minutes. 'Could I take your name please?'

'Goodenough, Jerry Goodenough'

Thank you, Mister Goodenough; your address is eighty-three Park Crescent, is that correct?'

Margaret Goodenough shouted from her vantage point. 'Tell them to hurry; it's spreading really fast.'

Jerry ignored his wife. 'Yes, that's correct.'

Could you tell me what type of property it is sir?'

'Three storey detached house.'

'Thank you. Do you know if there's anyone inside the property sir?'

'No; I mean no there isn't as far as I'm aware. It's been empty for a few months; unless they've got burglars or squatters. There's been some comings and goings in recent weeks but I don't think anyone is actually living there.'

'Do you know the names of the owners Mr Goodenough?'

'Well it was owned by Robert Cole, Bob Cole he was Deputy Chief Constable, until he committed suicide.'

'Oh yes, I know the story.'

'So with his wife being murdered and his son killed in Afghanistan, I don't know who owns it now.'

'Thank you for the call Mr Goodenough. Please do not attempt to enter the property. It could be extremely dangerous.'

Jerry had no intention of even crossing the road let alone playing the hero; besides Margaret would never allow it.

Nineteen

When the Chief Constable arrived at Woodlands Farm she was confronted with a scene reminiscent of the aftermath at the Water Mill bombing. The emaciated prisoners were being stretchered into a fleet of ambulances; five lifeless bodies were laid out in the barn, covered by blankets; fire fighters were running extraction hoses from the cellar along with air intake pumps in the opposite direction. No attempt was being made to protect the integrity of, what was now, a crime scene; to do so would have been futile and impeded the emergency services in doing their job. The four detectives were standing outside the rear of the barn, there was little they could do to help in the circumstances; best left to the emergency services.

'Hell of a situation,' said Pauline Crompton to Pullman.

'Appalling ma'am,' he replied. 'If DI Proctor hadn't come up from London, over the possibility of Johnston running a paedophile ring, we'd probably never have found them.'

'Where are they from?'

'Best guess is Thailand. DI Proctor thinks she recognised the language. They're certainly from that part of the world.'

Crompton shook her head and exhaled a weary sigh. 'How the hell did they get here? She knew Mike Pullman didn't have the answer.

'Haven't a clue at the moment; don't even know if they all came together. Hopefully we'll get some answers when we question them.'

'Where's the wife? She must be involved.'

'For sure ma'am; we've informed the Met but we don't know exactly where she and Peak were heading. We've still not been able to contact him.'

'Do you think he's involved too?'

'It's looking likely. He knew the couple very well and he was a bit too quick to get Mrs Johnston away from here.'

'But you don't think there are children or youngsters involved here.'

'Not as far as we can tell; we'll know more when they've been examined. Some of them look pretty young but whether they're under age, I can't tell.'

'So, people trafficking then.'

'Looks like it. They are mainly female, so I'm guessing the sex trade or mail order brides.'

'Is there a difference?' asked Crompton with a resigned shake of her head.

'Not a lot. There are computers and files down there in another room; we'll examine them once the place is clear of people. The Johnstons weren't expecting their secret to be discovered, I doubt they had time to wipe the hard drives or dispose of evidence.'

'So Mrs Johnston ran off and left them to die. Jesus, Mike; a maniac bomber; people trafficking; a paedophile ring; unresolved murders, what the hell next.'

'Just one unresolved murder ma'am and we're closing in on Claude.' It was somewhat of an exaggeration but a necessary one. 'I've spoken with DS Barnes and we're stepping up the house to

189

house on the search for the stolen mini. As for a paedophile ring, it could be that there isn't one, if this is all they were up to...'

'All!' interrupted Crompton. 'This is more than enough.'

'What I meant ma'am was...'

'I know what you meant Mike.'

'DI Proctor is going to speak with the UK Human Trafficking Centre back at the NCA; she'll get their advice on how we proceed from here.'

'Doesn't she know? I thought that was part and parcel of her remit.'

'She comes across child trafficking as part of her job but investigating adult trafficking is not her main role, she thought it best to speak to her colleagues. In any case we needed to report it to them. She and her DS will stay up here until we can establish if there's any child abuse involved.'

'If there isn't, what then?'

'I haven't discussed it with her but I presume she'll head back to London. Adult slavery isn't her specialism.'

'It's not exactly ours either,' said Crompton.

'Exactly ma'am. I reckon we could use all the help and advice we can get, if that's okay with you; we've got more than enough on our plate as it is.'

'Nothing inside the house to point us in the right direction I suppose; no clues to how they got into the country?'

'We only carried out a cursory search; we weren't expecting to find this lot; we need to have a proper look inside the house, as well as this place; if the budget will stand it.'

'Budget? What budget? That went out of the window weeks ago.'

'Some of the victims have been taken to Doncaster Royal Infirmary and some to Hull; as far as we can tell, most of them don't speak any English so we'll also need an interpreter or two when we start the debriefings.'

'Great,' she sighed looking around at the organised chaos. 'Ah well, I guess we'll have to find the money from somewhere. It's not just the money though; personnel are spread too thinly as it is, now we have the trafficking to contend with as well, it will stretch our manpower to breaking point; it would help if we could find Claude and the sooner the better.' She gave Pullman a pleading glance. 'How about you Mike, can you cope?' she meant it from both a professional and personal level.

'No problem.' The past few weeks had taken him to some very dark places but not as dark as the place in which he'd been during his time on compassionate leave. 'It'll be a stretch but I've got a good team and we'll get some results soon.'

Crompton forced a resigned smile. 'I do hope so.'

When the last of the captives had been transferred to hospital, the team, along with three SOCOs, set to work examining the room to the left of the dungeon. Cartright got to work examining one of the two laptops that had been left behind; drawers were searched; files sifted through. Amongst the items in a drawer Sperring found an electric branding iron. The business end of which bore the double H logo.

'I'm pretty sure this wasn't for use on the cows, when it was a functioning dairy farm,' she said, holding up the device.

'More for branding human cattle,' said Pullman examining the implement. 'Tattooing presumably took too long and the women wouldn't have sat still.'

Sperring looked perplexed. 'But if that symbol is about a paedophile ring; why are they using it on these people, they're adults?'

191

'Until they're examined we don't know that they have been branded. Could be that the Johnstons were operating both a ring and trafficking from here.'

Although the air pumps were in operation, the smell in the airless room was still overpowering. Pullman decided to place everything they could find into evidence boxes, to be removed to Howden Police Station, where the local police were establishing an incident room and the air was somewhat fresher. The SOCOs could endure the aroma in the dungeon for a while longer before they turned their attention to the main house.

There was still no word from Claude; which was both a relief and a worry for the Operation Alligator team. House to house interviews had so far drawn a blank. It was as if he had disappeared off the radar; no sightings; no mini; no clues. DS Barnes and DC Sharpe had re-checked the army records again, without any luck. No soldiers had gone AWOL; none were on compassionate leave. Perhaps the link to the army was spurious; perhaps they had got themselves fixated on one line of enquiry. It seemed that they were heading down a cul-de-sac after all.

'Looks like we've drawn a blank here,' said Steph Barnes.

'Yeah, looks that way,' said Sharpe.

'Where did we get to with ex-employees of the Deep?'

'We dropped that when we went down the army route. An ex-employee could possibly apply to the explosion at the Deep but if it was someone with a grudge against them, it's a bit of a stretch for that person to be pissed off with the church and clubbers as well.'

'That means were back with ex-council employees or a lunatic resident; someone with a vendetta against the City.'

'But it would have to be someone who meets the profile; someone experienced with explosives; flying model planes; all that shit,' said Ash.

'Think we need to update the DCI,' said Steph. 'I wonder when he'll be back from Howden.'

'Shall I give him a call?'

'No I will,' replied Steph; she was after all the senior of the two.

Pullman took the call. 'I'd have put my mortgage on Claude being in the military,' he said, after DS Barnes had explained their current impasse. 'Are you sure he's not?'

'We've been over and over the lists sir; unless we're missing something obvious. If we are, neither I, nor DC Sharpe, know where to look.'

'Have another word with your contact at the regiment and see if he's got any thoughts on any other avenues we could explore.'

'Will do.'

'I'll be back in tomorrow; there's not much more I can do here; Lynne will work out of here for a while longer; she can have the fun of interviewing the Thais. Are you and Sharpe okay to work tomorrow; Sunday?'

'No problem for me.' Steph would be pleased to have an excuse for not being at home. Jack was going through one of his black mood periods. She checked with Ashley Sharpe; he was keen to demonstrate his commitment once again. 'Yes that's okay with both of us.'

'Appreciate that; we need to get this guy off the streets. See you in the morning.'

'See you then sir.'

193

'One other thing Steph; I haven't had any word on the whereabouts of DS Peak have you heard anything?'

'No sir. But to be honest I haven't asked.'

'Would you please Steph; and if there's any news let me know.'

All that remained of seventy-eight Park Crescent, the once splendid Georgian home of DCC Bob Cole, was the outside walls and a section of gable end. Fire Services had fought the inferno from the front and rear of the property. A farm track running between the rear garden and the farmland it over-looked, enabled one fire engine to gain access to the back of the property; simultaneously two fire appliances fought the flames from the front. As well as the intense heat of the fire itself, the firefighter's efforts were hindered by a large explosion, which all but destroyed the detached garage together with a large section of the ground floor. It was thought that either a vehicle or gas canisters had exploded in the pre-cast concrete structure.

It took over an hour and a half for the three fire tenders to bring the blaze under control. Jerry Goodenough observed the proceedings from the vantage point of the step ladder, with the aid of a pair of binoculars.

Graham Nattley, Chief Fire Investigation Officer for the East Yorkshire Fire Service, was treading gingerly through the still smouldering embers of the remains. He needed to establish the cause of the fire before the building tumbled or was demolished; once that happened the cause may never be known. As it stood, there was precious little left to examine in any case. The first priority was to establish that there had been no loss of life. The

194

house was said to be empty but that didn't rule out the possibility that squatters had occupied the premises nor that human negligence had caused the blaze.

The seat of the fire appeared to be the lower ground floor or basement, as it would have been called in less grand dwellings. The rooms at that level, once used as servant's quarters, stretched under the entire area of the house; now they were acting as a reservoir for thousands of gallons of water pumped onto the blaze by the fire crews. Fire Officers carefully sifted through the rubble, wading up to their thighs through the basement lake, searching amongst the floating debris for any clues as to the cause of the blaze; within two hours they had determined, to Nattley's satisfaction, that no human remains were present. Photographic records and physical samples were collected for examination in the labs. It was doubtful that, given the conditions, there would be sufficient forensic evidence upon which to base conclusive findings. Nattley would return the following day to complete his examination.

Twenty

Sunday 16th November

Iain Thwaite was already in the Chief Constables office when Pullman joined them. Pauline Crompton was pouring coffee; she waved the pot towards Pullman as he entered.

'No thanks ma'am.'

Crompton handed a cup to Thwaite before sitting down at her desk. Neither she, nor her ACC were used to being in the office on a Sunday, but these were exceptional circumstances. 'Mike before the current situation swamps us completely, I think we need to review exactly what we've got on our hands here and allocate resources accordingly.'

'Ma'am.' Pullman nodded in agreement.

'Our number one priority has to be Claude. He threatened to kill again and we must do all we can to prevent that happening. I want you to focus all your attention on tracing him and getting an arrest.' Despite his protestations that he could cope she could see that her DCI was looking almost as world weary as he did when he returned from compassionate leave. 'The fact that we haven't heard from him for days could mean that he's planning something even bigger than before.'

Pullman nodded again. 'Yes ma'am I think you're right; it's not as though we've stopped working on finding him but every avenue has so far closed on us.'

'That's why I want you to give it your undivided attention; find new avenues Mike.' She took a deep breath the way people do before they deliver unpleasant news. 'I'm going to assign DI Brookes to the trafficking investigation.' She looked at Pullman waiting for the anticipated reaction; she didn't have to wait long, his reaction was instant.

'Tch, Brookes ma'am.' His tone of voice was questioning; his look said *are you sure.*

'I am well aware that the two of you have crossed swords before but the trafficking inquiry is a separate case; once you've brought him up to speed, there's no need for you two to have to work together. Although the pair of you really do need to bury the hatchet, understand.'

The mixed metaphors were building quite a nice little armoury. All she needed to do now was tell him not to put the knife in, rattle his sabre or look daggers at Brookes and he'd have more weapons than he could shake a spear at.

'Understood ma'am.' Brookes was the kind of copper that even coppers didn't like; the man was bigoted, a closet homophobe and had long since passed the borderline racist reputation. The unfortunate victims of the trafficking were in for a rough ride. 'But could I suggest that he doesn't interview any of the victims; that we let DS Sperring do that, then she can brief Brookes to take it from there.'

'I'll suggest it to him; I know he has a somewhat brusque style of questioning but if he insists on seeing them, I won't stand in his way.'

Brusque style of questioning; had she read his record? The memory of Brookes beating the life out one of the Asians, they had discovered in a container in Goole docks, still lived with him. Brookes had completely lost it with the man; just went berserk;

197

punching and kicking the unfortunate illegal immigrant into a pulp. The poor sod was now back on the sub-continent somewhere, looking at the world through one barely functioning eye and trying to survive without a spleen; not exactly an ideal health benefit in a region where the immune system needs to work overtime. Brookes had been suspended; to this day, he still blamed Pullman for ruining his career by reporting the incident and giving evidence to the IPCC. Like most violent bullies, nothing was ever his fault.

'Fair enough ma'am; could I also suggest that we let Sperring continue on the Wethersby case, as it's probably separate from the trafficking.' He knew that wasn't true but the less involvement Brookes had, the better it would be for Lynne.

'Is it? Was the headteacher's murder because of the suspected paedophilia or the people trafficking or both; were his links to Wethersby connected with either? If Johnston was involved in both, was he involved in anything else? For all we know he could also have been into drugs or some other organised crime.' Crompton was making this sound a lot more involved than finding Claude; Pullman was beginning to think he'd got the least interesting end of the deal. 'Now the media have got hold of it, we need to be seen to be doing all we can; that means having an SIO of Brookes level.'

Pullman was disappointed that the CC didn't buy his feeble attempt at snookering Brookes. He didn't disagree with her assessment but was peeved that once again the power of the media seemed to be Crompton's motivating factor. 'You're right of course ma'am,' he couldn't say anything different.

'I know I am. So first thing tomorrow morning, bring DI Brookes up to speed and then let go. Apply your skills to finding Claude; that's an order, clear.'

The Chief Constable could not have made her instructions any clearer; Pullman wouldn't disobey her order, yet was confident that Lynne would keep him up to-date. He'd been involved for too long now to fully step away. DS Steph Barnes and DC Ashley Sharpe were now his primary force in the hunt for Claude.

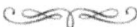

'Unless we've got lucky and he died from his head wound Claude must be close to striking again,' said Pullman. He didn't really mean it; they needed to find him alive and see him brought to trial; he was a sociopath completely lacking a moral compass; devoid of a social conscience. There was no way that the maniac would terminate his campaign without at least one final flourish. Pullman was sitting, with his team; at a highly polished, mahogany table in conference room three, reviewing progress in the investigation so far. This would now be their hub of activity until they made an arrest. Files littered the table top; laptops were booted and ready for action; a wipe board stood at the head of the table in front of the windows.

'He said he'd give us a week so we've got three and a half days.' Pullman opened the conversation.

'He gave a date last time sir but he didn't stick to it,' said Ash.

'All the more reason to find him asap.' He looked at Steph. 'So the regiment didn't come up with any other suggestions as to how we could identify him.'

'None sir; they say we've now got the name of every soldier in the past three years who's left the regiment due to injury, psychological discharge, redundancy, court martial or who simply wanted out of their own volition.'

'We've been through every list twice now; some three times,' said Ashley Barnes. 'I'm buggered if I can see anything.'

Pulman drummed his right hand on the table. 'So if he wasn't in the military, what the hell was he in? Why did he have a military tattoo on his arm? Where did he learn to use explosives and what's his bloody beef with Hull?' Pullman sucked his teeth. 'What are we missing?'

'I researched the tattoo to see if anyone else used the phrase and all I could come up with is a cult group called the Devils Disciples; they had an album out in the late nineties called Fortes Fortuna Adiuvat. They were a heavy metal rock band so it's possible that matey was into them and had the tattoo done as a fan.'

'Pullman gave a non-committal nod. Steph said. 'Maybe Claude was an actual member of the band; a devil's disciple; he's certainly acting like one.'

'Let's not discount it,' said Pullman. 'We've got to explore every possibility no matter how crazy it may seem. Not that I think you're crazy Ash.' Pullman said, with a reassuring grin. 'I've never heard of them but find out all you can about them; where they are and what they're up to now. Sound as if they could be in the right age group.'

Ash nodded. 'Although they are American, so it's a long shot.'

'We've only got long shots,' said Pullman, who would have given his right arm for a short shot. 'Let's review the CCTV footage at the hospital again; see if we can spot anything that might help. Also the hotel tape; maybe we missed something first time round. What else?'

'We could re-interview the nurses that looked after him, maybe there's something they've remembered that they haven't bothered to tell us about,' said Steph.

'Okay'

200

'The drone; we could see if we can trace where it was purchased,' suggested Ash.

'I suppose so,' said Pullman. 'But we didn't find enough of it to positively determine what colour it was let alone what type. We don't have the manpower to trace every model aircraft sold in the last, god knows how long. Besides, unless he paid by credit card, which I very much doubt, we'd still have nothing to identify him.'

'He might have built it himself; we'd never trace all the components,' said Ash.

'He's smart enough to have done that,' said Steph.

'I don't understand why we can't trace the mini; it can't have vanished into the ether; wherever that car is, our man won't be far away. If we can find that, it will narrow the search area. First thing tomorrow morning we'll step up the house to house.'

'What about sending him a message on Facebook sir,' suggested Ash. 'If he doesn't reply maybe we have got lucky,'

'If he does, then maybe you could push him into giving something away,' said Steph Barnes.

'Nothing to lose; he's gone very quiet. Although I'm not sure I want to awaken the Kraken,' said Pullman. Nevertheless he decided to contact Claude; he changed the draft several times before hitting the enter key to transmit the message:

Claude how's the head? We're close to finding the mini you stole and when we do we'll be closer to finding you. Just a matter of time. So why not make it easier on yourself and quit while you're ahead; you've made your point so now it's time to tell the world who you are and why you did it. You want to be famous and make a point don't you? If you don't want the world to know just tell me; your friend. Mike.

Pullman hoped it would be enough to stimulate Claude into a dialogue but not so much that it would trigger another premature attack. It was over an hour before he got a response:

Mike so nice to hear from you. The head's doing fine thanks, I've had a lot worse headaches; the vinegar and brown paper helped lol. It's a bit too late to be looking for the mini. Even if you had found it you would have been disappointed. Don't worry about my fame Mike I'll have a lot more than my 15 minutes soon enough. You really shouldn't be working on a Sunday; you need your rest Mike, you deserve it. I said you'd hear from me in a week Mike so there's still a few days to go; don't be so impatient. Relax, sit back and enjoy some Roxy Music. Claude

So he was still alive and kicking. 'What does he mean too late to find the mini?' posed Pullman.

'Abandoned it somewhere,' said Steph.

'Blown it up more likely,' said Ash.

'Let's get uniform to check out quarries for recent abandoned cars; check out car scrappers to see if they've had a mini dumped on them. He'd have needed the log book to sell it so he couldn't have done that.'

'I'll see if there's been any reports or sightings of cars going over the cliffs or the quayside,' said Ash.

'Why tell me to listen to Roxy Music?' They haven't done anything for years. Why them? Strange choice; that can't be random.' Pullman furrowed his brow. 'He's playing a game; dropping clues. The bombings are no longer enough stimulation; he wants to taunt us.'

'Perhaps it's a red herring sir; trying to divert our attention,' suggested Steph.

'Yeah, maybe,' Pullman wasn't convinced.

'I'll check out their albums and see if there's anything in the titles that'll give us a clue; I'll check the singles as well while I'm at it.'

'At least he doesn't sound pissed off. His underlying tone was quite calm didn't you think? Pullman added, 'So maybe we have got until Thursday to stop the bastard.' Pullman slapped both his hands gently on the table. 'Right let's concentrate on finding that car.' He was feeling optimistic 'I've got a good feeling about this.'

Twenty-one

Monday 17th November

DI Eddy Brookes strolled through the open door of Pullman's office with a distinct swagger. 'Morning Mike.'

Pullman looked up, slowly, from the file he was reading. 'Detective Chief Inspector or sir will do just fine,' he said.

'Oooh, touchy,' said Brookes.

'Oooh touchy, SIR,' emphasised Pullman. It was plain that the two men's antipathy towards one another was as strong as ever.

'Sir.' said the DI reluctantly in a tone that was more of a snarl; it was a battle of wills that he was not going to win, given Pullman's superior rank.

'Take a seat Detective Inspector; the sooner we get this over and done with, the better, for both of us.' Brookes sat down as instructed. 'What do you know about the situation?'

'That you found a load of chinks in a basement....'

Pullman jumped in, 'Are you looking for another disciplinary; haven't you learnt anything since the last one?'

Brookes sucked in a lungful of air. 'That you discovered a number of human beings of oriental or far eastern appearance who may or may not be illegal immigrants, sir.' the statement was heavily ladened with mockery.

'You really are a piece of work aren't you?'

'I get the job done; if those people don't want to be treated like the scum they are, they shouldn't come over here, should they.'

'You're treading a very fine line Detective Inspector; a very fine line. Believe me I won't hesitate to report you again if you make one more racist remark.'

'Well it's thanks to you Detective Chief Inspector,' Brookes said the rank with deliberately invective tone. 'That I have a blot on my record the size of a North Sea oil spill.'

Pullman stood up; went over to the door and closed it before turning to Brookes. 'Listen fuckwit; you are a despicable excuse for a human being. How you made it this far in the job defeats me. You are an intolerant, bigoted little shit and if I didn't have to be in the same room with you, I wouldn't be. If there was some way I could get you kicked off the force I would do it in a heartbeat. I failed last time but trust me, I won't fail again; just give me one more reason and I'll nail you to the wall. Do I make myself clear?'

'Are we done, sir?'

'No we're not.' Pullman took a deep breath to calm his anger. 'Unfortunately I have to brief you but don't let me hear that mouth of yours make one more snide remark, understood.' Pullman didn't wait for a response. He fully briefed Brookes on the situation with the illegal immigrants and handed over the case notes. He purposely did not tell Brookes of his working relationship with Lynne Sperring; it was going to be tough enough for her anyway, working with this moron, without him venting his spleen on her.

'Don't forget that you are still reporting to me on this but I don't need to know every detail. I've got my hands full with our bomber.'

'Yes I heard that was going really well.' Brookes smiled sarcastically; very pleased with himself.

Pullman let the remark go; he opened the door for Brookes to leave; the two protagonists made no attempt to shake hands.

205

DS Peak had not phoned in. 'I think we can safely assume that he's gone walkabout.' said Pullman to Lynne Sperring, when he called her to give the heads up on Brookes. 'I'll get an air and ports alert put out for him; chances are that he and Mrs Johnston will be trying to leave the country, if they haven't already done so. I'm sorry Lynne; I should have listened to you earlier.'

'No sir, I thought he was acting a bit odd but I didn't think he was involved in anything criminal; just thought he was protecting his friend.'

'From what? If he didn't know what the Johnstons were up to, what did he think he was protecting them from? I reckon he's in this up to his jugular and I'm going for it.'

'What do you want me to do sir?'

'Stick with it Lynne, until you can determine if the paedophile ring and the trafficking are connected or if there is actually a paedophile ring at all. Could be this whole thing is about the trafficking not child abuse. See what DI Proctor has to say about it before she goes back to London.'

'She's certain that the double H is connected to child abuse as it crops up with everyone involved, plus we found the branding iron at the farm, it seems that we could be looking at two sides of their activities.'

'Yes I agree it's looking that way. If you have any trouble with Eddy Brookes let me know and I'll deal with it. Don't let him wind you up; he's not worth getting het up about. Good luck.' Pullman replaced the receiver. Having told her not to get het up about Brookes, he knew he, himself, would find it difficult to avoid allowing the DI to enter his thoughts. Bit like Claude blaming his

206

campaign of mass murder on his demands not being met; no comprehension that he was responsible.

Although the researchers were fully trained and experienced at identifying points of interest on CCTV recordings, Pullman decided to check the critical timelines on the tape himself. It proved to be a waste of time; the researchers had done their job well; nothing was visible that they had not already noted.

DS Barnes re-interviewed the nurse who had spoken with Claude during the spell he was conscious. 'What kind of an accent would you say he had?'

'Ordinary; local I'd say; east coast at any rate.'

'Were there any specific words or phrases he used that stand out; something you thought it strange he should say?'

'Don't think so, he was confused from the concussion. When I said that he was lucky to be alive he said Terry couldn't finish him off so the mugger wouldn't either; or something like that.'

'This Terry did he have a surname?'

'Not that he mentioned. He was dazed; not really with it.'

'And you're the only person who spoke to him,' asked Steph

'I think so; he was unconscious or sedated most of the time.'

'We know he had scars on his shoulder and leg and a tattoo on his upper arm; did you notice anything else? Any other scars or birth marks that sort of thing?'

'No nothing that I can remember; he was already wrapped up when I came on duty on the Sunday morning. It was a pretty bad night; everyone was rushed off their feet.'

'Okay, we'll leave it there, thanks.'

'Sorry I haven't been more help. I hope you catch him; it's terrible, what he's doing.'

207

The sixteen captives taken to Doncaster Royal Infirmary, for examination, had been held overnight in a makeshift dormitory in Wheatley Village Hall. Lynne Sperring was at Doncaster Royal Infirmary, with DI Proctor, discussing the findings with the consultant leading the team that completed the examinations.

'The patients are all women; according to the interpreter they claim to be between seventeen and twenty-eight years of age and are all from the Hua Hin province of Thailand. Their health is not good, neither physically or mentally, but the most important part of their physical condition is that they are all in the early stages of pregnancy; between eight and twelve weeks.'

'What all of them!' gasped Sperring.

'Are you sure?' asked DI Proctor.

The doctor was taken aback that the diagnosis should be questioned. 'Quite sure; the interpreter confirmed that all the women were aware of the fact.'

'Where is the interpreter now?' asked Proctor.

'I believe she's at the village hall with the women,' he said.

'We need to speak to her,' said Sperring looking at Proctor. 'Was there anything else about them that we need to know?'

'Presumably you know that they had been branded or had a symbol burnt onto their buttocks; some of the wounds were quite inflamed.'

'Was it a kind of double H symbol?' asked Sperring.

'Yes, I believe so, although it was not terribly distinct; human flesh does not react in quite the same was as cow hide.'

'Thank you doctor. We'll get over to the hall now; we need written confirmation of your findings please.'

'Of course. What will happen to them now?'

Sperring shook her head. 'That's a good question doctor; we'll get it sorted somehow.'

'They can't stay at the hall and we certainly don't have enough beds here for them but, in my opinion, they will need medical supervision for some time yet.'

On the way over to the village hall DI Proctor rang Hull Royal Infirmary, where the other detainees had been taken. The medical team there recounted a similar story. All but three of the seventeen women taken there were also at similar stages of pregnancy.

'Damn,' said Proctor.

'What's that?'

'We kind of knew these things existed but I've never actually uncovered one before.'

'Sperring was puzzled. 'You knew what things existed?'

Proctor thought for a second or two. 'I think what we have here is a baby farm.'

'A baby farm; what you mean like a puppy farm.'

'Yep.'

'Jesus; you think these women are being used like breeding bitches or brood mares.'

'That's exactly what I mean. For years families in third world countries have been surviving extreme poverty by selling their kids to rich westerners but demand outstripped supply, so we believe that, for some time now, children have been specifically produced to meet the demand.'

'Like a production line; babies produced for sale to childless couples.'

'Those babies are the lucky ones. What really concerns us is that the unlucky ones aren't being sold to childless couples but being shipped out to paedophiles.'

'Oh my god you're not serious.'

'I wish I wasn't.'

'And this is happening in Thailand,' asked Sperring with increasing disbelief.

'Don't know for sure. The Thai authorities are doing all they can to stamp out so called sex tourism but...'

'But this isn't sad men going abroad to pay for sex or satisfy their perversions; this is...' Sperring searched for the words. 'erm organised baby trafficking; it's unbelievable that something like this could be going on.'

'It's a bloody awful world we live in Lynne; this kind of shit is happening in other parts of Asia, Africa and now Eastern Bloc countries, according to our intelligence.'

'And here too; if you're right about these women.'

'It's the most likely explanation. Question is; are they pregnant when they're imported or are they impregnated here.'

'Imported! God you make them sound like coffee or cars or something.'

'That's the way the so called gangmasters treat them; they're just a commodity to be traded; there's no moral code, it's all about money.'

'What can we do for them?'

'I haven't got a clue; that's way beyond my remit. They're undoubtedly illegal immigrants so I guess they could be sent back home, where they will no doubt be rounded up by the gangs again and shipped somewhere else; and so the circle continues.'

'I'm sorry you're probably used to this but it's a whole new world to me; nothing like I've ever experienced before or want to again.'

The conference room was barely above twelve degrees; the central heating system had failed and two convector heaters were struggling to make themselves felt. Pullman, Barnes and Sharpe were huddled around the table; hands enveloping steaming mugs of filter coffee.

'I've checked out the band members of the Devils Disciples, as far as I can from here sir, but if you'd like me to go to the States I can probably find out more,' said Ashley Sharpe impishly.

'You wish,' said Pullman. 'Just tell me what you've got so far.'

'Ain't got diddly squat, as they say,' said Ash in his best southern American drawl. 'Zilch. One got shot dead in a bar in New York in,' he consulted his notes. 'Ninety-eight; one is an Indie producer in LA and the other one is a Pentecostal preacher, out in the sticks somewhere. I haven't checked with immigration but I wouldn't think any of them have ever been to Hull, not even to play the New Theatre.'

'Well we knew that really, didn't we; so we can forget that. While we're into the music scene; what about Roxy Music?'

'Nothing that I can see sir,' replied Ash. 'Been through all of their albums and singles, can't see anything to connect them to the bombings; nothing obvious anyway. They played Hull twice but unless they didn't get paid I can't see what...'

'Neither can I,' said Pullman interrupting his young DS. 'So why did Claude mention them?' He was not expecting an answer; he didn't get one. 'Any progress with the drone?'

'No sir. I spoke to the British Model Flying Association and, understandably, without a description of some kind they really couldn't help; there are loads of different makes of quadcopters, or multi-rotors as they're called, and any number of them could have delivered matey's payload. He might not even have bought it, or the components, in the UK; so I don't think we're going to get very far down that runway.'

'What about the hospital; there's nothing new on the tapes; anything with the staff?'

Steph leaned forward. 'Not really. I spoke to everyone who had been in contact with him. Only one of the nurses could add anything to previous statements; she said that he had a local accent.'

'We know he could adopt different accents,' said Pullman.

'Yes but he'd just regained consciousness when she spoke to him so it's possible that he was speaking normally because he was confused and unaware of the situation.' It was a reasonable assumption to which Pullman nodded agreement. 'The other thing she said was that when she told him he'd been beaten up by a mugger he said that Terry had tried do him in and failed so a mugger wasn't going to succeed.'

'Terry who?' asked Pullman.

'Claude didn't mention a surname apparently; the nurse said he was still concussed so I don't know what credence we can give the comment.'

'Right then; all we've managed to add to the profile, is that he's probably local and knows someone called Terry. Brilliant. Let's hope they have more luck with the door to door.'

Twenty-two

Detective Sergeant Raymond Nathaniel Peak was arrested at the Thai Airways check-in desk in Terminal 2 at Heathrow; he made no attempt to resist arrest. A check on all other passengers boarding flight TG911, to Bangkok's Suvarnabhumi Airport, resulted in the detainment of Anchali Sukhasvasti travelling under her Thai passport; her British passport in the name of Anchali Johnston was found in her travel bag. The two detainees were kept in separate interview rooms, pending instructions from DCI Pullman. Instructions came within the hour for the prisoners to be driven, in separate cars, to Hull the following day for questioning.

Pullman briefed Lynne Sperring on the arrests, when she called to tell him about DI Proctor's baby farm theory. Pullman was astounded by that news but not with news of her reaction to the arrival of DI Brookes.

'He's a moron,' she said with controlled outrage. 'When we briefed the new SIO on the pregnancy situation with the women he said, and I quote, *that's all we need; another load of illegal whores dropping their sprogs all over the place.* The guy's a chauvinistic, racist prick, sir.'

'Detective Sergeant Sperring, is the moron you're referring to by any chance a superior ranking officer, namely Detective Inspector Brookes?' Pullman emphasised the ranks.

'Yes sir, sorry sir,'

'Good 'cos you're right he is a racist prick.' He could sense Sperring's relief. 'He needs reporting but don't you do it; ask DI

213

Proctor to report it to her boss and get her to ask whoever that is, to contact the CC direct with a complaint.'

'Couldn't you do that sir?'

'Unfortunately, DI Brookes and I have history. I didn't want him on the case but the Chief Constable, in her infinite wisdom, insisted; if I go to her with this she'll just think it's sour grapes; best it comes via someone else. If Proctor has a problem with that, I'll have a word with her. Tell you what I'll have a word with her anyway.'

'Okay sir; but I don't think she'll have a problem with that; from his look of disdain when he met her I don't think there's any mutual admiration. She had a go at him about his attitude herself; especially when he said he'd stick them all in a container and send it back on a slow boat to China. Apparently all Orientals are Chinese as far as he's concerned.'

'If he used the word Chinese, he was being more polite than usual. Anyway enough of him; when you can wrap things up there, I'd like you to come back and sit in on the interviews with Peak and Mrs Johnston.'

'Thanks. I'll get Sue...erm... DI Proctor.'

'It's alright Lynne I wasn't being too serious about the rank thing.'

Proctor came to the phone. 'Hello sir, Lynne said you wanted a word with me.'

Pullman explained the situation with Brookes and she agreed to the complaint route. She didn't think the women were in any kind of emotional state to cope with the Brookes; even though most of them wouldn't understand a word he was saying, the venomous tone of his questions and comments would be perfectly clear. Pullman asked if she could arrange to stay up there for two or three days longer. She said she'd already got clearance on that and had also arranged for the women to be taken to a hostel, when they were discharged by the medics. The Home Office would decide what further arrangements needed to be made. She told Pullman that Cartright might have found some interesting stuff on the Johnston's computer that she would discuss with him when they met. She had already informed London, as this was now clearly a national, rather than regional, matter.

Pullman was relieved that the issue of the baby farm was being taken out of their hands but the murder was still a local matter and one he intended to deal with, regardless of the CC and Brookes.

'Peak and Johnston will arrive here later tonight; first thing tomorrow morning you, me and Lynne will meet in my office prior to interviewing them. Okay.'

'Sounds like a plan,' said Proctor.

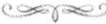

Pullman was about to call it a day when Sergeant Carter popped his head around the conference room door. 'Got a minute sir.'

'Sure Sarge; your boys got something from the door to door?'

'Not sure sir but you know me; I like to err on the side of caution.'

'It was you who spotted that Claude was the mugging victim Sarge so if your instincts have picked up on something else, I'm all ears.'

'One of my WPOs covering Park Crescent mentioned that the DCCs house had been gutted by fire...'

'Bob Cole's place you mean?'

'Yeah.'

'Bloody hell how much shit luck can one family have?' It was a rhetorical question. 'Not that it matters much to the DCC now.'

215

'No sir.'

'So what about it?'

'Just out of curiosity I got hold of the Fire Officer's assessment report, just to see what caused the fire; as I say, just out of curiosity.'

'And?' said Pullman, urging Carter to get to the crux.

'Well the upshot is that the house was empty, had been since...well you know; they don't know how or where in the house the blaze started; there wasn't much left by all accounts.'

'Your point is, Sergeant?'

'There was a car destroyed in the fire; completely burnt out; the report doesn't say what make or model it was so I've taken the liberty of asking them to find out sir, just in case.'

'Good man Sarge. Did you ask them to get the VIN while they were at it?'

'Yes sir.'

'Do me a favour, get someone to contact the owner of the mini and get the VIN off the registration doc; should have done that before now.'

'Sorry sir, didn't think.'

'Not you Sarge, me. Beginning to think the Chief Constable was right I was spreading myself too thinly; missing the details.' He shook his head and sucked his teeth. 'Glad you're on the ball; thanks.'

'Might not be anything; might not even be a mini; might be the DCC's Jag.'

'Might be a Routemaster bus for all we know but it's worth checking out.'

216

Tuesday 18th November

Pullman was in his office bright and early. His sleepless nights were few and far between since Claude had started his campaign. Events had pre-occupied his mind to such an extent that he could ward off the moments of sadness which, less and less frequently, filled his thoughts. He could now talk to Jane's parents and friends without his voice breaking up; he could recall past memories without the emotional turmoil that had previously accompanied them. Time, the great healer, was doing its work; he had to make sure he didn't pick at the scabs.

Iain Thwaite, still ACC, entered the office. 'Morning Mike.'

'Morning sir.'

'Just to let you know that DI Brookes has been taken off the trafficking case.'

'Why's that sir? he asked, feigning ignorance.

'Request from London; they want their people to handle it.'

Up yours Brookes thought Pullman. 'I can understand that sir,' he said. 'Probably linked to wider trafficking issues.'

'Probably; how's everything else going?' asked Thwaite.

'Did you know that Bob Cole's house had been destroyed by fire?'

'No. Hell's bells, no one told me.'

'Only found out myself late last night; we're getting a copy of the damage report sent over.'

'Is arson suspected?'

217

'No idea; normally I wouldn't take an interest but apparently there was a burnt out car at the scene so we're just checking that it wasn't our missing mini.'

'I see. I'd like to take a look at the report when you've done with it.'

'Sure thing,' said Pullman. Thwaite left the room. Pullman was pleased that his ploy to get Brookes taken off the case had been successful; he was sure Brookes wouldn't be feeling the same way.

Sperring and Proctor arrived within minutes of each other and joined Pullman in his office. He informed them that Brookes was no longer on the case; subdued euphoria broke out.

DI Proctor said, 'Blimey that was quicker than I thought.'

'Quicker than any of us thought, thankfully,' said Pullman. 'Do you know what's happening with you Sue?'

'Yes sir, I'm staying up here for as long as it takes to close this one down.'

'Excellent. So bring me up to-date,' said Pullman.

'Cartright is convinced that the evidence of trafficking is on the laptop but most of the entries were in some sort of undecipherable code; we're having the laptop couriered down to London for our cyber unit to take a look at.'

'I remember the receptionist at the college telling me Trevor Johnston was some sort of computer whizz kid,' said Sperring. 'She called him a genius.'

'Well apparently it took some kind of genius to put together the encryption on the laptop, so I guess she was right,' said Proctor. 'It will need our own version of Alan Turing to crack it.'

'From past experience with the National Cyber Crime Unit I'm sure they'll get it sorted,' said Pullman, looking at Sperring for confirmation. She smiled and nodded agreement. He turned to

Proctor. 'What about this baby farm thing then; it's not something I've ever come across before?'

'Nor me; we've had reports for some years now that such things existed in parts of Asia and Africa but this is the first time I've actually seen the evidence; and here in the UK.'

'Are you sure that's what it is?'

'There's no other explanation, sir; thirty odd women, all but three of whom are pregnant and that doesn't count the five fatalities; the post mortems on those haven't been done yet. The big question is not whether the babies were for sale but to whom they were being sold.'

Pullman shook his head. 'How did they get pregnant,' he asked, then quickly added, 'I don't mean the birds and bees; I mean was it here; wherever they came from or some other place.' He shrugged.

'They're all pretty traumatised so it may be a few days before we get the full picture but it seems, from what we've managed to ascertain so far, that twenty-three of them are Thai and the others are Malay; they were held in a camp of some sort in southern Thailand where they were subjected to sexual abuse several times a day over a period of weeks before being transported by road for several days. Eventually they were put into a container. We don't know how long they were in there for but we do know that it takes at least forty days for a container ship to sail here from that region; it would have been impossible for them to survive that long, so they must have been driven a lot closer, probably somewhere on mainland Europe.'

'Jesus, how the hell did they survive all of that?'

'We don't know how many of them did, sir; we know how many arrived but not how many started the journey.'

219

Sperring said, 'The bodies we found were recent deaths, they could have disposed of the bodies that died in the container days or weeks ago.'

Proctor agreed. 'I think we need to search the farmland for signs of a mass grave sir.'

Pullman nodded to show agreement. 'Yes I was just thinking the same thing myself.' He slapped the palm of his hand on the desk. 'Container lorries,' he said, as if experiencing an epiphany. 'That would explain all that deep rutting on the farm track up to the house; obviously caused by heavy vehicles; it struck me as odd at the time, because it wasn't a working farm, so now I'm thinking they were caused by a container lorry or lorries.'

'Of course sir,' said Sperring. 'Blast, after all the ambulances and fire engines we'll never get any recognisable tyre prints.'

'No, too late for that,' said Pullman. 'Right then time to see what Peak has to say for himself; I'll get him brought up to the interview room.' He had a change of mind. 'No, no I won't; he can stew for a while longer. Lynne, grab a couple of uniforms and get over to Peak's place; have a look around; let's see if we can find anything that ties him in with the trafficking.' Sperring gave him a sideways glance of disapproval. 'Don't fret Lynne I'll get the warrant organised but there won't be anyone there to argue the toss; okay?'

'Okay,' Lynne said with reluctance; she was a stickler for procedure but instantly calculated, in her mind, that there was minimal risk in following orders on this occasion.

'Pullman pointed at Proctor. 'You and I will start with the Johnston woman.'

'Sounds like a plan,' said Proctor; she didn't notice the curl of disdain on Pullman's upper lip at the use of her pet phrase.

Sergeant Carter wrote down the number of the VIN as the nurse read out the digits over the phone. 'Great, thanks very much; yes I'll let you know if it turns out to be your car.' He replaced the receiver and picked up the Fire Officer's report. He smiled with satisfaction as he saw that the numbers matched. 'Bingo!' He couldn't wait to tell Pullman that a hunch of his had once again proven to be correct; he had to curb his enthusiasm because the DCI was in an interview.

Anchali Johnston (nee Sukhasvasti) sat motionless, head bowed; eyes fixed on the table in front of her. Pullman and Proctor watched her through the one way window. 'Right, let's get this show on the road,' said Pullman. He opened the observation room door to be confronted by a medical examiner. Pullman was startled.

'Morning DCI there's something you ought to know about the woman you have in custody.'

'Don't tell me she's pregnant.'

'No chance; I can absolutely guarantee that.'

'What about her then?'

'She isn't.'

'Okay, I take your word on that; so if she's not pregnant?'

'She isn't a she.' The medic raised his eyebrows but not as much as Pullman and Proctor raised theirs. 'She is, or rather he is, male; a ladyboy is, I believe, the term used.'

Pullman managed to raise his dropped jaw. 'Let's step back in here a minute.' They re-entered the observation room. Pullman pointed at Anchali Johnston through the glass. 'You're telling me that she's a man.'

'She has male genitalia.' The medical examiner handed a folder to Pullman. 'He or she was, understandably, very reluctant to undergo a medical examination but we got there eventually.'

'So the ...erm...' Pullman made a cupping motion on his chest.

The medical officer smiled. 'Implants.'

'Shit; you wouldn't know would you.' said Pullman.

'She's hardly the Mona Lisa but... a man,' said Proctor.

'I presume Trevor Johnston knew.'

'If he didn't at first it wouldn't have taken long to find out.'

Pullman took a deep breath. 'Right then, we'd better have a word with her... him; what do we call him/her?'

Proctor smiled at the DCI's embarrassment. 'If we stick to Anchali we won't go far wrong.'

'Good thinking,' said Pullman. 'Bloody good job Brookes isn't here; Christ knows what he'd have said.'

They interviewed Anchali Johnston over two sessions; the first lasted forty minutes; the second thirty-five. Throughout both sessions she never uttered a word; never diverted her eyes from the desk and never showed any signs of emotion or reaction to the questions; it was if she had entered a trance like state. As they left the interview room Pullman was once again startled. This time by DS Steph Barnes.

'I wish people would stop doing that.' said Pullman.

'Ooops,' said Barnes by way of apology. 'Sorry sir, the Chief Constable would like to see you and DI Proctor in her office in half an hour and I thought you might like to know that Sergeant Carter was right about the car at Bob Cole's house.'

'It was our missing mini then.'

'Sure was.'

Pullman checked his watch. 'Excellent. Let's go to the incident room.' He turned to DI Proctor. 'Sue, I just need to sort this; see if you can get hold of Lynne and see how she's doing at Peak's house; use my office; then join us in conference room three; just down there on the right.' He indicated the direction. 'Then we'll go see what the CC wants.'

As he and Steph walked to the incident room he asked. 'Don't suppose there's any hope of forensics?'

'Norfolk and chance,' said Steph. 'It was completely destroyed; the blaze was intense by all accounts.'

They entered the room. 'So what was it doing there?'

'No idea sir. When the fire service arrived at the scene, the incident tape was still in place across the entrance to the driveway; they ripped it down. No one had been to the house as far as we know since the suicide. No postmen, no circulars, no deliveries.'

'Claude must have broken in; removed and replaced the tape.'

'There is an access track at the back of the house. He could have driven along that and entered the garden from the rear. The fire brigade used that track, so it was well churned up.'

'Are there any other vacant properties in the street?'

'Don't know sir.'

'Check it out Steph; might help if we determine if the choice of squat was Hobson's or chosen for a specific reason.'

'I'll get uniform to check that out.'

'We need to get forensics in there too. Now we know the mini was there, they can check for any other signs that matey was operating from the house. The fire assessor wouldn't have been looking for traces of our explosives. I don't suppose there's any chance he...'

'Died in the fire? No sir, there were no human remains found.'

223

'Get that double checked as well,' instructed Pullman. 'Suddenly I'm feeling lucky.'

'Can't get too excited sir; the fire was Saturday you were on Facebook with him yesterday; I don't believe in ghosts.'

'Damn, nor do I. Oh, check out all the Cole's relatives, perhaps someone had the keys.'

DI Proctor entered the room and looked around at the incident boards and piles of files. 'Someone's been busy,' she said.

'The accumulated results of weeks of enquiries; none of which is getting us very far at the moment. What news from Lynne?'

'She's on her way back; she says Peak has been careless. She's found a baseball cap that matches the description given by the vendor of the Ford Focus; whatever that means, along with a set of keys that might be from the car as well, given that Peak drove to London in his. She also found bank statements showing very healthy balances in the names of John Freans and Penelope Ghent.'

Pullman laughed out loud. 'Stupid, arrogant bastard.' He chuckled again.

'Sir' said Proctor wondering what it was that had amused him.

'A little joke from Peak; you're too young to remember but there used to be a biscuit brand called Peek Freans – John Freans get it– and Penn-y-Ghent is one of the three peaks in Yorkshire – Penelope Ghent; he was having a little joke. Let's see if he's as funny when we interview him.'

'Okay sir,' said Proctor.

'I'm sorry Sue but I want to wait until DS Sperring gets back; she knows Peak and I think she should be in on the interviews.'

'Of course she should.'

Pullman turned his attention back to Claude; he prodded the wipe board where he had written *Terry couldn't finish me off* he asked Steph. 'Any thoughts on this Terry character?'

'None.'

DI Proctor said, 'Is there any possibility that this Claude of yours is in the army?'

'What makes you think that?' asked Pullman.

'My kid brother, well he's twenty four now but I always call him kid, anyway that's beside the point, he left on his second tour with the Paras in Afghanistan a couple of months back; when my mum was saying goodbye, all tears and hugs, telling him to be careful, I distinctly remember him saying that Terry didn't get him last time so he'd make bloody sure they didn't get him this time. Apparently it's what the boys out there call the Taliban – Terry Taliban.'

'You're having me on,' said Pullman.

'No, it's a nickname. I suppose it's like Germans being called Jerry or our troops being called Tommy. I don't know where it comes from but that's what they call the Taliban. Terry; honestly.'

Pullman looked at the board again *Terry couldn't finish me off* 'Bollocks!' he exclaimed. 'He *is* a bloody soldier; Terry couldn't finish me off; he *was* injured by the Taliban. Bollocks.' He looked at Steph and Ash with a pleading look in his eyes, as if to say are you listening to this; why the hell couldn't you find him. They were dumbstruck. Pullman was aware he had over-reacted. 'Okay, okay; let's think about this logically. We know he had an injury to the leg and shoulder; he has a tattoo of the Yorkshire regiment's motto on his arm so we assumed he was with the regiment. It was the logical thing to assume but we can't find a soldier who's been invalided out, or is still in there, who matches the profile of our bomber. So what are the options; one,' Pullman's left hand grabbed the index finger of the right hand. 'He is still on active service despite the injury.'

225

'If he was still serving, surely someone would know if he was missing for days at a time, especially when he was in hospital,' said Steph. 'Wouldn't think he's been on normal leave for this period of time either.'

'Okay. Two; he is or was in some other regiment.' He was now grasping two fingers.

Ash spoke. 'Then why would he have their motto tattooed on his arm.'

'Maybe he once served in the regiment and got transferred; maybe he is a fan of that rock group of yours, Ash; maybe he just likes the bloody phrase.'

Proctor interjected. 'Perhaps he's a frustrated wannabe soldier; didn't get accepted because of the injury you say he has; so he's now acting out his fantasies and sees the world at large as his enemy.'

'Good thought,' said Pullman.

Steph wrote it down; then looked up. 'Territorials,' she said. 'Maybe he's a part time soldier.'

'A Reservist, yes could be,' said Pullman. 'They're trained to normal combat standards. So maybe they've been to Afghanistan.'

'Or he just imagines he has,' said Ash.

'Okay let's pursue that line of enquiry; Steph, you and Ash concentrate on that but keep behind the forensic team at the fire site; if they discover anything, other than the mini, which links our man to that place I want to know as soon as they know.'

226

Twenty-three

The introductions over and done with, Pauline Crompton opened the proceedings. 'As Iain has already informed you, DI Brookes has been taken off the case.' She looked directly at DI Proctor. 'I believe that was at your request, Detective Inspector.'

'Yes ma'am.'

The Chief Constable looked at Pullman but asked Proctor. 'Off your own bat was it?

'Yes ma'am.' replied Proctor with a deadpan expression. She could almost hear the cogs turning inside the Chief Constables head. She felt further clarification was needed. 'I know I'd only just met DI Brookes but it was clear to me that his attitude towards the victims could have hindered the investigation; possibly even prejudiced the case. I mentioned it to my boss. I didn't know he had spoken with you until DCI Pullman informed me.' She really did believe that would have happened, which made her answer all the more convincing. Crompton had no alternative but to accept Proctor's version of events; nevertheless she was confident that Pullman had influenced Proctor's action. Pullman's face was expressionless. 'And to be frank ma'am his attitude towards me was unacceptable as well,' added DI Proctor.

Crompton refrained from pursuing the matter; her problem now was trying to find yet another assignment for Brookes but finding Claude and investigating the baby farm activities were the main priorities. 'Very well; where are we on finding out what was actually going on at the farm?'

227

Proctor sat forward in her chair. 'We know that in the final part of their journey, the women came in by container. They didn't spend too long on the road once they had been loaded onto a lorry so we are inclined to think that they came directly into Hull, which means we've ruled out Teesport.'

'Wise, it's a fair drive down from Middlesbrough and obviously you know that Immingham, Howden and Hartlepool don't handle containers.'

'Yes ma'am that's one of the things I learned from discussing it with the HTC.'

'That's the Human Trafficking Centre,' said Crompton, pointlessly demonstrating her knowledge.

'Yes ma'am; as you know I'm with CEOP, so my experience is in investigating child exploitation and abuse; this case has now overlapped into human trafficking, which is outside my remit, so I needed to ask my colleagues for guidance.'

'What advice have they given you?'

'To work closely with the local team on the ground...'

'That's interesting considering you've had my appointed SIO taken off the case.' Touché.

'Ma'am it's not for me to question your appointments...'

'Quite right, it isn't.' Crompton said with the disarming smile of a coiled cobra. 'Fortunately ACC Thwaite here, was heavily involved in uncovering several cases of illegal immigration and domestic slavery over the past few years; he will be able to guide you through the local maze.'

Pullman was feeling frustrated; he wanted to get stuck into Peak so he interrupted the fencing match. 'Ma'am, do you think I could be excused from this discussion, I really need to get back to looking for Claude.'

Crompton said, 'Of course but I would have thought that you would have wanted to interview DS Peak, considering we have him in custody downstairs.' Pullman reacted like a child who'd been caught with his with his hand in the biscuit barrel. 'I'd like a word first Mike. Iain do you think you could take DI Proctor to your office and continue this conversation there.'

'Of course.' He and Proctor left the room.

'Mike, contrary to popular opinion, I do actually know what's going on in my own force.' Pullman stood like a schoolboy being admonished by the headteacher. He suddenly wished that he had the foresight to put an exercise book inside his keks; he felt sure he was in for six of the best. 'I am perfectly well aware of DI Brookes' shortcomings; I had hoped that this case would have put him in the spotlight. Unfortunately I need more than a mild complaint, from a visiting DI, to enable me to take disciplinary action. I was rather hoping that DI Brookes would metaphorically shoot himself in the foot; which I am quite certain, he would have done, given a little more time. That's why I appointed him and why I distanced you from the investigation; I didn't want any proceedings to be tainted by personal animosity between the two of you.'

Pullman felt like a fool. Not only had he been caught red handed but the biscuits had been poisoned. He instantly decided it was the CC's fault for not taking him into her confidence but then that thought was quickly transplanted by the realisation that, had anyone else known, she could have been accused of entrapment. He owed her an apology. 'I'm sorry ma'am; I let my personal opinion of Brookes cloud my judgement.'

Crompton nodded sagely in agreement. 'Right let's leave that aside for another day. I hear the missing car was found at Bob

Cole's house, at least what remains of it; any idea how it got there?'

'No ma'am; we're checking for forensics and re-interviewing the neighbours to see if they saw any comings or goings; I'm also having the Cole's relatives checked out; could be that one of them had access.'

'I met a lot of them at the memorial service, can't say any of them struck me as odd, but worth a check.'

He repressed his urge to tell her that they were re-examining the soldier route; there would be time enough if they reached a positive destination this time round.

'I've got a meeting with Peter Monkton tomorrow; he's getting a little bit edgy that Claude is still on the loose.'

'I suppose he has every right to be nervous; none of us want another incident.'

'He's edgy because he's up for re-election in a couple of months. The only incident he's concerned about is losing and, to be fair, I'm concerned too; his main opponent isn't exactly a friend of ours and he has the most appalling halitosis.' Crompton wrinkled her nose at the memory.

Iain Thwaite was more than happy to share his local knowledge with DI Proctor. He had been involved in several cases of possible illegal immigration during his career on Humberside but not once had they managed to gather any irrefutable evidence to enable a successful prosecution. 'It's probably best if I take you out to the terminal, so you can see the scale of the operation for yourself.'

'Sounds like a plan.'

'It really is vast; the site covers over thirteen acres, they handle something in the region of three hundred thousand containers a year and growing. It's impossible to examine that volume, so the best we can do is the odd spot check. The operators are pretty vigilant but there's only so much they can do, if they're going to run an efficient business.'

'We can't be sure they came into Hull anyway sir.'

'From what the unfortunate victims told you, I think it's a pretty safe assumption but proving it won't be easy; believe me.'

'Let's hope that between the seized computers and, DCI Pullman's questioning of the people known to be involved at the farm, that we can put together a case; with or without finding anything at the container terminal.'

'Hope was all that was left in Pandora's box,' said Thwaite.

Pullman and Sperring studied Peak through the observation room window. He sat with his elbows on the table; hands raised in a praying formation, tapping his fingers together. He looked relaxed; unconcerned about the situation.

'How are we going to handle this sir,' asked Lynne Sperring.

'Like he's just taken unofficial leave and we want to know why. We'll keep our find at the farm in reserve and hit him with it when he's feeling even more relaxed than he appears to be at the moment.'

'Doesn't look as if he's got a care in the world, does he.'

'He's about to get more than he can handle.'

231

The two detectives entered the interview room. As they did so Peak jumped to his feet. 'Why the hell have I been arrested?' he demanded to know, in a manner that belied his calm exterior.

Pullman sat down motioning to Peak to retake his seat. 'Have you been read your rights Detective Sergeant?'

'No I bloody well haven't.' Peak sat down.

'Then you haven't been arrested have you; eh? You know the drill; you're simply here, voluntarily, to answer a few questions regarding your conduct over the past few days. We need to establish if there is a disciplinary to face.'

'I don't recall volunteering.'

Pullman ignored the remark. 'Tell me, why did you think it necessary for you to personally accompany Mrs Johnston to London?'

'I said I would make sure she was safe with her relatives. You agreed.'

'You said she had relatives in London and that you would make contact; that's all I agreed to. I did not agree to you taking her to London.'

'She was too distressed to go on her own, I was just being...'

'Sir Galahad.'

'I discussed it with DS Sperring.'

'You didn't discuss it, you just told me you were on your way,' said Sperring defensively.

Pullman leaned forward. 'So, mind telling me what were you doing at Heathrow? Her relatives work there do they?'

'No. Her cousins were on holiday, back home in Thailand, I couldn't leave Mrs Johnston in London on her own so I offered to take her out there.'

'I'm sure she's capable of flying on her own.'

'I was worried about her mental state.'

232

'Like I said, Sir Galahad.'

'If you say so.'

'Tell me does Sir Galahad always carry his passport with him?'

'Yes, as a matter of fact he does. I always keep it in my overnight case to make sure I never forget it, as I have done in the past.'

'Overnight bag; so you intended to stay in London did you?'

'I was just covering all eventualities; I had no idea what was going to happen when I got down there.'

'Who paid for the flight?'

'I did, so you can't accuse me of taking bribes or gifts.'

'That's a very expensive gesture. Tickets must be... what seven hundred pounds?'

'Five hundred and eighty actually; can get them cheaper in advance but not on the day.'

'Return?'

'Single,' replied Peak without thinking.

'Single, meaning one way?'

'That's the usual meaning.' Thinking quickly he said. 'That's all we could get; it was too complicated to arrange returns.'

'We were in the middle of a murder investigation and you didn't think to call in to let us know what you were doing?' said Pullman

'I didn't think DS Sperring would need my help. We weren't getting very close to Wethersby's killer.'

'I was referring to the murder of Mr Johnston.'

Both Pullman and Sperring noticed Peaks pupils dilate. 'I thought it was a hit and run.'

'So did we at first because that's what we were meant to think but the killer laid in wait or should I say, parked in wait, for Johnston to leave the house and then deliberately ran him over.'

233

'Why would anyone want to kill him?'

'I was rather hoping you could tell me.'

'Me? Why would I know?'

Pullman leaned his head to one side in a conspiratorial manner. 'Was he gay?'

'No.'

'Was he bi-sexual or bi-curious as they call it these days?'

'How would I know,' said Peak with an exaggerated gesture of bewilderment and indignation.

'Were you having an affair with Mrs Johnston?' asked Pullman holding back a smile.

'No bloody way,' snapped Peak with even more indignation.

'You were all very close; did you not fancy her?'

Peak began to realise why Pullman was asking questions about Anchali Johnston. 'You know don't you.'

'What?' replied Pullman.

'That Anchali is transgender.'

'I know that she's a ladyboy.'

'That's just for the tourists; it's not confined to Thailand. There are plenty of transgender people in Britain; girls who wannabe boys and boys who wannabe girls but they're not called ladyboys or boyladies here.'

'Is there such a thing as a boylady?' asked Pullman. 'I've never heard that before.'

'Probably not; I was just making a point,' said Peak.

'Did Trevor Johnston know before the wedding? Or was there a wedding; was it arranged to get her into the country?' Pullman didn't wait for an answer he knew that the chances of it being truthful were remote; instead he changed the subject. He slid a clear evidence bag across the table towards Peak; it contained a blue baseball cap. 'Do you recognise this?'

Peak looked at the cap in silence for a few seconds while he thought of an answer. 'Yes' was all he came up with.

'Is it yours?'

'Could be; I've got one like it but I couldn't say if this one is mine.'

Sperring spoke up. 'I can say it's yours because I found it at your house along with these keys.' She pushed another evidence bag towards Peak. 'They belong to a Ford Focus, sold on an auction site to a man wearing this cap, the day before Johnston was murdered.'

'If you're accusing me of murdering Johnston I want a lawyer.'

'Are you accusing him of murder Lynne?'

'No sir.'

'Am I accusing him of murder Lynne?'

'No sir.'

'Don't know where you got that idea from Detective Sergeant; I am however saying that you purchased the Ford Focus, that was found, burnt out, last week and which was, we believe, used to kill Mr Johnston.'

'I never bought a car on Ebay and there must be hundreds of those caps sold every day.'

'I didn't mention Ebay,' said Sperring.

'Yes you did.'

'No, I said an auction site but you're right, it was Ebay.'

'That means nothing, these days Ebay is generic for auction sites; you don't auction something, you Ebay it; just like no one says search engine anymore they say Google it or say iPad for a tablet; just shorthand, we all do it.'

'The vendor has identified you as the purchaser from photographs.'

'Good job he sold his car then cos with eyesight like that he shouldn't be driving.'

Pullman intervened. 'Look Peak we've got eye witness identification; we found the keys in your house and we've got forensics. You bought the car that's rock solid.'

'You've got some guy who, let's say, I once cautioned; now he's got a vendetta against me so he's lying to stitch me up; you've got a set of keys I found in the street but, what you haven't got is any forensics to tie me in with that car or the scene of the accident of that I'm sure. In total that all adds up to fuck all. So unless you've got something else, I'm out of here.' Peak had a look of confidence about him; he stood up.

'Sit down, Detective Sergeant.' Peak did as he was told. 'I've got more than enough to hold you for further questioning and I will place you under arrest if I have to; you won't be going anywhere for a while.' Pullman's grumbling stomach was telling him that it was lunchtime; he checked his watch. His stomach was accurate as always. 'We'll take a break at this juncture.' He called in the uniformed officer. 'Take our guest back to the cells and see that he's fed please.'

When Peak had left the room, Pullman said softly to Sperring. 'Arrange for Peak's clothing to go for forensic examination.'

'He won't have been wearing that when he murdered Johnston surely.'

'Unfortunately not but while he's stripping off they can check him over for the double H tattoo. I'll put my pension on him having one somewhere; we need something to tie him into the Johnston's activity. It's not proof, I know, but it will help convince me that we're barking up the right tree.'

DI Proctor was sitting with Steph Barnes when Pullman and Sperring reached Monks Cafeteria, although most users still called it the canteen. Fancy names, a designer logo and new furniture, had not changed the range or quality of the fare on offer. The new arrivals selected pre-packed sandwiches and coffee before joining the incumbents at their table.

'Steph looking after you then,' said Pullman.

Proctor smiled. 'Yes thanks. How are the interviews going?'

'Slowly, very slowly but we'll get there. What about you? ACC sorting you out?'

'He's taking me over to the container terminal after lunch so I can get a feel.'

'While you're in the car with him, make sure *he* doesn't get a feel.' Pullman gave a knowing look.

Sperring said. 'Don't listen to him. Thwaite's a bit of a flirt but he's harmless. The indecent exposure allegations were never proven.'

Proctor was agog. 'You're kidding right?'

All three locals laughed. 'Yes of course,' said Steph.

'Just winding you up.' Pullman took a sip of coffee. 'Where's Cartright? Haven't seen him today.'

'He actually took the laptop to London last night. We wanted to make sure it got there in one piece; it's potentially far too valuable to risk losing.'

Sperring answered her mobile. 'Sperring. Hi Rick..... Did you, bloody hell......sounds horrific.....When you've checked it all out get the report to me as soon as you can. Call me with the top line if there's anything crucial. Thanks. Yeah see you.' Her three colleagues looked at her for clarification. 'That was Rick.'

'We gathered that much,' said Pullman. 'New boyfriend?'

237

'Good god no, although I wouldn't say no if he asked, he's rather....err no, he's one of the forensic team over at the farm. In the dungeon, they've discovered a concealed room which they think has been used for deliveries judging by the amount of foetal matter they found.' Her companions all winced to show disgust. 'There are all kinds of medical instruments and a small armoury of knives and cleavers; goodness knows what they were used for.'

Steph said. 'Doesn't bear thinking about.'

'Cleavers you say?'

'Meat cleavers, I think he actually said; perhaps they cut up some of the babies, you know, if they were still born or deformed; maybe they killed the mothers once they'd given birth?' said Sperring.

'That's an unfortunate possibility but can you get back to your boyfriend...'

'He's not my boyfriend!'

'Whatever; ask him to bag up the cleavers and get them over to Denise Morrison at the pathology lab; then ask her to check them for any traces of Wethersby's blood or DNA.'

'Wethersby? said Sperring.

'Yep. Just a thought; we're pretty sure Wethersby knew his killer; the Johnstons and Peak all knew Wethersby and now we know they had access to the kind of weapon that was used to kill him. Probably co-incidence but worth checking out.' He finished his coffee. 'Right time to rattle a couple of cages I think.'

'I'll make those calls while I finish my coffee sir, if that's okay; then I'll join you in the interview room,' said Sperring.

'Okay I'll nip into my office on the way. Nothing from Claude was there Steph?'

'Not up to lunch sir,' she said. 'We're monitoring your Facebook; Ash would have let us know, had there been any posts.'

238

Twenty-four

Mike Pullman sat at his desk; elbows on the surface and hands covering his eyes; he was, once again, looking through the darkness they created, to focus his thoughts. He was clear in his own mind that Peak was involved in the goings on at Woodlands Farm; it was looking more than likely that Peak had killed Johnston. If he was capable of that, then he was just as capable of being involved in Wethersby's murder; but was he involved? Thinking did not necessarily make it reality and, if it was reality, proving it was a very different thing; how could he get Peak to incriminate himself? And how was he going to get Anchali Johnston to open up? Not in the biblical sense.

'You all right sir?' asked Lynne Sperring.

'Yeah fine. Just thinking; I always look this bad when I'm straining my undersized brain.' He smiled and stood up. 'Right, time for round two.' On their way to the interview room Pullman popped his head around the conference room door. 'Anything?' he said. Steph and Ash looked up and shook their heads; Pullman gave a disappointed nod but was inwardly relieved that Claude had not resurfaced; he had enough on his plate currently.

As Pullman opened the door of the interview room, a uniformed officer handed him a note; Pullman read the note and looked through the open door at Peak, sitting at the table dressed in a police issue overall, before handing the note to Sperring. The note simply read; double H tattoo on top right bicep. The two detectives sat down facing the anxious man.

Peak said angrily, 'What the hell are you doing with my clothes; if I had committed a crime, do you really think I'd be so bloody stupid to be wearing the same gear a week later? For Christ sake, I've been a copper for twenty five years; I know the score.'

Pullman let him finish his rant. 'Lynne tapes please.'

Sperring opened two new audio cassette tapes.

Peak crossed his arms and snorted with derision. 'About time you went digital isn't it.'

Sperring said by rote 'This interview is being tape recorded. This is an interview with...' she looked at Peak. He was well aware that he should state his name, having gone through the procedure many times.

Eventually he said. 'Detective Sergeant Peak.'

Lynne shook her head. 'State your full name please.' She emphasised the word full.

Peak reluctantly complied with his full name followed by his address and date of birth as required. Sperring completed the formalities by stating that she and Pullman were also present.

Pullman opened the recorded conversation. 'I'm now going to refrain from calling you detective sergeant because you're not fit to have the rank and I'm going to prove that you are a murderer, a human trafficker and a paedophile.'

'Don't you call me a fucking paedophile,' screamed Peak.

'Then why have you got that symbol on your shoulder?'

Peak instinctively rubbed his right shoulder joint. 'It's just a symbol of brotherhood.'

Sperring said. 'You mean like a tong or the masons.'

'Yeah something like that, just a sort of club; there's nothing to it, harmless really.'

'Then why did you deny knowing what it was?' asked Sperring.

'Because it didn't have any relevance to the case and I didn't want to complicate the investigation.'

'You didn't want to be implicated you mean.'

'Whatever.'

Pullman said.' According to our colleagues from London that symbol represents an international paedophile ring and as far as I'm concerned the fact that you are wearing it like a badge, makes you part of that ring.'

'I told you, I may be many things but I'm not a nonce.'

'Ah so being a murderer and trafficker you don't deny then.'

Peak took a deep breath to recompose himself. 'That's it I'm done; not saying another word until I get my solicitor here.' He stood up.

Pullman remained seated, looked straight into Peak's eyes. 'I'll decide when you get a solicitor.'

'For fuck's sake Pullman, I'm not some sixteen year old you've pulled in for glue sniffing. I've been in custody for over twenty-four hours; voluntarily in custody that is; so unless you're going to arrest me on one of your ridiculous charges, I'm out of here, tapes or no tapes.'

Silence reigned while Pullman weighed up the change of character from the lack lustre local cop to the hard-nosed villain. The hiatus was broken by Pullman. 'If you do know your job you'll know that you've only officially been in custody since you arrived here last evening.' Pullman checked his watch. 'What shall we say, no more than twenty hours?'

'Not another word until I get a solicitor.'

Pullman shrugged. 'Suit yourself; okay Lynne, we'll start with murder.'

Lynne Sperring stood up to face Peak. 'Raymond Nathaniel Peak, I am arresting you on suspicion of murder; you do not have

241

to say anything but, it may harm your defence if you do not mention, when questioned, something which you later rely on in court. Anything you do say may be given in evidence.'

Pullman also got to his feet. '*Now* you can call your solicitor.'

The third interview with Anchali Johnston went the way of the first two; she never uttered a sound; it was as if Pullman and Sperring were not even in the room. No acknowledgement of their presence; no change of expression; no body language, not even a discernible eye movement. For a fleeting moment Pullman thought of handing the questioning over to DI Brookes; he'd beat the shit out of her until she talked. That thought evaporated in an instant; instead Pullman applied for forty-eight hour custodial extensions for each prisoner; both were agreed by Pauline Crompton.

'He was pretty incensed at being called a paedophile,' said Sperring. 'So maybe the double H symbol is about the trafficking and not child abuse.'

DI Proctor said,' It's cropped up in too many other areas not to be; besides if Peak was involved in the production of babies for paedophile rings then it makes him one in my book.'

'If that is what they were up to,' said Sperring.

'There's no way he was that close to the Johnstons without knowing what was going on at the farm,' said Pullman. 'We've got his prints in that side room; so he's definitely been down there and no doubt we'll find them in that delivery room as well; should have enough to satisfy the CPS on that score. He's already proven that he's a flight risk so we should have no problem keeping him under lock and key.'

'But we arrested him on suspicion of murder, not trafficking or child abuse; we'll have to charge him with something we can prove or he'll walk,' said Sperring. 'All the evidence for Johnston's murder is circumstantial. We can't prove it was him who bought the car or that it was him who mowed down Johnston. He thinks the seller identified him because that's what we told him but we know it's not true. So all we've got is a set of keys and a common baseball cap to tie him in to the car.'

Pullman said, 'The keys are enough; why else would he have them?'

'He'll say we planted them.'

'He's already claimed he found them in the street.'

'Yes but that was before we started recording the interview; unless he admits it, which is not very likely, I don't see that we'll make it stick. A good lawyer will brush it away like a piece of fluff.'

'Then we'll charge him with the trafficking.' He looked at Proctor. 'Do you think any of those women will be in a fit state to identify him?'

'Yes; if he was there.'

'Okay arrange a parade asap. We know he was there; we've got enough forensics to prove that, so identification will nail him to the wall.'

DC Ashley Sharpe knocked on the office door and entered without waiting for an invitation. 'Sir, there's a message from Claude on your page.'

'Bollocks, that's all I need.' Pullman sighed wearily. 'Okay I'll be there in a minute. Lynne, you and Sue charge Peak with trafficking, false imprisonment and anything else we can make stick; then put together a case for the CPS; review the evidence on the hit and run; see if there's anything we've missed. I'll see what our maniac bomber's up to and then I'll catch up with you.'

Steph Barnes and Ashley Sharpe were waiting eagerly for Pullman to arrive in the incident room. 'All set up sir.' said Sharpe. The message was being projected onto a screen for ease of viewing.

Hi Mike I'm guessing that you've discovered the mini by now. Like I said I hope you weren't too disappointed with its condition. Pity about the fire it was a rather convenient place to work from. Never mind I have all I need with me here. My next event will I think be my final performance. It will however be spectacular even if I say so myself. I hope you haven't got plans for the weekend. Claude

'Shite this weekend; final performance; what does that mean – a suicide bombing? What the hell does he mean by spectacular?' said Pullman.

'At least we know for sure it was him using the Cole's house sir but where the hell has he gone now?'

'Good question; let's get a search going of all unoccupied properties including commercial premises within, say, half a mile radius to start with. It's possible that the choice of the house wasn't chance; that our man had pre-knowledge of the property?'

Steph opened a file on the table. 'We've interviewed all the Cole's relatives that we can get hold of; there aren't that many. Nothing out of the ordinary there; mostly women anyway. We've spoken to their solicitor; probate hasn't been granted yet so the executors have not been able to deal with the will. The solicitor has a set of house keys but he's not Claude, I'm sure of that. No limp and if he lost five stones he'd still be the man who ate all the pies.'

'What about friends?'

'Wouldn't know where to start sir.'

Ash spoke up. 'Just a thought sir; why don't you ask Claude why he was at the house?'

Pullman's instant, inward reaction was incredulity; then he thought why not; he had nothing to lose. 'Okay Ash I will; maybe that's not as daft as it first sounded.'

Claude I was planning to take a break this weekend but now you've spoilt it. Don't you think your last mass murder was spectacular enough? You've got nothing else to prove; we all know how good you are at what you do. I was wondering why you chose the Cole's house to squat in. Did you know the owners? Nice guy Bob Cole. If you don't feel like answering on-line, don't worry I'll ask you personally when we arrest you.

Pullman hit the messaging button. 'Don't suppose he'll bite but hope springs. What about the TA's did you check them out?'

'I'm still working on it,' said Ash. 'About a thousand reservists, as they are called, have been involved in serving in Afghanistan. It'll take a while to check them out.'

Claude responded:

Sorry to spoil your weekend Mike – I don't want to rock the boat. Do yourself a favour and stop trying to find me. I don't exist. ☺

As expected Claude had not answered the question. What did he mean by I don't exist? Pullman responded.

You kill a lot of people for someone who claims not to exist. Are you on some kind of hallucinatory drug?

The one line response pinged back almost instantly.

Love is the drug Mike. AFK

'What the bugger does he mean by that?'

'AFK sir, away from keyboard,' explained Sharpe. 'It means he's not going to respond...'

'I know that Ash, I'm from the middle ages not the Jurassic period. I meant, love is the drug.'

'Probably nothing sir; just loves murdering people and he's hooked on it.'

'No it means something; he's trying to be clever again.'

'Got a sort of feeling there was a film a few years back called something like that.'

'Do your Google thing Ash. Check what it was about.'

Sharpe checked it out. 'It was about American teenagers sir; don't see what that's got to do with our man – he's not American. Hang on there was also a song by that title; guess who by...' The look on Pullman's face indicated that he was in no mood to play party games. '...Roxy Music, released in nineteen-seventy-five.'

'Get the lyrics up,' ordered Pullman.

Sharpe did as requested. They read them through on the screen.

'*The toll of a bell*; church maybe, but he's already done that. *Downtown red light place...*'

'Somewhere in the Hessle Road area maybe,' said Steph.

'*Singles bar* any of those down there?'

'I'll find out,' said Ash.

'*Park my car* maybe he's planning a car bomb this time,' suggested Steph.

'Or maybe he's just pissing about with us,' said Pullman. 'On the other hand that's twice he's mentioned something to do with that group. You said it was released in nineteen-seventy-five, Ash; that means he would have been about a year old, if our descriptions are correct, don't get it. There's no timing logic and what did he mean by I don't exist?'

'Beats me,' said Steph.

'I suppose I'd better tell her ladyship, so she can arrange another *what if we all waste some more friggin time* meeting. He realised that he shouldn't be criticising the Chief Constable in open forum but he couldn't stop himself. 'Strike that.'

'Strike what sir?'

Pullman nodded to show appreciation.

Denise Morrison emailed over a report stating that traces of Wethersby's DNA had been isolated in blood stains on a cleaver found at the farm; as well as on a paring knife. This did not prove that the implements were used to kill the teacher but there was a strong likelihood. His probable involvement in events at the farm could mean that his blood found its way on to the weapons there; at least that is what a defence council would no doubt argue in a court. Nevertheless, it gave Sperring the tiniest lever to activate in her interrogation of Johnston and Peak. With three distinct lines of enquiry in this case, it was difficult to know which crime to focus on with which potential perpetrator.

247

Sperring also found it very difficult to refer to Anchali Johnston using feminine pronouns, now that she knew the Thai national was transgender. She triggered the tapes and announced herself and DI Proctor. Johnston remained mute. 'Anchali you are not helping yourself by remaining silent. We have all the evidence we need to charge you with human trafficking, child abuse and murder. Do you wish to say anything?' The silence was deafening. 'For the purposes of the tape the defendant has made no sound or expression.' Sperring officially arrested Anchali Johnston on suspicion of human trafficking, as a specimen charge, and read her the statutory rights before stopping the tape and having the woman taken back to her holding cell.

'We're going to have to get Peak to implicate her unless the captives will identify her and recount events,' said Sperring.

'Shouldn't be a problem with identification, provided she was actually involved; I can't believe she wasn't. You couldn't live at that place and not know.' Proctor broke off to answer her mobile. She listened intently and nodded before, finally, breaking into a smile and giving, a puzzled, Sperring the thumbs up sign. 'That's brilliant Ben; excellent stuff. A couple of days I would think. I'll see you when I get back. Thanks again.'

'Got some stuff off the laptop have they?' asked Sperring.

'Yep. Hundreds of names and addresses, images of newly born babies as well as toddlers; container shipment details, bank account details; the whole nine yards. The NCA are disseminating the information and circulating it to the relevant forces to take the appropriate action. Ben did say there were some very interesting names listed.'

'Any evidence that they were part of a paedophile ring?'

'Apparently there are a lot of names on the list that we've been monitoring for some time.'

'Anyone you can mention?'

Proctor thought for a brief moment. 'Well the story's going to break soon anyway; Drey Gillespie.'

'You're joking. I used to love him on Wishing Well when I was a kid; he's a ...'

'Yep. He's not only a paedophile but, we also suspect him of being involved in infanticide; we're still gathering evidence and don't want to spook him until we have conclusive proof; he really is a nasty shit.'

'I nearly went on that programme once; glad I didn't now.'

'Do you remember the Kiddie Kuddles game he used to play; where he and the kids used to get in that big sack?'

'Jeepers you just don't think about it do you; just seems so innocent at the time.'

'There were numerous stories that he was groping the kids while he was fooling around in the sack but they got brushed off as accidental contact, until finally, the Beeb cancelled that section.'

'Just never know, do you. Such a pity; there's some really kind people out there that get tarnished by people like him.'

'Yeah, well now we've got the laptop, we might find out that some of them are not as innocent as they look.'

Twenty-five

Wednesday 19th November

As Pullman feared, Crompton arranged a meeting of minds to coincide with her pre-arranged meeting with PCC, Peter Monkton. They along with Muriel Hudson, Frank Delaney and Iain Thwaite were already seated, patiently awaiting Pullman's tardy arrival; he apologised with transparent lack of sincerity.

Crompton and Thwaite had already been briefed by Pullman and the CC in turn had outlined the situation to the others, when convening the meeting.

'Quite frankly, I see little point in producing a list of possible actions Claude might take,' said Crompton; much to Pullman's surprise and relief. 'It didn't get us anywhere on the previous two occasions but, just to be on the safe side, is anyone planning a wedding or a birthday party?' She looked directly at the Lady Mayoress as she spoke.

'To be candid all we can do is heighten security at all public places and events over the weekend,' said Thwaite.

Monkton sighed and shook his head. 'Every public meeting, media interview and event I attend these days I'm asked the same question – when are the police going to catch the maniac. So let me ask you the same question.'

'Mike.' Crompton effortlessly passed the buck.

'We're closing in; it's just a matter of time.'

'Too much time I would have thought,' said Monkton. 'And it's fast running out.'

'We'll do our best to arrest him before your next election.'

Monkton ignored the slight. 'I'm not worried about elections; I'm worried about more innocent people losing their lives; which might not happen, if you can catch him before the weekend.'

'Hear, hear,' said Delaney, whose local council elections were also looming on the horizon.

'We're doing everything we can. It might help if I wasn't sitting in meetings instead of... '

Crompton leaned forward. 'Okay Mike, tether your hobby horse in the stable. You can get back to the team; we'll continue here.'

Pullman didn't need a second invitation. He rose to his feet, nodded to the meeting and disappeared out of the door before she could change her mind.

Pullman felt like Stretch Armstrong, being pulled apart in opposite directions. It was infinitely more certain that Claude would kill again before the two culprits he had in custody. Yet he still had no idea of Claude's identity or to where he had decamped; on the other hand, the two suspects in custody, he was sure, were murderers and he knew exactly where they were. If he could put those two to bed quickly, he could concentrate on Claude.

He decided to put the heat on Peak; it seemed unlikely that Anchali Johnston would be pressurised into making a statement, given that, so far, she had said less than Sooty.

Peak was waiting confidently in the interview room, alongside his solicitor, when Pullman and Sperring entered the room. Sperring conducted the formalities for the tape during which the solicitor introduced himself as Theo Brockman of Brockman

Ghyll, unnecessarily adding, for clarity, that he was representing Mr Peak.

'Detective Chief Inspector could I advise you of my client's right to...'

'You're here to advise your client Mr Brockman not me.'

'I was merely going to...'

'Save it. Now Raymond we have conclusive evidence to convict you of the murder of Trevor Johnston...'

'Detective Chief Inspector might I know what this conclusive evidence is that you claim to have?' asked Brockman.

'You'll get full disclosure in due course; and if you must keep interrupting, could you shorten it to DCI or we'll run out of tape. However, I would prefer it if you didn't interrupt at all. Thank you.' Pullman smiled mockingly at Brockman before turning his eyes to Peak. 'We have found the weapon that was used to murder Thomas Wethersby; it has his blood and your DNA on it.' Peak's DNA was not found on the cleaver but it was worth a punt.

'Oh no it doesn't,' said Peak firmly.

Oh yes it does was Pullman's mental pantomime response but he refrained, saying, 'We know you killed Johnston and we have every reason to believe that you murdered Wethersby.'

'You don't have to say anything,' said Brockman.

Peak ignored the advice. 'I didn't kill Wethersby; I knew nothing about it until afterwards.'

'So if it wasn't you, who was it?'

'Him and her.'

'Do you mean Anchali and Trevor Johnston?'

Peak nodded. 'For the benefit of the tape Mr Peak has nodded affirmation,' said Pullman. 'The thing is Raymond; Trevor Johnston is dead so we can't question him; maybe that was your intention when you ran him over.'

252

'You can question Anchali.'

'We will.' And a fat lot of good that will do, Pullman and Sperring thought simultaneously. 'Her DNA was on the weapon too, but then she was murdering babies and mothers, wasn't she?' Peak said nothing. 'You see Raymond, if we believe that you didn't kill Wethersby, we have to assume that you played a part in killing the poor, unfortunate wretches that were kept in that cellar.'

Peak stared at Pullman. 'My DNA can't be on any weapons because I never touched them. I've cooked loads of meals at the farm so I have used one or two kitchen knives but I've never used a cleaver, never.'

'What cleaver? Did I mention a cleaver?' said Pullman smugly.

'I think you're forgetting I was on the murder team; I know what weapon was used.' The look on Peak's face said; shove that up your arse, Pullman. Even Brockman had a smile on his lips.

'Why did you kill Johnston then? So you could run away with his wife? Was he blackmailing you?' The little red demon on his shoulder wanted to ask Peak if he liked women with dicks but that was just the kind of inappropriate comment that had got Brookes into hot water. He mentally brushed the demon aside.

Peak was experienced enough to know that Pullman had a pretty good case against him for causing Johnston's death. It was now a matter of attempting to mitigate the circumstances; without consulting his solicitor he said. 'I didn't mean to kill him.' Wow, Pullman wasn't expecting a confession that easily, neither was Brockman. 'I admit, I meant to injure him, I thought that if I could get him into hospital it would give me the chance to free the women in the pens.'

'Ah! I see, so it was an act of heroism. You were the Schindler of Woodlands Farm; the white night riding up on your charger to free the women in distress.'

Brockman put his hand up in an attempt to stop his client from incriminating himself further. Peak brushed it away.

'I thought you said I was Sir Galahad. Yes, I wanted to free the victims; Johnston was getting completely out of hand. What started as one off adoption of an unwanted baby became a production line. He'd gone crazy. He was selling babies all over the country; some to mainland Europe. I went along with the original deal because Johnston had got his maid pregnant and I helped him get out of the situation but once he knew how easy it was, he ran out of control.'

'You're a copper; why didn't you stop him?'

'I was in too deep by then; he threatened to take me down with him. I had no choice.'

'There's always a choice. So you're not a murderer then; it was an intended act of kindness that went wrong. You just wanted to get him out of the way for a few days.'

'Yes; I didn't mean to kill him. I just panicked and got rid of the car.'

'So you're thinking manslaughter then?'

'Yes, it was unintentional.'

'I could buy that,' said Pullman. Peak somehow managed not to exhale a deep breath of relief. 'I could buy it,' Pullman paused for effect. 'If you hadn't run over him three times before getting out of the car to check that he was dead. That's not the act of a white knight, Peak, that's the act of a cold blooded killer; it's murder and you're going down for it.'

Peak's relief subsided. Brockman advised his client not to say anything further.

Pullman continued. 'You're looking at ten to fifteen which, as an ex copper, locked up with some unsavoury characters, will seem like a lot longer; so why not come clean with the full story.'

'You offering me a deal?'

254

'You know I can't do that. But maybe we can influence where you spend your time; no deal, no guarantee, just a maybe,' said Pullman. Peak sat in silence; the cogs turning in his head. 'Your call. It would save us a lot of time that we could better spend catching our bomber; maybe even save a few lives, so you could be a white knight after all.'

The cogs were now working overtime.

'Tell you what; have a think about it while we have a chat with Anchali. If she co-operates then it will save you having to make a decision.' Pullman knew it was unlikely that she would speak but maybe Peak was wise enough to open up first, in the hope that life behind bars could be made a little easier.

The interview was terminated. They left Peak in the room with Brockman. In the corridor Sperring asked Pullman. 'What happened there?'

'Don't know; it was almost too easy. Perhaps he thought that our case was stronger than it is and if he admitted to the murder or manslaughter, as he'd like it to be seen, then we'd believe him on the other stuff.'

'Wethersby you mean.'

'Yeah that, and everything else at the farm. Anchali may be a bloke but she doesn't look strong enough to wield a cleaver with the ferocity required to sever a head; although she could have used the knife.'

'But if the murderers were Peak and Johnston what about the SOC connection?'

'Probably another red herring; we've been there before, haven't we. Has that line up been arranged?

'Yes tomorrow morning; DI Proctor is doing the necessary.'

'Good, the sooner we can pin down exactly what part Peak played in all this, the sooner we can put the bastard away.'

255

'But how are we going to get him for Wethersby?'

'I don't know Lynne. If Anchali won't talk and Peak continues to deny involvement, we have a stalemate. Even if she does talk it'll be her word against his. We can't even be sure that the blood on the cleaver got there as a result of the murder.' Pullman stopped before entering the incident room. 'Lynne, I'll nip in here and see where we're up to with Claude; you see if you can get hold of Sue Proctor; between you, start mapping out what actual key evidence we have against everybody involved, dead or alive. It's all getting a bit confusing; and I don't do confusing.' Pullman had a sudden thought. 'Lynne did we search Johnston's office, at the college, after his death?'

'No sir, there was no reason; we didn't suspect him of anything then. Shall I get it organised?'

'Yeah, do that.'

'What are you hoping to find?'

'Don't know. Just an instinct that the man was careful enough to have covered his arse, and conceited enough to have thought he was above suspicion; besides I don't suppose he was expecting to die for a while, so maybe he left a loose end or two.'

Pullman was, once again, struggling to balance the two cases but didn't want to admit that to himself, let alone, the Chief Constable. He wished he could compartmentalise his brain; to have two distinct hard drives that he could boot up in his head as he switched between the two cases. Such was his pre-occupation with the complexities of assimilating and analysing the information that he hadn't even remembered that today would have been Jane's 43rd birthday. In fact the only times he felt her loss was when he'd arrive home in the evenings to an empty house and silence. An all engulfing silence that served to remind him how much he missed his best friend; how empty his existence was. Fortunately for his sanity, those moments were fleeting. He had learned to control those emotions; switch off the feelings through determination and distraction. Only once in the previous three weeks had he allowed the emotions to overwhelm his self-control; only once had he shed a tear; only once had he had to pull back from the brink of self-destruction. Today he was thinking of nothing but putting Peak and Anchali Johnston behind bars, whilst simultaneously finding and arresting Claude, before further lives were lost.

'How's it going?' asked DS Barnes as her boss entered the incident room.

'Don't ask,' said Pullman, waving a dismissive hand. 'How you two doing, got any further?'

Pullman poured himself a coffee. Steph began to fill him in on progress. 'We've been checking out the references in the song lyrics. There are three singles bars within half a mile of the red light area; Pullers on Penn Street; One-to-one, which is at one-two-one Garaways Road and Jack and Jill's in Mirren Mews. None of them are very big, two of them are known to be pick up places for sex workers and none of them look like potential bombing targets.'

'Unless he's got a particular beef with one of them; maybe against a particular girl. No strike that; can't believe this whole campaign is to cover a bloody bust up with a prostitute or the price of imitation champagne.'

'We can't see any other connection with the lyrics; we might be looking for something that doesn't exist.'

'Like Claude you mean; still can't fathom why he would say that, he's frugal with his words, so there has to be a reason.'

'Uniform has checked out numerous empty houses and commercial premises but nothing so far. Ash has had no joy with the TAs.'

'That's right sir. I've spoken with the top honcho, a Major Wanker.' Sharpe shook his head and smiled to indicate that wanker wasn't his actual name. 'I've looked through as much detail on the thousand or so records as I can, nothing jumps out that could relate to our man. I'm still on with it but it's not looking hopeful.'

'Jesus, it's one cul-de-sac after another. What about the Cole's friends, did you go down that road?' It was always difficult to abandon a metaphor.

'I've spoken to neighbours, it seems the Coles were both members of the tennis club, played bridge and the DCC was a member of the Hull Sailing Club and Ganstead Golf Club.'

Ash said. 'Makes you wonder how he found time to work.'

'Did he own a boat?' asked Pullman.

'Apparently so,' said Steph. 'According to one neighbour ...' she consulted her notes. 'It was a "bloody great thing" he once sailed across to the Balearics.'

'Where does he keep it?'

'Don't know.'

'Then find out, and the name while you're at it.'

Steph raised her eyebrows. 'D'ya think Claude could be on it?'

'He's somewhere; he could have found the keys or whatever while he was squatting in the house.' Pullman wagged his index finger towards Steph Barnes. 'Every stone until we find him.' Then the lightning bolt hit Pullman right between the eyes. 'Shit!' he yelled. 'Ash get his last message up on the screen.' Ash complied. *Love is the drug Mike. AFK.*

258

'Not that one; the message before that.' Ash scrolled down and highlighted:

Sorry to spoil your weekend Mike – I don't want to rock the boat. Do yourself a favour and stop trying to find me. I don't exist. ☺

'There. I was hooked on *I don't exist* and missed *I don't want to rock the boat*. That's it. The smart arse thinks he's being clever. Why else would he use that phrase? Look it's out of place; doesn't fit, does it? Find that boat, now.' Pullman punched the air. 'We're coming for you matey boy. I'll rock your bloody world, let alone your boat.'

Barnes grabbed her coat and car keys and was on her way out of the door; to see the neighbour she had spoken to, when Ash called to her. 'Steph what about the solicitor he should know the name I bet the boat is part of the estate. Shall I call him?'

Steph stopped in her tracks. 'Good idea.'

'Pullman intervened. 'Go anyway Steph, just in case he doesn't have the information; you can always turn back; we don't want to lose any time.'

As it turned out the solicitor knew only that the boat was called *Cuprum* but not where it was moored. The neighbour on the other hand, knew the name and that it was usually moored in Hull Marina; he'd been there several times with Bob Cole and their wives. He told Barnes that *Cuprum* was Bob Cole's little joke; cuprum being the Latin for copper and also that it was moored in berth 29, the atomic number for copper on the periodic scale. Bob had to wait over two years to get that specific mooring. The good neighbour was also able to let Barnes have a photograph of the craft, even though he was embarrassed that he and his wife were modelling the Titanic pose on the bow.

Concurrent with Steph Barnes obtaining the information, Pullman had despatched four unmarked cars, each complete with two unmarked police officers, to the marina; including himself and DC Sharpe. Uniformed back up, in the form of a transit load of fully equipped fire arm officers, was standing by, out of view, in Wellington Street. Steph joined them at the scene.

'Steph you and Sharpe take a stroll along the pontoons; hold hands, as if you're on a lunchtime stroll,' said Pullman.

'He's a bit too young for me sir,' said Steph with a smile.

'You can carry it off,' replied Pullman with a wink. 'Just stroll down there and see if there's any signs of activity. No heroics just stroll down, observe and come back.'

'Sir.'

Barnes and Sharpe linked arms rather than hold hands. They strolled casually along the walkway pretending to happy together in each other's company. They stopped at the third spur of moorings and hugged so that Steph could look over Ash's shoulder, along the row of craft. Pullman was watching through binoculars as the play unfolded.

'Can't see properly from here; need to get closer,' she said to Ash. She broke free from the hug and sauntered along the jetty, breaking into a carefree spin with arms outstretched. The movement would have looked natural on a warm summer's day, or if Maria had performed it on an Austrian mountain, but on a chilly, late November morning, it was completely incongruous. She need not have worried about the play acting, berth 29 was vacant. Cuprum was not there.

'You look happy,' said a disembodied voice emanating from the Daisy May; a large, white motor cruiser, moored in space 28.

260

Steph was startled; she looked up to see a middle aged woman holding a can of brass cleaner and a cloth. 'Oh, hello; have you been here long.'

The woman smiled. 'Since yesterday morning; just getting her ready the weekend's little shindig.' Mrs Daisy May was joined by her inquisitive husband.

'Was there another boat here when you arrived?' Steph pointed to berth 29.

The man said, 'Yes but it went at high tide last night. We were still debating whether or not to call the police.'

'Oh why's that?'

'Nothing in particular; it doesn't matter,' said the man. 'Better get on. Nice meeting you; I think your boyfriend is getting lonely.'

Steph looked back at Sharpe. 'He's not my boyfriend, he's a colleague.' She took out her warrant card and held it up for the couple to see. 'Detective Sergeant Barnes and he's DC Sharpe,' she said waving for him to join her. 'So why were you thinking of calling us?'

'Well the boat belongs to a couple called Cole, Margaret and Bob Cole; we met them when we first moored here a year ago.'

'Nice couple,' said the woman mournfully.

'Tragic story, they're both dead now but anyway, when we arrived yesterday a young man, well young compared to us, was loading boxes onto the yacht. I said hello but he ignored me; sullen sort of character. He could see I was paying interest in what he was doing, so he pulled up one of those hoodie things, on top of the baseball cap he was already wearing. He told me he had inherited the boat and was going to do some maintenance work on it. He looked down when he spoke; never actually looked directly at me. Appeared a bit shifty but, as I knew Bob had died, I thought it was plausible.'

261

'So why were you thinking of calling us?' Steph asked again.

'Just something about him really; nothing concrete.'

Steph knew that the world was full of well-meaning people who never actually carry out their good intentions; when push comes to shove they just don't want to get involved. Mr Daisy May was just one of them; he would never action his thoughts. She managed to get a vague description out of him although with insufficient detail to brief an artist He was adamant that he would not be able to recognise the man in the flesh or from photographs. He was however, pretty sure that the man was local because he'd said he wanted to cast off before it started "siling down", a term for rain that was mainly used locally. Mrs Daisy May claimed even less recall of the man.

So, had they just missed Claude? Pullman decided on the balance of probabilities that they had. The mystery man had said he'd inherited the boat yet, according to the solicitor, the will had not yet been read. He was apparently doing his utmost not to be recognised but, if his story was true, why was he concealing his identity? Claude had threatened a spectacular act; if this man was Claude, he would not have sailed too far away from the place of performance. All local forces from Whitby, in North Yorkshire, down to Grimsby, in Lincolnshire, were put on alert to find the Cuprum.

Pullman was seething that for the second time they had come so close to catching Claude. Close but no cigar.

262

Twenty-five

Thursday 20th November

Abortion in Thailand is illegal except in cases considered necessary, if the pregnancy is endangering the health of the mother or in cases where it is due to a sexual offence such as rape. Even then, it is permissible only if performed by a qualified medical practitioner. The women found at Woodlands Farm certainly fell into that category, some into both. The Home Office had already decided that the women would be repatriated; all those under 24 weeks term of pregnancy would first be offered an abortion before they returned home. This decision was withheld from the women until they had taken part in the parade to identify Peak. Six of the women volunteered to take part; each took an individual turn to study the line-up, from behind the two way window mirror. All six identified Peak as being involved in their imprisonment and abuse. The case against him for human trafficking, kidnapping and false imprisonment was conclusive; Pullman was sure that the CPS would accept the case for trial. Peak and Anchali Johnston were remanded in custody. The charge of child abuse, involving the sale of babies, was dependent upon the examination of the information retrieved from the confiscated laptop. It seemed likely that those investigations would dovetail nicely into Operation Oakwood.

The forensic search of the farmland, at Woodlands, had uncovered a multiple grave. Forensic archaeologists were in the process of examining the remains; the exact number of skeletons was still to be determined, however, the skulls so far recovered

263

indicated that more than twenty adults and infants were involved. It was doubtful if Pullman could prove conclusively that Peak was involved in any of those murders; guilt by association was purely circumstantial and such a charge would easily be swept aside by any self-respecting defence barrister. He was absolutely convinced that Peak was involved in the murder of Thomas Wethersby; nevertheless, with Anchali maintaining her continued silence and Peak denying involvement, he knew there was little chance of obtaining a conviction.

Mike Pullman decided to re-focus his full attention on the search for Claude. With less than two days to go before the weekend, it was imperative that the maniac be found before his self-proclaimed final performance.

Captain Lawrence Hidgem, Hull Harbourmaster, stood in front of the large detailed map of the estuary that adorned the wall of his office. 'As you can see the Humber from the estuary right upstream, until it becomes the river Ouse, has a great many coves, bays and mooring places; your boat could be moored-up, out of sight, in any one of them.'

'The Cuprum, we believe, is around fifty-five feet long, would that narrow it down,' asked Pullman. 'That's right isn't it? He said looking at DS Barnes.

'Yes sir.'

'A little, but it would still leave in the region of a couple of hundred hidey holes; that's always assuming that your man hasn't sailed out of the estuary, in which case he could be anywhere along the coast. Alternatively he may have sailed further upstream to Goole or beyond.'

'How far could he have got on the open sea?' Not that Pullman thought Claude had gone off the radar.

'Depends what type of craft; the diesel tank capacity and the speed he was doing of course. Just like a car really; the faster you go the more fuel you use.'

'We're waiting for those details to be phoned through,' said Steph. 'Shall I give Ash a chase sir?'

'Give it another ten minutes; he'll call as soon as he's got something,' said Pullman. He addressed Captain Hidgem 'We do know that it's capable of sailing to the Balearics although I'm more inclined to think that he'll have stayed within easy reach of the city.'

Steph's mobile rang; she moved away from the group to take the call. She jotted down some notes, thanked Ashley Sharpe and cut the call. 'The Cuprum is an Ocean Alexander fifty-four built in nineteen ninety-one in Taiwan, would you believe; it has a top speed of twenty-two knots and a fuel capacity of five hundred and sixty gallons.'

'So what does that make its range captain?'

'Well I doubt that he'd go flat out for long, so let's assume he does an average cruising speed of say sixteen knots.' He began pressing keys on his calculator whilst mumbling figures to himself. 'You say he set sail about eighteen hours ago.'

'About that,' said Barnes.

Hidgem resumed mumbling and pressing. 'He shouldn't have got more than say eleven nautical miles, about twenty kilometres, away; twenty three tops. Enough time to get him to Goole and back several times.'

'We've got land forces searching for signs of the boat so I'll be asking for support from the river police and possibly the lifeboat crews, if they're not otherwise engaged.' said Pullman.

'They're going to be otherwise engaged this weekend with the pageant.'

'What pageant?'

'Hull History Society have organised a two hundred strong flotilla of boats to mark the seventy-fifth anniversary of the death of Captain Cecil Murdoch, at the Battle of Narvik.'

'That's what she meant by a little shindig,' said Steph Barnes.

'Who did?' enquired Pullman.

'The lady on the Daisy May at the marina; she said they were getting the boat ready for a little shindig.'

'Let me get this straight,' said Pullman. 'This weekend there will be upwards of two hundred boats on the river, having a parade, like the Queen's jubilee.'

'That's the minimum number expected.'

'Why didn't I know about this?' it was a rhetorical question. 'More to the point why wasn't it mentioned at the friggin meeting?'

'There has been full liaison with all the relevant parties including the police. Would there have been any reason for someone of your rank to know?'

Pullman realised that Captain Hidgem was right, there was no need for him to know; more than that, he hadn't seen a newspaper or a news broadcast for days. He'd been too absorbed in his own microcosm to be concerned about the world at large. Surely the Mayoress would know or Delaney but nobody thought to mention it. Perhaps if he, himself, had told the meeting that Claude was on a stolen boat, someone may have put two and two together. He was as much to blame as them. 'Where exactly will the boats be?'

266

Hidgem pointed at the map again. 'A few will converge from the estuary, that's the larger ones, but most will sail up from the Trent and Ouse. They will congregate in this area around Read's Island, west of the bridge. That way they'll keep clear of the terminal.'

Barnes asked. 'What kind of boats are we looking at?'

'Private, ocean-going yachts right down to narrow boats and everything in between; the Royal Navy is deploying HMS Stamford as the focal point of the flotilla.'

'Is that a battleship?'

'Hardly; she's a River Class patrol boat, but at about eighty metres long, most onlookers will think she's a war ship; it's going to be quite spectacular.'

'Oh, I hope not; spectacular is something we don't need.'

Chief Constable, Pauline Crompton turned slowly from her contemplative gaze at the horizon, through the incident room window. 'Are you sure it's not a flight of fancy?'

Pullman had briefed her on the turn of events and felt a touch insulted by the question. 'I'm not given to flights of fancy, ma'am. Given everything we know, it's the best scenario we can come up with.'

'Could he be setting us up; leading us in one direction while he goes in another?'

'He doesn't know that we know, he's on the boat; if he has been deliberately dropping us clues, to ensure we do know he's on the boat, then he thinks he's cleverer than us and that, we can't stop him doing whatever he has planned. Either way he's being over confident; we have to out think him.' Pullman took a deep breathe;

267

what he was about to suggest next was contrary to every fibre of his being. 'Ma'am we need a joint meeting with everyone involved but I don't think we need councillors or the PCC.'

Crompton nodded agreement.' Very well; I'll have to re-arrange a meeting.' She checked her watch. 'I suggest we grab sandwiches or whatever and reconvene here in an hour.'

'If it's okay with you ma'am I'd like to invite Captain Hidgem, the harbourmaster to sit in and also Chief Superintendent Parker.'

'Good idea but I happen to know that Chris Parker is on leave this week, so it will have to be someone else from the marine section; I'll sort it.'

Pullman smiled inwardly, Parker was no fool; a major event taking place on the river this weekend and the man responsible for the day to day management of the Operations Support branch was on holiday. No doubt he was sunning himself on some far away beach or, ironically perhaps, he was on a cruise. Ultimately, of course, the Chief Super reported in to ACC Iain Thwaite, head of Operations, but given a preference, Pullman wanted the involvement of a front line officer.

'Okay ma'am; what about the coastguard.'

'Once we've agreed what action we need to take, we can decide if they need to be involved. They and the lifeboat service will have their hands full as it is. Right, an hour then.'

Starr Signs on the Brighton Street Industrial Estate, Hessle, was busy producing countless 'Sale' and 'Winter Sale' banners for the post-Christmas retail period. Nevertheless, they delivered on the *any sign in one day* promise, upon which their long established business had been founded. As it happened, it had been a simple enough request – two signs with just the words Sea Lion printed as one conjoined word with two capital letters. The font required was a bold script digitally printed in a silver colour ink on white, self-adhesive vinyl, one point five meters in length and point eight of a metre deep. The man, who collected the signs, was pleased with the result, paid cash and did not require a receipt.

Crompton had mixed feelings when Mike Pullman asked if they could postpone the meeting for an hour. On one hand she had rearranged her meeting with some inconvenience but on the other hand was encouraged that Anchali Johnston wanted to make a statement. She had to be interviewed while she was compliant and, of course, Pullman had to be there; that was a no brainer.

Pullman and Sperring sat facing Johnston and her female solicitor; a smartly dressed, mixed race woman in her mid-thirties with jet black, glossy hair, swept back into a neat bun. Immaculate make-up applied to disguise the elliptical shape of her eyes. She introduced herself as Nicha Jepsom; Pullman had been informed that she was attached to the Thai embassy to represent the interests of Thai nationals in the UK. Pullman started the tape, went through the formalities and reminded Anchali that she was still under caution. 'Well Anchali it's your show.'

Johnson's gaze was firmly fixed on the desk in front of her. Jepsom spoke first, in a formal, Cambridge educated voice. 'Detective Chief Inspector, for the benefit of the tape my client wishes to receive confirmation that her requirements for making this statement, will be met. Namely, that she will be returned to

269

Thailand for any trial or custodial sentencing that may or may not ensue from this discussion.'

Pullman had been fully briefed. 'It has been agreed by the Home Office that your client, Anchali Johnston, will be handed over to the Thai authorities for trial provided she co-operates fully and answers all the questions put to her, during the course of this interview.' Pullman had been initially incredulous, when he had been informed of the granting of her request by the Home Office; he'd always been under the impression that the regime in Thai prisons was somewhat less hospitable than those in UK prisons; that she should want to endure such conditions was a surprise to him. It had been explained to him that a Kathoey, as transgender women, and overtly effeminate men, are known in Thailand, would be sent to a male prison. That was accepted by them and everyone understood the position. Most were comfortable with the situation. In fact there had been documented cases where Kathoeys engaged in the sex trade actually felt a place of belonging in prison and some even came out of prison richer than when they went in; unfortunately some came out with terminal illnesses as well as money. Many of those released were known to re-offend so that they could be sent back, into their comfort zone. The Home Office was more than happy to comply with the request; it both solved the conundrum of whether she should be sent to a male or female prison and saved the cost of keeping her there.

'Very well, my client will answer your questions.' Jepsom gave an encouraging smile to Johnston.

Pullman wasted no time. 'Could you please tell me what your involvement was in the trafficking of young women and the subsequent sale of babies?' Anchali looked at Jepsom and they exchanged words in Thai. 'In English please.' said Pullman.

'My client was asking me if she should tell you everything.'

270

'I hope you said yes.'

'I did.'

Anchali composed herself; she did not alter her focal point; her voice was soft, little more than a whisper. 'My husband and me first met about seven years ago in Bangkok; I was working in a bar. Most of the men who seek my, our, company, are either drunks looking for a different sexual experience or are gay and just looking for a one night stand. It is the way we survive. Trevor was looking for a longer term relationship. Very few men are actually confused and think we are natural females, despite what they may claim afterwards. Trevor was well aware of my gender and I believed he was gay. He asked me to move to England with him and eventually I agreed; we arranged a marriage so that I would be allowed into the UK, and I was. It wasn't until I was over here that I found out why he had been in Thailand in the first place.'

'Why had he been there?' Pullman felt he had to say something, if only to demonstrate that he was listening.

'When I got to the farm he showed me the room where the girls were kept; I couldn't believe it. He told me the girls were brought into the country to provide babies for European couples. He said they were prostitutes who had got pregnant and, rather than have abortions, which are not permitted in Thailand, they voluntarily came to the UK to give birth, so that the babies could have a better life. I soon found out that he was not telling the truth. The girls were kidnapped from home, forcibly made to have babies which were then adopted by couples who could not have children of their own. He said it was humanitarian work but I know it was slavery. After two or three pregnancies, the girls were sold to other men.'

'Did you know that most of those poor babies were sold to paedophiles? That they would suffer horrendous abuse.'

'I never knew that; I thought they were going to good homes.'

'Even so why didn't you do something; go to the police.'

Johnston snorted contemptuously. 'I was little more than a slave myself; besides the police were part of it.'

'Peak?'

'Yes, he was the worse one of them.'

'Who's them? Who else was involved?'

'The teacher.'

'Thomas Wethersby?'

'Yes. He liked the youngest ones. Peak would rape anyone.'

'And you just stood by while all this was going on,' said Pullman

'I was dependent on him.'

'Drugs?'

She nodded. 'Trevor kept me supplied. He also threatened that I would end up in the pit with the others.'

'By pit, I presume you mean the mass grave we uncovered; he threatened to kill you and bury you with the other victims? Johnston nodded. 'Please say yes or no.'

'Yes,' she said.

'Do you know who murdered Wethersby?'

'Trevor and Ray.'

'That's Raymond Peak.' Pullman had to make it quite clear for the tape.

'Yes.'

'Why?'

'They had a big row when Tom raped the two girls at the school. Trevor was really angry; said he had put the whole operation at risk. He told Tom that the girls would withdraw the complaint for one thousand pounds each and he was to get the cash.'

'Was it Trevor or Peak that actually killed him?'

272

'I don't know; they were both there, I wasn't.'

'Peak says you were there; that you and your husband killed him.'

'He's lying. It was him and Trevor. I didn't know anything about it until they got back to the house that night.'

'Didn't they talk about it afterwards?'

'Not to me. I knew it had been done but that's all.'

'You knew they had committed murder yet still you did nothing about it.'

'I should risk my life for a filthy pig like Wethersby; I don't think so.'

'Your husband was the headteacher at a school. He worked during the day. Peak was a policeman, he worked during the day. You had more than enough opportunity to get away from the farm yet you didn't even make an attempt. Am I supposed to believe that you were so scared of Johnston and Peak that you didn't dare escape?'

'I really was terrified; besides I too was locked up during the day.'

Pullman shook his head in disbelief. 'What about your husband's death? Were you and Peak in that together?'

'I didn't have anything to do with it. I was shocked. I honestly thought it was an accident.'

'So Anchali, you'd have us believe that you were an unwilling participant; knew nothing of what was going on until after the events; that you had no involvement in trafficking, child abuse or murder; that you are a pure as the driven snow and will ascend to heaven as an angel.'

'I know I am not a good person. I have made many mistakes and bad choices in my life but I am not responsible for any of those things.'

273

'Then why were you running away? Why were you fleeing the country; going home?'

'Another mistake; Ray made me panic. I was frightened you wouldn't believe me.'

'Well guess what, I don't.'

Twenty-six

Pullman took the lead in the meeting. He stood before the screen upon which was projected a detailed map of the Humber Estuary. 'The flotilla will be milling about in this area here,' he said indicating the area from the bridge, west to the confluence of the rivers Ouse and Trent. 'I understand that upwards of two hundred boats are expected to attend the event and we believe that our man will be amongst them. His yacht is called the Cuprum, there's a photograph in the files you have. Now as far as I can see there is only one thing that could be described as a spectacular target; the Humber Bridge itself. There's nothing else along that stretch of the river that would meet Claude's requirements to finish on a high. Although having spoken to the profiler, who helped us a few days ago, he does not believe that he will end his reign voluntarily; despite his comment to the contrary.'

Pauline Crompton asked. 'Mike, what if you're wrong and he's not on a boat; what if he's not on the river at all?'

'Then I've made a huge error of judgement,' said Pullman. 'But I don't believe I have; all of his word games lead towards him being on that boat. The fact that it left the moorings, means that it has been stolen and the prime suspect for that has to be the person using the Cole's house as a bomb factory; that we know to be Claude.'

'Does all your team share that belief?' asked the Assistant Chief Constable, Iain Thwaite, glancing towards Barnes and Sharpe.

Pullman could hardly believe that the ACC would ask his subordinates if they supported their boss.

'One hundred percent,' said Steph Barnes.

'Absolutely,' said Ashley Sharpe.

'Good,' said Thwaite.

Pullman would have expected nothing less than their total commitment, even if they actually thought he was wrong.

'What's your suggested plan of action then Mike?' asked Crompton. 'What resources will be required?'

'It is a question of observation ma'am. We have forces scouring every creek and inlet for the boat, as far upstream as Goole. It could be that we locate it before it sails with the flotilla. If we don't then we need to set up observation points along both banks. On the South bank, here at Whitton, here at Winteringham South Ferriby and on the Far Ings nature reserve. On the north bank at Blacktoft, Faxfleet, here at Crabley Creek, here at Brough Haven and further along at North Ferriby. Also of course at three places on the bridge, observing in both directions. I would like air support with choppers, primed and ready, here at Brough Aerodrome, along with high speed launches but I'll take advice from the river boys and Captain Hidgem as to their strategic location. If all else fails we'll have HMS Stamford armed and ready to blow Claude out of the water.' That raised a few eyebrows amongst the audience. 'Only a last resort ma'am,' added Pullman with a grin.

Captain Hidgem raised his hand. 'Is your man a scuba diver?'

'I have no idea,' said Pullman, looking towards his team. Barnes and Sharpe shook their heads and pulled 'no idea' faces. 'Why do you ask?'

276

'I'm not an expert in these matters but, from what you've told me about this Claude character and from what I've read, it seems to me that he plans meticulously; if that's the case, it occurred to me that your man might have already have planted explosives on the bridge, ready to detonate on the day.'

'Yes, you're quite right Captain, that's just the sort of thing he might have done. Which is why, as we speak, we have a team examining the super structure of the bridge above and below the waterline.'

'Good. I had this image in my mind of him detonating his device just as the fireworks reached their crescendo.'

'Fireworks! There's going to be fireworks?'

'Yes, quite a big display in the evening.'

Pullman looked at Barnes. 'Steph, there's still time to vet the people installing the display; get uniform to supervise the installation; make sure there are no interlopers.' She nodded. That would have been the perfect cover; Claude could have replaced the roman candles with half a ton of Semtex; some crescendo that would make.

'If the bridge is his target, we must stop him at all costs,' said ACC Thwaite.

'Absolutely; it would be catastrophic for the city,' said Crompton. 'I'll cancel all leave immediately; call in all the specials and re-deploy as many officers as I can. We'll lock the area down.'

'We need to do all the above ma'am but, if that's his intended target then, he must have considered that we would take every precaution to prevent its destruction; it's reasonable to assume therefore that he's planned a way around all of that.'

Steph Barnes said. 'We've got the river covered but what about the air? He bombed the night club with a drone; perhaps he'll do the same with the bridge.'

277

Pullman nodded thoughtfully. DS Sharpe said. 'From the research I did at the time sir, I don't think there's a drone capable of carrying a big enough bomb to destroy the bridge in the same way as the club.'

'Check it out again Ash, to make absolutely sure.' Pullman looked at his Chief Constable. 'Ma'am, do you think we could deploy marksmen, at one or two points on the bridge and approaches, who could take down a drone; if that scenario occurred?'

'Little bit fanciful, don't you think Mike.'

'Maybe but as the ACC said, that the bridge must be protected at all costs.'

Crompton nodded. 'I'll discuss it with the firearms section and see what can be done.'

'There is an alternative,' ventured Iain Thwaite. 'We could just cancel the whole event and ban all boats from that stretch of water. Then we'd have no problem spotting the maniac.'

'Yes Iain, it had crossed my mind too but, if we thwart him by doing that, he might just turn his attention somewhere else; by letting the event take place as planned, we are at least containing the situation into an area we can police.' Thwaite did not feel slighted; that was what 'what ifs' were all about. The problem was that few optional scenarios existed in this particular case. 'Right then, we've got twenty-four hours to get this implemented; I suggest we get to it.'

The meeting broke up. Pullman and Barnes were on their way for a comfort break when they were stopped in the corridor by a female uniformed officer. 'Excuse me sir, DS Barnes has had a call from a Mr Barraclough; says he met you at the marina this morning.'

278

'Must be the guy I spoke to on the Daisy May,' said Steph. 'What did he want?'

The officer checked the note she was carrying. 'He said it was probably something and nothing but he would like a word with you. He left his mobile number.' She handed Steph the note.

'Call him right away,' instructed Pullman.

'Alright if I just...' she jabbed a thumb towards the ladies toilet and went to it without waiting for a response.

Suitably relieved, Steph Barnes keyed in the mobile number she had been given. A man answered. 'Hello this is DS Barnes; you wanted to speak to me.'

'Yes Detective Sergeant, thanks for getting back.'

'What can I do for you?'

'As I said to your colleague, this might be something and nothing but I thought you'd be the best judge of that.'

'Okay, go on.'

'I was talking to Jack Simms, he owns the Blue Marlin, lovely boat, anyway he's been mooring here for years and knew the Cole's well. I was telling him of your interest in the Cuprum and he told me that he thought he recognised the man I had seen loading things on to it.'

'Okay, did he give you a name?'

'Well that's the thing he said the man bore an uncanny resemblance to Barry Cole.'

'Barry Cole, the son?' Steph thought she'd misunderstood.

'Yes. I never met him but Jack knew him quite well and he said if it wasn't Barry then it was his doppelganger.'

'But Barry Cole is dead.'

'I know; a tragedy.'

Barnes' mind was whirring. She could hear a voice talking but she wasn't receiving the audio. 'I'm sorry could you repeat that, Mr Barraclough.'

'I said, Jack was quite insistent and although we know it couldn't possibly be Barry Cole, I thought it would give you a good description of the man you're looking for.'

'Yes thank you; that's very helpful. I might need to get back to you if that's alright.' They exchanged farewells and she replaced the receiver. Barry Cole, they didn't even have a picture of him from which to get the description. Steph relayed the content of the call to Pullman.

'Get on to the Hull Daily Mail, they're sure to have covered the story, they're bound to have an archive photo,' said Pullman. 'As far as I remember his body was never recovered. It was the thought of his remains rotting in some hell hole in Afghanistan that tortured Mrs Cole.' Pullman suddenly slapped his forehead. 'Wait a bloody minute; *I don't exist,* isn't that what he said? *I don't exist.* We all think he's dead. Supposing he didn't die.'

'But the Taliban released a video of him being executed; shot in the back of the head.'

'Where's the file from the hospital.' Steph sorted the file and handed it to Pullman; he flipped through it. 'Here look; Claude has a deep scar on his clavicle, shoulder blade. Supposing they shot him from behind but missed the target; shot him through the shoulder and assumed they'd killed him; as did everyone else. Then just left him for dead.'

'Is that likely,' said Steph.

'Why not? It would explain his presence at the Cole house; his knowledge of the boat; why we couldn't find the army connection.'

'We never checked on dead soldiers.'

'Exactly; we didn't think of looking for a ghost. It would also explain his vendetta against Hull. He was let down; no negotiation for his release from captivity.'

'But that was the government, not Hull council.'

Supposing he channelled his paranoia on the city. He had to pick somewhere, so why not his home town. The home town that allowed his mother to be murdered and ultimately his step-father to hang himself. His whole resentment focussed on the city.' Pullman waved his palms in a downward motion, in a calming fashion. 'Right let's think.' He took a deep breath. 'Steph get on to Corrine Browne at the Look North studios and see if they've still got archive footage of the execution, they're bound to have a still too, save you going to the Mail; try not to tell her why we need it but if you have a problem tell her we'll give them the exclusive, if it turns out we're right, provided they keep a lid on it until we're ready. They've played ball so far so it shouldn't be an issue.'

'Okay sir, I'll get right on to it.'

'Perhaps I ought to take young Ashley's advice again and just ask Claude if he's Barry Cole.' Pullman booted the laptop; went on to his Facebook page before typing:

Hello Claude or should I call you Barry? Nice to know you're still alive. I'm looking forward to the weekend and meeting you when we arrest you for multiple murder.

Pullman had no way of knowing if Claude was still monitoring his Facebook page but if he wasn't, he might get a nudge via email. He stopped short of pressing the 'post' key to reconsider his actions. Would informing Claude that they knew he was Barry, serve any useful purpose. He considered it for ten seconds. What the hell. He posted the message.

Pauline Crompton had hardly taken her seat before Pullman told Ashley Sharpe to roll the video. He had filled her in on his hypothesis which she, at first dismissed, but had since come round to his way of thinking.

'I suggest we just let it roll first time round, then replay it at slower speed if necessary.'

The video had been spliced with a count-down sequence for studio transmission purposes. It showed a man wearing a balaclava standing behind Sergeant Barry Cole, who was kneeling. The hooded man raised a hand pistol, pointed it towards the kneeling captive and said *"You have failed to comply with our demands to release our brave comrades and this man will now pay for your imperialist atrocities against Allah."* He pulled the trigger; blood sprayed onto the camera lens and, through the smudges, Cole could be seen to fall forward. The tape went black.

Pullman said. 'That looked pretty straight forward. Nothing too ambiguous there. Okay Ash, run it again.'

Sharpe ran the tape again.

After the second viewing, Pullman said. 'I'd say that the terrorist with the gun is fairly young; judging by his voice and the eyes. He appears nervous; I think his hand is shaking slightly. Could be that the nerves and the recoil of the pistol caused him to miss the back of the head; shoot Cole in the upper neck stroke shoulder area instead, producing plenty of blood and causing Cole to collapse. Then they mistakenly left him for dead.'

'So it's possible that a friendly face found him and nursed him back to life; is that what you think?' said Crompton.

'We don't know for sure that Claude is Barry Cole but it's a reasonable hypothesis.'

282

'Well whoever it is you think his target is the bridge,'
'Yes, I do.'

Sharpe said. 'I wonder why he didn't tell you to listen to 'Bridge Over Troubled Water' by Simon and Garfunkel, sir or 'Under the Bridge' by the Red Hot Chilli Peppers or 'Love Can Build a Bridge' by the Judds.

'How long have you been working those out,' said Pullman? 'Smart phones are not just for calls and texting,' said Sharpe, holding up his IPhone to show the Google pages.

'I agree it makes sense but instead he chose Roxy Music. Anything about bridges in their stuff?'

'Not that I can see sir.'

Crompton stood up. 'Very well let us assume for one minute that our man is Barry Cole and now we know what he looks like – it's not bringing us one step closer to finding him, is it. We need to find that boat, then we'll find the man; whoever he is.'

Twenty-seven

Saturday 22nd November

It is said that everyone alive at the time, knows where they were on the 22nd November 1963; the day president John F Kennedy was assassinated. Would the same apply to this day; would this be remembered as the day that Claude created history with his spectacular finalé? Not if DCI Mike Pullman, and his colleagues on the Humberside Police force, had any say in the matter.

Operation Alligator had maintained complete vigilance throughout Friday. Every officer available was on duty, in case the unpredictable maniac brought forward his planned atrocity. Despite their vigilance or maybe because of it, nothing happened. Craft of all shapes and sizes had begun to assemble in the designated area. As night fell the Humber became a floating disco with parties on numerous boats and music filling the still night air. Even the moon played its part, illuminating the scene from a cloudless sky. Several craft had moored close to Read's Island in order that crews could take short dinghy rides to the shore, to light barbeques and hold beach parties; all ignoring the numerous signs prohibiting the landing of craft on the nature reserve. A gradual hush fell on the river, in the early hours, as the revellers welcomed Mr Sandman to their dreams.

As the first bluish, grey glow of dawn crept over the horizon, a crisp, white icing of frost coated the landscape. Uniformed observers shivered in the bitter morning air. The night had seemed long; how they wished they, too, had been snuggled up in the warmth of even the tiniest cabin. Slowly the traffic volume on the bridge built as the city began to stir. Pauline Crompton had made the decision, in conjunction with the usual members of the 'what if' committee, that they would allow business as usual. They could not allow Claude to intimidate them into locking down the city. Life would go on; the pageant would go on.

Film crews from both the BBC and ITV began preparing for the early morning news bulletins; they would remain present for the entire event, transmitting regular up-dates and live broadcast at the height of the pageant. Neither they, nor the few journalists in attendance, had any reason to think that the police presence on the bridge itself was excessive, for the size of event. However, had they known just how many officers had been deployed along the river banks and other vantage points, they may have thought differently.

The control room of the Humber Bridge Board was a little busier than usual with additional staff monitoring the CCTV. They were anticipating increased vehicular activity, as well as vastly increased numbers of pedestrians, both on the bridge itself and in the leisure areas and nature reserves on either side. They had been issued with a picture of Barry Cole, albeit with little hope that he would be recognised from their screens; besides which, he had already proven to be an expert at disguise. However they were able to zoom in on any suspicious individual they deemed to be acting out of place.

The hum of police launches, criss crossing the river, could be heard above the hubbub of traffic. On board the leisure craft the inhabitants began to stir; going about their morning routines, oblivious to the scrutiny they were under. The search for the Cuprum had so far drawn a blank but the hunt would continue throughout the day ahead.

Out in the boisterous North Sea, HMS Stamford had ceased her patrolling duties to begin her journey to the estuary for her PR visit to the pageant. The crew of 42, who spend some 300 days a year on the high seas was looking forward to the short sojourn.

The Coast Guard Search and Rescue helicopter was already on standby at Brough Aerodrome, as too was the police search helicopter and the Yorkshire Air Ambulance. All leisure flights from the airstrip had been grounded for the day. DS Barnes was overseeing things at the airfield to make sure that no aircraft ignored the ban and that no unauthorised flying machines, of any size, took to the air.

DC Sharpe was mingling with the first of the arrivals at the nature reserve to the east of the bridge; he was accompanied by a young WPC in plain clothes. It is a sad fact of life today, that a single man wandering amongst families with children would be viewed with suspicion.

Mike Pullman, along with Lynne Sperring, who had pigeonholed the Peak case for the day, was about to board a police launch, to start the day-long patrol of the river.

The Chief Constable was due to arrive shortly in the observation room on the bridge. ACC Iain Thwaite was making his way towards the larger of the 3 marquees, due to house local dignitaries, representatives of the Royal Navy and descendants of Cecil Murdoch, the person, in whose honour the whole event had been organised. An event which, having been planned as a family fun day out, had now, unbeknownst to onlookers, become the biggest police operation ever implemented by the Humberside force.

Pullman had not been born with the gift of sea legs. The undulating motion of any boat bobbing on water caused him to feel nauseous yet he had managed short sea trips on more than one occasion. His biggest failure was when he and Jane were in Malta; she had persuaded him to take a boat ride, along the coastal area where Robin Williams had filmed 'Popeye'. Mike, may well have lasted the trip, had it not been for the fresh sardine lunch they enjoyed just prior to embarkation. That was the time he and several fellow passengers, discovered that vomiting, like yawning, had an involuntary contagious effect. Today, purely as a safety precaution, he had only consumed toast for breakfast along with 2 travel sickness pills to quell any possible uprising. So far so good.

'There's a few hundred thousand quid floating around here' observed Pullman looking at the assembled fleet. 'And some that don't look seaworthy to me.'

'You wouldn't get me on that blue thing over there; looks in a worse state than the Marie Rose when they found it.' said Sperring.

'It's a fantastic sight though, isn't it?' Pullman was studying the flotilla through binoculars; the launch lurched to starboard causing him to stumble forward, grasping the guard rail to steady himself. Three brightly coloured, two person kayaks paddled into view, dwarfed by a craft that bore all the hallmarks of being a converted trawler. Pullman was however, only interested in spotting larger yachts; those with a specification close to that of the elusive Cuprum. There were far too many that met the description for his liking. 'I didn't expect so many big boats as there are,' he said. 'But I can't see our target; can you?'

'No, but I've seen a target I quite like,' she said; looking at a sea bronzed group of thirty-something men aboard a Day-Glo yellow, offshore powerboat. 'Wouldn't mind dropping anchor there.'

Pullman followed her gaze. 'Shady types, probably drug smugglers,' he said with a broad grin. 'You'd more than likely end up having to nick them.'

287

'The one in front would look pretty good in cuffs.'

'Think you've been reading too many erotic books young lady.' He was still smiling. 'Do you think you could tear yourself away from your fantasies and concentrate on the task in hand?'

'Yes sir; spoilsport.'

More and more craft were arriving on what, had now become a crisp, sunny autumnal day. Out of Pullman's and Sperring's view, on the estuary side of the bridge, a procession of ocean going craft was making its way past Queen Elizabeth Dock, HMS Stamford was at the vanguard. They eventually made their way under the mighty bridge to join the corral. The Cuprum was not amongst them.

As morning turned into afternoon and afternoon turned into early evening, dignitaries began congregating in the marquees; champagne corks were popping and ritual shaking of hands was taking place; the Chief Constable, sans champagne, had joined the throng. Peter Monkton, avec champagne, sought her out.

'Good afternoon Pauline; everything seems to under control.'

'Yes Peter; hopefully it will remain that way,' she commented; as she spoke, her eyes were scanning the scene. 'We've got every available man jack looking out for a spectre that may, or may not, be at the feast.'

'Very necessary, I'm sure.'

'You're not going to like the overtime bill though.'

'You cannot put a price on public safety.' A well-rehearsed line from his forthcoming election speech. 'It would do us all a lot of good if we could arrest the lunatic sooner, rather than later.'

An ear splitting electrical, squeal resonated over the public address system, as the Lady Mayoress, Muriel Hudson, was introduced to the assembled gathering. In the failing light, the ceremony had begun.

288

The squeal could be heard on the police launch. Surely if Claude was going to strike it would be during the speeches or as the fireworks erupted immediately after; when public attention would be focussed on the brightly illuminated marquees or fixed on the promised, dazzling display of exploding incendiaries in the twilight sky.

Every movement of every craft was being scrutinised. Nothing. Four of the large motor yachts had moored, amidst an armada of small boats, close to the bridge for a grandstand view of the pyrotechnics. On the far bank DS Sharpe and his 'girlfriend' were nervously vigilant. He looking to his right; she to the left.

'Here comes Bryan,' she said having a perfect view of the Pride of Bruges making its way towards King George's Dock terminal.

'Who's Bryan?' asked Ash.

'Not who, what. I used to come down here a lot with my mum when I was little and whenever one of these ships came into dock she'd always say "here comes Bryan"; it was just one of those things I'll always remember about her.

'Okay.' said Ash but feeling he ought to ask the inevitable question he asked, 'Why Bryan?'

'Because it's a ferry and my mum had an enormous crush on Bryan Ferry, the lead singer with Roxy Music.'

The penny hit Sharpe so hard it could have been a sledgehammer. 'Fuck,' he shouted. Parents and children turned in surprise at the foul language. Sharpe held up his hands in an apologetic gesture. 'Shite; that must be it.'

'What must be it?'

'Long story.' He pulled out his mobile phone. Hit the quick dial for Pullman; he answered. 'Sir, it's the ferry.'

'I can hardly hear you; what did you say?'

'The ferry, Claude's going to hit the ferry.'

289

'What makes you think that?'

'Roxy Music. The lead singer was Bryan Ferry. Remember he said we should listen to Roxy Music. Why else would he say that?'

'Stay on the line.' Pulman looked around; a plethora of boats was floating between the launch and several larger craft towards the bridge. He scanned them through the binoculars. He panned from Silver Lady, Jetstream, Lucky something, the rest of the name was obscured by the bow of Perfect Day and furthest away Sea Lion; the latter of which appeared to be sailing away from the rest, heading under the bridge. 'Ash there's a large yacht moving under the bridge.'

'Yes I see it.' said Ash. 'It's picking up speed.'

At that moment Pullman knew that the Sea Lion was set on a collision course with the mammoth Pride of Bruges ferry finishing its journey from Zeebrugge. He dashed to the control room and screamed at the helmsman. 'Get this thing over to the bridge now with every ounce of speed it's got.' It was an order without scientific basis but the helmsman did as instructed. 'Don't hit the blues until we're on top of it; he might put his foot down, even more.' The launch was hindered by the formation of anchored boats; it was impossible to generate sufficient speed to run down the Sea Lion. Pullman thought quickly 'Take us over to the gun boat. That bugger will get there quicker than we can.' The helmsman swung the launch ninety degrees and headed the short distance towards HMS Stamford. Pullman grabbed the microphone for the loud haler system; when they were close enough, he opened the mike. 'Ahoy HMS Stamford this is Chief Inspector Pullman of Humberside police. We need assistance.'

The Stamford responded. 'Are you in trouble?'

'No, we need to stop the yacht Sea Lion cruising on the other side of the bridge. We believe he's carrying explosives with the intention of sinking the ferry coming into port.'

'Is this a joke?'

'Anything but; please stop that boat; stop it at all costs.'

'Do you want to come aboard?'

'Haven't got time. Just stop that boat. Whatever it takes; lives depend on it.'

The Stamford's two Ruston 12RK 270 diesel engines powered up with a mighty roar; simultaneously ropes were released, from buoys, fore and aft and the anchor retracted in a well-practiced drill. In under a minute the armed patrol boat, travelling at twice the speed of its prey, was in pursuit of the Sea Lion. Pullman got himself patched through to the captain of the gunboat. Sperring called the port authorities in an attempt to get the Pride of Bruges to reverse engines and get the hell out of range. Confusion reigned. From the shore onlookers assumed they were being treated to an impromptu display; cheering and waving flags as the Stamford sped past.

Captain Williamson, more used to tackling illegal fishing vessels, hailed the Sea Lion. 'Attention Sea Lion this is Royal Navy patrol boat, HMS Stamford. Heave to immediately; we wish to board your vessel. I say again, heave to immediately and stop engines.' Barry Cole ignored the command, maintaining the speed and position of the newly named Sea Lion; his eyes fixed firmly on his chosen target as he negotiated Sammy's Point, where The Deep was still undergoing repairs. He had not anticipated the involvement of the navy vessel. He knew he could outrun the police launch but had overlooked the presence of the superior vessel. His heart was racing. He would not allow his grand finalé to be interrupted.

Williamson repeated the warning, to no avail. He spoke to Pullman. 'The Sea Lion is not responding; repeat the Sea Lion is not responding. What action do you wish me to take?'

Pullman did not hesitate. 'Captain, that boat is packed with explosives; if it collides with the ferry there will be huge loss of life. He has already killed over fifty innocent victims. There are over nine hundred passengers on board the ferry and one man on the Sea Lion. The man's actions are tantamount to an act of war; what would you do in a similar situation.'

'Are you requesting me to fire on the vessel?'

'Nine hundred versus one, no contest. Stop him by whatever means it takes.'

The Stamford was armed with a 20 millimetre cannon and 2 machine guns. The gunners were ordered to disable the Sea Line. The fore and aft machine guns burst into life, firing an illuminated dotted line of bullets towards the stern of the target vessel. A huge cheer went up from the crowds on the Humber Bridge as the spectacle unfolded; it was, they assumed, an unannounced addition to replicate the Battle of Narvik. The stream of bullets perforated the hull of the Sea Lion; piercing the fuel tank and igniting the contents; within seconds the craft was engulfed in flames. Despite Barry Cole, AKA Claude, planning this suicide attack as his farewell performance, when death stared him in the face, his military survival instincts kicked in; he leapt from the burning boat just as the chemical bomb on board exploded. He was too late. The explosion mushroomed fifty feet into the air. The sound of a collective sharp intake of breath resonated as the spectators gasped in awe at the show; thirty thousand pounds worth of fireworks began their sequence, lighting up the darkening sky. The crowd burst into spontaneous applause.

It was an ironic end to a campaign of terror. Like the victims of his first bombing, he was blown to pieces; kibbled. Now it could be said – Claude truly did not exist.

Loose Ends

The search of Trevor Johnston's office uncovered a number of discs and memory sticks in a wall safe, concealed behind a framed degree diploma. A full analysis was carried out by the computer forensics department. The data contained in the files was passed on to the Operation Oakwood team; this information incriminated a stream of men and women, both in and out of the public eye, resulting, not only in a string of high profile prosecutions but also in the government establishing an independent commission into child sex abuse in the UK.

More than thirty young children were traced and taken into care; many had already suffered physical, mental and sexual abuse.

The evidence against Anchali Johnston became more than circumstantial, due to her own confession and to her identification by the women freed from the farm cages. She was remanded in custody pending her deportation to face trial in Thailand. Further investigations by the Thai authorities pointed in the direction of Anchali Johnston, not Trevor, being the main player in the nefarious operation. If this was proven, she would stand trial for human trafficking, occasioning rape and murder; the latter two charges carrying the death penalty. If found guilty Anchali would be transferred to Bang Kwang Central Prison in Nonthaburi

Province, just to the north of Bangkok, where death sentences are carried out by lethal injection; although, no executions had taken place, in Thailand, since 2009.

The case against Peak was solid even without his confession; the CPS decided that he should be charged with the pre-meditated murder of Trevor Johnston; his plea of manslaughter was disallowed, but would be re-submitted by his defence council at his trial. Peak was also charged with rape and human trafficking offences. It would be difficult, if not impossible, to prove that either he, or Trevor Johnston, was responsible for the murder of Thomas Wethersby so the case was officially marked as unsolved; nevertheless Humberside Police did not be seek anyone else in connection with the killing.

Detective Inspector Sue Proctor completed her investigations in Humberside, subsequently returning to the NCA in London.

Those investigations had led to the arrest of two container terminal employees together with the operators of a private container haulage company in East Yorkshire. Humberside police would continue the investigations and surveillance at the ports.

Locating and shutting down so called 'baby farms' in the UK and abroad became a number one priority for a multi taskforce initiative involving CEOP, Interpol and police forces across the globe.

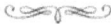

ACC Iain Thwaite was made Deputy Chief Constable.

Frank Delaney was re-elected as Chief Executive of Hull City Council and Peter Monkton served a second term as Police and Crime Commissioner.

A police review into Barry Cole's campaign of bombings was conducted alongside a team of psychologists and cognitive behavioural therapists. As was expected, it concluded that his actions were the result of Post-Traumatic Stress Disorder following his capture, torture and subsequent failed execution in Afghanistan. The later death, of the mother he idolised, was considered the final trigger point. His step-father's suicide came after the bombings would have been formulated and were, therefore, deemed to have had no influence in his psychosis.

Sufficient body parts were retrieved from the river to enable the pathologist to confirm death.

An official enquiry into the part the police and Royal Navy played in the death of Barry Cole was commissioned by the Home Office. Gerald Smenton QC was appointed to lead the enquiry team with a clear, un-written, brief to exonerate both parties and deliver a conclusion of death by misadventure. He duly complied and, as had been intimated, was knighted in the Queen's birthday honours list.

www.ingramcontent.com/pod-product-compliance
Lightning Source LLC
Chambersburg PA
CBHW071258170626
46809CB00001B/274